FROM PROVENCE, WITH LOVE

ALISON ROBERTS

B

Boldwood

First published in Great Britain in 2025 by Boldwood Books Ltd.

Cover Design by Lizzie Gardiner

Cover Images: Shutterstock and Adobe Stock

A CIP catalogue record for this book is available from the British Library.

Paperback ISBN 978-1-83617-316-8

Large Print ISBN 978-1-83617-315-1

Hardback ISBN 978-1-83617-314-4

Ebook ISBN 978-1-83617-317-5

Kindle ISBN 978-1-83617-318-2

Audio CD ISBN 978-1-83617-309-0

MP3 CD ISBN 978-1-83617-310-6

Digital audio download ISBN 978-1-83617-313-7

This book is printed on certified sustainable paper. Boldwood Books is dedicated to putting sustainability at the heart of our business. For more information please visit https://www.boldwoodbooks.com/about-us/sustainability/

Boldwood Books Ltd, 23 Bowerdean Street, London, SW6 3TN

www.boldwoodbooks.com

For the Maytoners
From me, with love xxx

PROLOGUE

Five minutes.

It wasn't a very long time at all.

But, when the rest of your life could depend on what happened at the end of that five minutes, it felt like a very long time indeed.

Laura Gilchrist put the cap back on the plastic stick and put it on the cold porcelain edge of the bathroom basin. She set the timer on her phone to three minutes. Then she glanced in the mirror over the basin.

It was automatic to smooth a single stray hair back into place so that her sleek, red-gold, shoulder-length bob was as perfect as it usually was.

How good would it be to be able to smooth away the visible fear she could see in her eyes?

Laura hadn't seen herself look like this since she learned how to hide fear when she was no more than about nine or ten years old. When she'd learned how to control her own emotions so that she could protect the people who were the most important in her life.

Her family. Her mother. Her younger sisters.

She turned her back to the mirror. It was too disconcerting to see that everything she had worked so hard for in life – her control, success, independence – could be slipping away from her.

She stood very still. And waited. She jumped at the sound of the timer and turned it off instantly. As she reached to pick up the stick, she realised she had known all along what she was going to see in the tiny plastic window.

Two lines.

She *was* pregnant.

How, in God's name, had this happened?

A sound that was probably closer to a sob than the intended huff of laughter escaped Laura's suddenly dry lips.

She knew *exactly* how this had happened.

She also knew that this was entirely her own fault.

Had she, on some deeply hidden level, *wanted* this to happen...?

PART I

1

'Look out!'

The urgency in her sister's voice was enough to make Laura freeze in the heartbeat before she pushed open the driver's door of the car. A millisecond later, a huge, black motorbike roared past within what seemed like only an inch or two of her fingers, still curved around the latch.

Both women stared as the engine noise changed to a protest of gears being rapidly downshifted. The back wheel locked enough to provide a subtle but still dramatic skid as the rider came to a halt just ahead of them, one booted foot coming down at the last moment to stop the huge bike from tipping too far.

He'd stopped right in front of the destination Laura had programmed into the GPS of the rental car – the highly recommended Provençal estate agency, Dufour Immobilier.

At least the distraction provided a means to wind down a rather intense conversation Laura had been having with her sister about the direction her life was going – or not going – in. Changing the subject might even be enough to stop Ellie getting out of the car while they were still at odds with each other.

'Has to be a courier,' she said, as if the identity of the bike rider was what they'd been discussing. 'Nobody else would drive that badly on a bike at home. He's got a satchel over his shoulder, so he's probably delivering a sales and purchase agreement that the agent's holding his breath for.'

'Doesn't look very professional,' Ellie said. 'There's no signage on the bike. What is it, a Harley-Davidson? That's kind of cool. Maybe he's a client.'

'I'd be double-checking his references if he wanted to rent something from *our* agency. You wouldn't want to find a commercial weed-growing operation under lights in the garage.'

Ellie snorted. 'You're so *judgy*, Laura.'

Laura was silent. Perhaps she was but, to be fair, she was harder on herself than on anyone else. She'd probably said too much already, but Ellie could do with taking a leaf out of her book and acknowledging what *she* needed to change in her life. How else were things going to get better? Life wasn't easy. Or fair. Sometimes you had to work very, very hard to get to where you wanted to be.

Like she had...

They could only see the back of the man as he pulled his helmet off and carelessly slung the strap over the handlebars of the powerful bike before walking into the agency's office building. His shaggy, dark hair was long enough to be brushing the collar of the leather jacket he was wearing and there was a smear of dirt on the faded blue denim of his jeans. Laura couldn't see the top of the boots he was wearing but she was deeply suspicious that they might have those curved tops and embroidered stitching popular with cowboys.

'On second thoughts,' Laura said, 'my guess is that he's a handyman or a gardener. He probably gets employed to do maintenance or repairs on rental properties.'

'Maybe he'll be the person who does the work on our house.'

'Let's hope he's better at his job than he is at riding motorbikes, then. He shouldn't have been anywhere near that close to a parked car.' Laura turned her head to check the road behind before finally opening her door. 'It's two o'clock. Time to do what we came here for.'

To finish what they'd come to the South of France for.

They'd gone straight from the airport in Nice to the house in Tourrettes-sur-Loup that morning. Laura had never driven on the right-hand side of a road before but it was exactly the kind of challenge she thrived on, having discovered long ago that a mix of focus, control and confidence could get you through most of the stickier situations life could throw at you. You just had to be able to rise above the emotional reactions that could undermine what you were trying to achieve.

It was Laura's independence and ability to problem solve that provided the building blocks of her continuing career success, working as an estate agent. Adding an international property offering to her portfolio might be a new direction but it was one she was more than willing to embrace.

Especially for a stone-built, quintessentially French cottage that was so picturesque it was more than Instagram-worthy, a terrace with a view to the rocky foothills of the Alps that looked like mountains in their own right, forests and a tantalising glimpse of the Mediterranean Sea in the distance. Even a lemon orchard! It would be far more desirable, mind you, when the damage and dust that had accumulated over too many years of neglect were sorted. There were bats residing in the one of the bedrooms. Electrical issues and broken shutters. A garden that was a complete wilderness.

Which was why the partnership she intended to cement with this local agency was the missing piece of the puzzle. They would be able to access tradesmen without being ripped off. They would also be in a position to connect with people who wouldn't necessarily consider buying a holiday home in the South of France but were here on holiday and found themselves falling in love with the region.

The Gilchrist sisters had an appointment scheduled with the managing director of this company – Monsieur Dufour himself. They went inside. From behind the reception desk an elegant woman, in a plain black dress with a white collar, gave an approving twitch of an eyebrow at the pale, olive-green linen dress that Laura was wearing, but her nostrils flared ever so slightly as she noted Ellie's jeans and tee shirt.

'*Bienvenue*,' she said, directly to Laura. '*Vous devez être Mademoiselle Gilchrist*.' She switched to perfect English. 'Welcome. My name is Blandine. Monsieur Dufour is expecting you both. Come this way, please.'

Both the younger women came to a halt the moment they were ushered into a large office.

They exchanged a glance with each other.

Ellie looked as if she was trying not to smile.

The man standing behind the antique desk was definitely smiling.

Laura had never felt less like smiling.

Because she was staring at the... *cowboy*. How on earth could someone who looked so... so... *disreputable* be the managing director of an estate agency whose outstanding reputation had reached well beyond the borders of his own country?

He had hazel eyes, she noticed in the briefest moment of eye contact that could be considered polite as she grappled with having to try and readjust her judgement of this man.

A dark hazel that was a golden-tinged shade of a brown that reminded her of, what... milk chocolate? Not quite as dark as his hair – or that designer stubble, for that matter – but it added up to a dark impression.

Sinfully dark...

And he was looking at her with such a blatantly admiring gaze. As if she was the most beautiful creature he'd ever seen in his life. With a crinkle at the corners of his eyes as if he knew perfectly well that the admiration was not being reciprocated but he was amused, rather than offended.

Good grief...

The confidence of that look was as disturbing as finding she needed to interact with someone so inappropriately dressed or groomed but, quite inexplicably, Laura had to dismiss an urge to touch her hair – like a teenager trying to get the hang of flirting? How ridiculous! Laura had never flirted deliberately in her life. She was far more comfortable taking the hand that was being extended towards her, in the wake of Noah Dufour's introduction, for a brief but firm handshake and another graze of eye contact that was short but to the point. This meeting was purely for business purposes.

Somehow, Noah Dufour managed to hold that moment of eye contact, however, and this time Laura had to stop herself snatching her hand, rather than her gaze, away from his, because it felt as though his touch was burning her skin.

Not that he gave any sign of having felt that heat himself.

'*Enchanté*,' he said, still wearing that undeniably charming smile. 'I am delighted to meet you both. Please... sit down. Can I get you some coffee? Water? Wine, perhaps...?'

'No. Thank you.' Laura shook her head as she sat down, smoothing her dress over her knees. She wouldn't have been at all surprised if one of the cupboards in this office was stocked with an extensive selection of wine. With time on his hands, she could imagine this man pouring himself a glass of a fabulous red wine, putting his booted feet up on the large antique desk, leaning back in his chair and possibly striking a match to light a cigarette to add the final touch to the image of a reprobate.

The man was not only charming, he was undeniably charismatic.

The kind of man that Laura Gilchrist would never dream of trusting. Certainly not on a personal level, anyway. She knew, too well, that if you did, they had the power to break your entire world when they broke that trust – and your heart.

Like her father had – for her entire family.

Charismatic, charming men were dangerous.

Laura pulled in a deep, steadying breath. She wasn't in any danger right now. This was disconcerting, that was all. She'd just been reminded that somewhere, buried so deeply it shouldn't even be accessible, that pull was still there, like the poignant whiff of a scent that evoked the memory of something precious you could never have again because it had been destroyed beyond repair.

She could still feel a residual warmth from that handshake – as if that match she'd imagined Monsieur Dufour using to light his cigarette was too close to the palm of her own hand – but it was nothing she couldn't handle. She could actually sense a mental door being slammed shut as she dismissed the visceral response she'd experienced that was both intrusive and unwelcome.

At least this estate agent's English was as perfect as his

receptionist's had been, the accent only adding more charm to the laid-back welcome they'd received.

'*Donc*...' Noah opened a file on his desk. 'I understand you have both inherited a property called La Maisonette in Tourrettes-sur-Loup? From your uncle?'

'Along with our other sister, yes,' Laura confirmed. 'Apparently we are his only living relatives.'

'And everyone is in agreement that it is to be sold as quickly as possible?'

'Yes.' Laura turned her head to include Ellie in the conversation. 'That's right, isn't it?'

'Pretty much,' Ellie agreed. She wasn't meeting Laura's gaze, however, and her voice was tight.

Was it because they'd gone ahead and made the agreement in the absence of their middle sister, Fiona, who had failed to respond to the invitation to the family meeting? Or was the lukewarm response due to the fact that this inheritance had come from an uncle who had been a complete stranger? They hadn't even known he existed until the solicitor's letter had arrived. Or that they had a French heritage of their own. This uncle's French mother – their *grandmother* – had only moved to Scotland years after her marriage and the birth of her two sons.

A grandmother they'd never heard of before who'd been born and raised somewhere around this part of France.

It made being here an unwelcome link to the father who had walked out of their lives probably too long ago for Ellie to have any lasting memories of him, but Laura had more than she wanted. Memories that could still surface in dreams that she had no control over – reminders of a dark side to that charisma and charm that could appear without warning and cause enough pain that the fear never quite went away. If her sisters ever had nightmares without understanding what might have sown the seeds, that subconscious awareness could well have created another layer of reasons why her youngest sister didn't really want to be here.

Laura wouldn't have chosen to come here with that new knowledge of their family history, either, but it had been logical for the eldest Gilchrist girl to take charge – she was an estate agent herself, after all, and it was quite likely that a property in a desirable part of the South of France would be snapped up as a second home to a buyer on their side of the English Channel. It had been their mother's idea that Laura brought Ellie along on the flying visit to see the house.

'*It might do her a bit of good, getting away for a day or two,*' Jeannie Gilchrist had said. '*Mebbe it'll take her mind off... you know... everything...*'

Of course Laura knew. They all did. But, so far, taking Ellie away from their home town of Oban, Scotland, didn't seem to be helping to distract her from what she'd had to deal with in the last few months, after the loss of her baby. Her youngest sister was still lost in a darkness that Laura couldn't begin to comprehend, possibly because she'd been so young when she'd learned that it wasn't going to help anyone, including yourself, to allow overwhelming emotions get the upper hand. You had to keep control.

Or you might drown...

She couldn't blame Ellie for not paying attention to all the information Noah was imparting about how complicated it was to buy and sell property in France, but it was a little annoying when she didn't answer Laura's query.

'Ellie?' Her tone was sharper than she'd intended it to be. 'Are you even listening?'

'Sorry... what?'

'Noah says he's got time to look at all the things that need doing to the house tomorrow, so I'm going to give him the key. You don't want to go back there, do you?'

'*No*...' Ellie's tone was emphatic.

Had she really hated La Maisonette that much?

Laura closed her eyes for a heartbeat as her breath caught in her chest. It really hadn't helped that one of the bedrooms had had a baby's cot in it. Thank goodness Noah had agreed to take care of whatever renovation and staging was needed for the presentation of this property to the market, but he was looking thoughtful as Laura handed over the huge iron key to the front door of the house.

'Are you sure you don't want to clean it up yourselves? It would save you a lot of money. Many hundreds of euros, I expect. Thousands, perhaps.'

Noah's smile was hopeful. Maybe he wasn't keen on the effort it would take to supervise an epic cleaning and restoration job. That didn't surprise Laura any more than the idea of him having a hidden wine cabinet in his office. There was a lazy quality to his smile that suggested he didn't let hard work interfere too much with his enjoyment of life.

The warmth of that smile seemed to be contagious. Laura could feel it seeping in to settle somewhere deep in her belly. Dousing it by tightening the well-toned muscles of her abdomen was an instinctive reaction. So was the firm tone of her voice.

'No. I'm afraid that's not an option.'

The disappointment in his face was simply part and parcel of that charm, wasn't it?

'*Pas de problème*,' he said. 'I will stay in touch.' He picked a business card from a holder on his desk and reached to hand it to Laura. 'Here's the agency number. If I'm not available, then just leave a message with my assistant, Blandine.'

It was only polite to give him one of her own business cards in return. His fingers brushed hers as he accepted it and Laura caught a glimmer of something very unbusinesslike in his gaze again.

'My private number is also on my card,' he murmured. 'Please call if I can be of any assistance.'

This felt far too personal. Almost an invitation? Laura shifted uncomfortably and broke eye contact.

'When do you leave?' Noah asked.

'Tomorrow. I wasn't sure how long things would take and the late flights were all full tonight.'

'I'm sorry I don't have the time to visit the property today but I have another appointment.' Noah's sigh was indeed regretful as he glanced at his watch. 'In fact, I really need to go. I'm rather late...'

'No problem.' That was an understatement, really. Having this man vanish could be the solution to a problem, in fact, because Laura could escape from whatever was causing this unsettling awareness of everything about Monsieur Dufour. 'We're planning to have a wander around the old town here,' she added. 'And then we'll go and find our hotel in Vence.'

She would be miles away from him by then.

Noah nodded as he got to his feet. He didn't seem bothered by the prospect of her disappearing from his life forever in the next minute or two.

'Leave your car here, if you wish. It will be easier to walk than find a closer parking place. You've got the Fondation Maeght just a bit further up the road if you're fond of art. It's a very famous gallery, and the Miró sculpture garden is just fabulous.'

One eyebrow, barely visible beneath the shaggy hairstyle, quirked just a fraction and a very different note made the tone of his voice richer. Warmer. The words were almost a caress.

'I would love to be showing you around there myself.'

Oh no… Laura didn't dare look at Ellie. Not just because she might be on the verge of giving her discomfiture away by blushing furiously. This was also awkward because Ellie had been an artist herself until the unthinkable had happened. Rubbing her nose into the fact that she'd lost more than her baby would be heartless.

'Maybe not today,' she said crisply, getting to her feet. She needed to escape for both their sakes now. 'We'll go and have a walk around the old town.'

* * *

There was no doubt about how magical the old walled city of St Paul de Vence was, but Laura was still puzzled, the next morning, about how that brief visit to the famous tourist attraction had achieved what she'd given up hope of happening anytime soon.

That Ellie would find something – *anything* – to hold onto that might help her find her way out of that dark space she was in.

Not that it mattered what had made Ellie change her mind about staying here to renovate La Maisonette herself. This was a huge step forward, and Laura was not only applauding it, she was quite prepared to cover any associated costs herself until the property was sold. It was an investment, after all – in both the real estate market and in her sister's future.

As a bonus, it was a totally new challenge for them both, and the need to make a plan and sort what was needed to begin that – all in a race against the ticking clock of Laura's flight to get back to Scotland – was energising. Exciting, even. Last night had been all about making lists. Laura couldn't wait for Ellie to finish her shower this morning so they could get on with what needed to be done.

Did Noah Dufour ever feel like this about his life, or work?

Laura doubted it. As she'd said to Ellie when they were walking towards the historic section of St Paul de Vence, if that man was any more laid back, he'd be horizontal. That an image of that shaggy hair on a pillow, framing those intense hazel eyes, appeared in her head so readily was even more irritating than the fact that she was thinking about him at all. Surely she'd got that out of her system when she'd been staring at the ceiling for far too long, trying to fall asleep last night?

It was too early to ring anyone else in the UK, but Mam was always up at the crack of dawn. The running water in the bathroom would make the conversation completely private, but Laura still stepped out onto the balcony of their hotel room.

Her mother was worried about Ellie not coming back when she needed to be out of her apartment so soon.

'I'll organise it,' Laura promised. 'I know a cleaning firm that will make it spotless as soon as we get her stuff out of there.'

'But what will we do with all her things?'

'I don't know, Mam... I guess we'll just store it. You'd have room for the cot in the attic, wouldn't you? We can fill it up with all the clothes and toys and suchlike.'

'Have you talked about that with Eleanor? Is this really a good idea?'

'No, of course we haven't talked about it.' Like everything

else that could cause painful reminders, they'd tiptoed around the logistics of Ellie taking any first steps away from the shattered remains of her old life. Laura closed her eyes for a heartbeat. 'But she said she's happy for us to clear the place out, and I don't think there's any need to remind her of the details of what she's leaving behind. This is the chance for a fresh start. A completely clean slate, in fact. Couldn't be cleaner – all she's got here so far is a change of knickers and her toothbrush.'

How impulsive would you have to be to do anything with no more than a change of knickers and a toothbrush? Laura couldn't begin to imagine doing it herself. She'd been as worried as her mother that Ellie might not have the emotional resources to put her life back together, but she didn't want her mother to undermine the courage Ellie was demonstrating in her decision to stay in France alone, and she heard her breath coming out in a heartfelt sigh.

'No... I'm not sure it's the best idea. But I think *she* thinks it is, and that's what matters, isn't it? Look, I'd better go, Mam. Ellie will be out of the shower any minute and we've got a ton of shopping to do before I head back to the airport. I can't miss my flight. I've got that awards dinner to get to this evening and it's the biggest night of the year in the real estate world.'

A text pinged into her phone as she ended the call.

> Bonjour, Laura. Can I help you with anything this morning?

Laura's heart actually skipped a beat. She'd given Noah a card that had her personal cell phone number on it but... she hadn't expected him to use it.

No... that wasn't true. She just hadn't been prepared for the tiny thrill it gave her that he *had*, even though his message couldn't have been any more professional, could it?

Tout est bien. Mais, merci beaucoup, Noah.

Laura had learned French at school. It had been one of her favourite subjects. She'd even spent a gap year in France. Not that she'd had any idea there was genuine French blood in the family back then, but it had been surprisingly pleasant to be able to brush some of the rust off her language skills at the airport and restaurants yesterday.

It didn't excuse her imagining that she could hear an echo of Noah's voice as she'd read that message from him, however. To be reading the words in her head with a French accent and hearing her name spoken with an inflection, the guttural growl on the letter *r* that made it sound so... good grief... sexy?

The sooner she left this sultry part of France behind, the better, Laura decided.

It was doing her head in.

2

Despite intense scrutiny, Laura could find no fault in the full-length reflection in the mirror on the back of her hotel room door.

She had bought a new dress for this occasion.

The plunging, sweetheart neckline was framed by two wide straps that almost formed sleeves because they somehow managed to hang at the very edge of her shoulders. The rest of her dress clung to her figure and finished just above the knee.

It was black.

It was, ironically, a French dress she had found in a Glaswegian boutique.

A necklace would have detracted from the way the design put the focus on her shoulders and collarbone, so Laura simply put her hair up into a neat chignon and wore long, silver drop earrings that had crystals sparkling like tiny leaves on a vine.

Even her make-up was flawless tonight. Had she, in fact, found the holy grail of freckle disguise in her new high-end mineral foundation?

The black stiletto shoes were the perfect finishing touch.

Laura was satisfied enough to take a photo of her reflection. If she ever found herself lacking in confidence ahead of, say, an important interview, she could take a peek at this image of a woman who looked like she had the whole world in her hands. A woman who was exactly who she wanted to be and where she wanted to be in life.

But maybe the shoes weren't quite the perfect finishing touch, after all. That would be when she was holding the premier award for sales as the regional winner. Could she dare dream of such a coveted achievement this year?

If that happened, she certainly wouldn't need to be taking selfies.

The Georgian architecture of this restored nineteenth-century building, with huge Romanesque pillars and elaborately decorated ceilings, was a sharp contrast to the tumbled edges of stone and the almost organic jumble of ancient buildings in the South of France. Far more Laura's style, however. Corporate and glittery – the kind of background that was perfect for the professional games of doing business and a world away from the kind of softness that whispered of romance and seduction. She approved of the military precision of the rows of wine glasses hanging by their stems above the bar, which were catching glints of light from enormous chandeliers, and the silver trays on the marble top of the bar with their sparkling crystal flutes of champagne already poured.

Let the games begin.

About to take a sip of her champagne, she put her glass down on the bar as she felt her phone vibrate silently in the small clutch bag she was carrying. Was it Ellie? Had she left her sister alone in a bat-infested house that she was too scared to sleep in?

There were two messages on her phone. The first was from her mother wishing her luck for the award ceremony tonight. The second was from a French number.

No...

Surely she hadn't somehow summoned the presence of Noah Dufour in a more concrete form than the random thoughts she was having trouble controlling?

Perhaps Ellie had needed to get a new phone?

But the message wasn't from her sister. It was a photo of what looked like a typical old French street – very like the ones Laura had been walking on only that morning – but she had no idea why it had been sent to her. Or who had sent it. There was a door, an unusual archway-shaped depression in a wall with strange decorations, and a sign that read La Farigoule.

Text came next.

> Bonsoir Laura. This is where I would have taken you to dinner if you were still here, as part of our marketing research. My favourite resto in Vence.

Laura blinked. Yes... on second glance she could see a wooden box on the wall which would have a menu behind a glass door, and the odd-looking decorations in the archway made sense now. There was a bunch of grapes and a mortar and pestle. Even an octopus...?

She pushed the phone back into her tiny bag. Why would Noah think that she would have gone out to dinner with him, anyway? His confidence was more like arrogance and it wasn't attractive.

It *really* wasn't.

She picked up her glass of champagne and took a sip. Maybe it would wash away the odd tickle, deep in her belly, that almost felt like the butterflies of being nervous.

Which she was, of course. She desperately wanted to win an award tonight and not just in the categories of outstanding property presentation or client satisfaction like she had last year. No... she wanted the big one this time. Regional Estate Agent of the Year.

In the meantime, there were people that Laura really should be networking with, including the CEO, Colin Armstrong. It wasn't often an opportunity like this presented itself and... was it her imagination, or was there more than polite interest in his gaze as he nodded in her direction?

Ah... hadn't she heard recently that his wife had left him?

Nobody had been particularly surprised. Colin was middle-aged, very successful and – it had to be said – more than a little boring.

But boring men were safe, weren't they?

Did it really matter if they were predictable and boring in bed as well?

Good Lord... where had *that* thought come from? The same place, perhaps, that images of shaggy dark hair, designer stubble and sinfully appreciative glances had been tucked away?

The images of a man who was reckless enough to ride a motorbike. Did he carry pillion passengers on the back of that overpowered machine? Women who would have to be pressed against his body and cling on with their arms around him?

Oh, *my*...

Laura took a much larger sip of her champagne but put her glass down as her phone buzzed again.

What if it *was* Ellie this time?

It didn't really surprise her that it was another photo, but the actual image made her catch her breath.

A garden courtyard with terracotta paving and a rough-hewn stone wall. Beams that were a playground for lush greenery overhead. The tables had white linen cloths and shining silver and glassware like the ones in the room Laura was about to go into, but this dining area had an understated elegance that was totally missing in the glitz and glamour of the event she was attending.

The restaurant in Vence offered pure romance, especially when the central feature of this photograph was a table for two. Tucked away in a corner, with shadows from candlelight on the stonework and leaves and the shelter of a nearby pillar with a flowering plant spilling from a hanging basket, it made a private oasis for lovers. It was an invitation that could make any woman breathe out a soft sigh of longing – the way Laura just had.

> Notre table, Laura. Une coupe de champagne pour toi, peut-être?

Clearly, it had been unwise to give Noah Dufour a business card that also had her personal cell phone number, but...

The idea that an inexplicably attractive man in France was thinking about *her* right now was...

Flattering, that's what it was. It gave her a sensation deep in her stomach that felt like the curl of an appreciative smile.

That he was dangling the seduction of pure romance in front of her was...

Oh... dear Lord... it was *tempting*, that's what it was. That feeling wasn't reminiscent of a smile any longer. It was more like a licking of lips.

Romance on this level was something that Laura had never

experienced and wouldn't trust anyway, but she had to admit that this photograph was exerting an oddly powerful pull. Laura did her best to dismiss the unsettling desire to be on the other side of the English Channel as the evening progressed. She really didn't want to be anywhere else, especially when it came to the highlight of the event.

Colin was smiling broadly. 'And the award for The Property Centre's Regional Estate Agent of the Year in Oban, Argyll and the Isles goes to... Laura Gilchrist!'

The applause was thunderous. Laura had to pose holding her trophy, and she had friends as well as the official photographer taking pictures. People forwarded copies to her as she accepted congratulations and celebrated with more champagne – because she wasn't driving home, was she?

One photo stood out because the angle made her dress look as stunning as it had on the exclusive boutique's mannequin and her smile made her look as if she was well aware of the significance of the award in her hands but wasn't as excited as a small child on Christmas morning. Laura thought she might have a copy printed to go in a discreet frame in her office but, for now, she was just going to forward the image to her mother. It was time to do some celebrating, and she could see Colin walking towards her, holding a bottle of champagne and two glasses.

Hurriedly, Laura opened the recent message from her mother to forward the photograph. The ping of an almost instant response made her glance at the screen as she slipped the phone back into her bag. It also made her frown.

Her mother never used emojis as a response to a text message. She was old school and preferred to use words. She would definitely not be sending a shower of hearts.

Oh, *no*...

No, no, *no*...

Colin was right beside her now. 'Congratulations, Laura. Tonight's award must be the icing on the cake for you right now. Someone's just told me that you've inherited a house in the South of France. I want to hear all about it. I'm thinking of getting into a bit of international real estate myself. And your award tonight! So well deserved. You must be very happy...'

Laura managed to dredge up a bright smile but Colin's words were little more than a background buzz. She wasn't happy.

She wasn't happy at all.

Had she accidentally just sent that photo of herself to Noah Dufour?

3

One of life's great pleasures, for Noah Dufour, were the combined aromas of strong coffee and tobacco smoke, preferably enjoyed alone in a place that allowed him to watch the world waking up around him.

This morning, however, he wasn't observing the activity in the square overlooked by the outside area of the café just outside the fortress walls of St Paul de Vence. He was scrolling through messages on his phone. More specifically, the messages that had been received and sent by Mademoiselle Laura Gilchrist.

Not that she'd responded to his initial contact with the restaurant photos, like the delightful food, so beautifully presented with its decorations of microgreens and tiny edible flowers. Even the picture of a single dessert with two silver spoons hadn't provoked her enough to comment, and Noah had almost given up trying to get through the barriers around the most stunning woman he'd ever seen, but then she'd sent him that photo...

It was clearly intended to remind him that their relationship was strictly professional. He'd zoomed in on the plaque she was holding that proclaimed her the winner of what had to be a prestigious award in the Scottish real estate industry.

Mais, oh là là là là...

He'd looked at this image a thousand times since and, if the intention was to create another barrier between them, it hadn't dimmed his longing one little bit. If anything, it had increased the impression that Laura Gilchrist was, quite simply, a goddess. A woman who deserved to be worshipped.

It had been a mistake to send the explosion of love hearts, of course – *trop peu professionnel* – but Noah had been far more circumspect since then. He'd resisted contacting her, waiting until he'd had an excuse, and that had been to let her know that the plumber he'd organised to attend to the hot water problem at La Maisonette had been successful. Mike was going to line up the other tradesmen that might be needed as well, like a glazier and a builder.

Her response had been brief.

Merci beaucoup

And then there'd been a tiny chink of light through that professional barrier.

How is Ellie coping, do you know? Is there anything that she needs?

I'll call in on her today and find out. I'm going that way. I want to send you a photo of La Chapelle du Rosaire in Vence. Henri Matisse considered the design and decoration of it to be his life's masterpiece. The house he lived in is nearby, too. La Villa Le Rêve.

Please do. Famous artists are of interest to many people.

Like restaurants?

Noah couldn't resist nudging that professional barrier again.

Were you tempted by La Farigoule?

The lack of response had been long enough for Noah to decide he'd pushed it too far, then his phone signalled an incoming message. When he'd become engrossed in something else, the sound had made his heart skip a beat.

You captured the romance of France very well. I'm sure one of those photos will end up in our brochure.

The smiley face at the end of the text had been a surprise. It felt like Laura was taking a step outside the realms of a professional relationship, too. A small step, perhaps, but it felt significant.

The frequency of messages had gradually increased. As July arrived and summer settled in, Noah had been able to reassure Laura that her sister was coping very well with her new life in France.

He'd added just a single heart that time.

He'd sent the photographs he'd taken of the chapel in Vence with the stained-glass windows and images painted on ceramic tiles, the pretty, two-storied house that Matisse had lived in and some links to more information. He'd waited for Laura to respond to that and he wasn't disappointed. She hadn't made him wait that time, despite the heart emoji he hadn't been able to resist adding again.

Fascinating. I read that Picasso visited him there. And that Marc Chagall lived in Vence even longer than Matisse?

Oui. There is a Chagall mosaic artwork in the Vence cathedral and his grave is in St Paul de Vence.

I wish I'd known. I'd like to have seen that.

It's not too late, ma chérie. Come back and I will show you everything. Did you know that Vence is famous for having the smallest cathedral in France?

There was no response to that but Noah wasn't bothered. It had been their longest text conversation so far and he had umpteen other local features of interest that were the perfect excuse to initiate further contact. Besides, he felt like he was getting to know this mysterious woman a little better now.

She needed time to feel safe.

And he had all the time in the world.

He signalled the waiter.

'*L'addition, s'il vous plaît.*'

He had work to do.

But maybe he'd swing past La Cathédrale Notre Dame de la Nativité in Vence to snap a photo of that mosaic on his way to view a potential listing in Grasse. If nothing else, when he checked the image it would give him an excuse to look at that photo of Laura that had been automatically added to his camera roll.

The one where her smile was reminiscent of all the seductive mystery of La Joconde. Where she was wearing the gorgeous black dress that left her shoulders bare enough to invite a kiss and showed off collarbones his fingers simply itched to trace.

* * *

It was past five o'clock in the morning and should have been daylight, but the dense cloud cover and pouring rain on the west coast of Scotland made it feel more like the middle of the night as Laura ran into the brightly lit gymnasium. It had, in fact, felt like summer had started fading weeks ago – almost as soon as she'd returned from that visit to France.

She was shivering in her designer Lycra leggings and matching crop top, but the first ten minutes on the treadmill were enough for her to ditch the sweatshirt she'd kept on and hit the next level for speed and incline. Another ten minutes and she would be warmed up enough to get stuck into her circuit routine. Maybe she'd feel a little more enthusiastic about it by then, although it didn't matter if she didn't.

This was her routine and it was paramount to stick to it. Routines – like boring men – were the threads that made up the safety net of her life and she wasn't about to take the risk of letting them unravel. Besides, doing things that were good for you felt like you were building a credit that could be spent on something more enjoyable, eventually, even if it wasn't so good for you.

Maybe *especially* if it wasn't good for you.

She had her phone strapped to her arm to give her some music to accompany her workout, so the sound of a text message arrived via her Bluetooth earbuds and, while it was still earlier than 7 a.m. in France, she just *knew* that it had come from Noah.

Or was she *hoping* it had?

Bonjour, Laura. I hope you will have a good day.

Laura used the rest of the thirty seconds of catching her breath to send back a two-word response.

You too.

She wasn't smiling outwardly as she went to the first station of her circuit routine and picked up a pair of five-kilogram dumbbells to do some single arm curls, but she couldn't deny it felt like she was smiling inside.

Okay, the guy was arrogant and overconfident and maddeningly persistent but... but she was getting so used to the contact that she'd stopped rolling her eyes and making him wait for any kind of response. They were working together, after all, and ideas for the brochure to help sell La Maisonette were coming together nicely. A lot of that professional contact was being exchanged via email rather than text messages now, with larger files full of photographs and property details being sent back and forth but, somehow, the habit of texting had become... just that. A habit. Only now, it was more personal. Sometimes, Laura even found herself pausing for a moment in whatever she was doing. Listening for the sound of a message arriving.

Hoping she was going to hear the ping?

Her biceps burning, Laura moved to the triceps pulldown equipment. She loaded up the weights, took hold of the rope loop, braced her abdominal muscles and tucked her elbows in. This was such an automatic routine that counting the reps in each set and even listening to music or a podcast didn't mean she couldn't have another line of thought ticking away in the back of her head.

Like her programme for the day, which included numerous viewings, a photo shoot for one of her new listings, a staff meeting in the Oban office and countless emails and phone calls to attend to.

The email Noah had sent the other day, with a link to the fabulous art gallery that was just up the road from his agency office had occupied her entire lunch break. The history of a fabulous hotel restaurant – the Colombe d'Or – just before the entrance to the historic part of St Paul de Vence had been another revelation. How amazing that she and Ellie had walked straight past it, oblivious to the story that Picasso and Renoir were rumoured to have paid for meals or accommodation there with paintings or sketches? She'd clicked on a link to the menus and barely tasted the quinoa, cucumber and chickpea salad she'd been eating while reading about quenelles of fresh salmon and roast beef with gratin dauphinois.

That was the day she'd sent the first text message that wasn't a response to one that Noah had sent.

> I think I need to go to the Colombe d'Or for dinner. Maybe I'll come back to visit when we do the photo shoot for La Maisonette.

His response had been instant.

> J'ai hâte ça.

He *hated* that?

So why had he sent one of those clever showers of hearts?

Laura had ignored the list of calls she needed to make to

confirm appointments in order to use a translation app to check the message. Noah didn't hate the idea at all. He was looking forward to it.

Couldn't wait, in fact.

It was ridiculous to feel this relieved, mind you, but there it was.

Maybe she couldn't wait, either.

She'd certainly been thinking about it ever since. She'd even gone online to see how you could do that sending showers of hearts thing. Out of curiosity, nothing more. She would never dream of doing something like that herself.

But she was thinking about it again now. About the dinner that Noah was looking forward to them having together – trying to focus on imagining the food rather than the man on the other side of a tiny table. An image of those thinly sliced potatoes, baked in double cream, with Gruyère cheese, garlic and thyme made her unconsciously put more effort than usual into her leg press set, pushing a foot plate so heavy it instantly made her whole lower body burn. The pain should have been a welcome distraction but, instead, Laura was letting her thoughts stray to another website she'd been on more than once recently.

The online presence of the Noah Dufour immobilier included a photograph of its managing director, and the image was disturbingly easy to retrieve from her memory banks. It looked like a studio portrait, and Noah was looking straight into the camera with a hint of *that* look. The one he'd bestowed on Laura when she'd first walked into his office.

The one that suggested she might be the most beautiful woman he'd ever seen.

In this photo, his face framed by unkempt curls, his lips were barely tilted with just a frisson of that lazy smile. Had the photographer been an attractive woman, or was that expression of appreciation simply the way this man approached life in general?

It made him look...

Ellie had called it 'rock star chic', which wasn't a bad description. Laura could imagine him holding a guitar, front and centre on a poster that countless teenage girls would want on their bedroom walls.

The pain in her leg muscles was unbearable now. Laura moved her feet from the plate to the floor and leaned forward to take several deep breaths. There was not enough to distract her, and the heat she could feel blooming deep in her belly couldn't be attributed to purely physical exercise. Neither could the groan that escaped her lips as she finished her workout and headed for the shower.

Where was this almost uncontrollable fascination with Noah Dufour coming from? Why was it so strong, and when was it going to wear off?

Ellie was planning to stay in France until the end of summer, which was officially the end of August, wasn't it?

Would she have to wait that long to quash this distracting new element in her life? Longer, even – perhaps until the house was sold and what had created the connection between herself and Noah Dufour would cease to exist.

Or could the process be accelerated? The photo shoot could probably be arranged to take place within a few weeks given the progress that Ellie was making on preparing both the house and the garden for sale.

It was her excuse to go back to France.

To see Noah again.

Ohh...

Yes...

The prospect was both terrifying and remarkably titillating, and the sensation was a whole new world for Laura, taking her back to another one of those possibly unanswerable questions.

What was making him so ridiculously desirable? Was it that he was so far towards the opposite end of the Laura Gilchrist spectrum for evaluating the suitability of men?

The opposite of a suitable man like Colin Armstrong, perhaps?

That suitability hadn't stopped her from politely declining the CEO's invitation to dinner that he *had* made in the wake of the awards dinner. Laura had used a prior engagement as her excuse for being unavailable, but Colin must have seen through her apology because that was weeks ago and he hadn't asked again.

And that had felt like permission to keep indulging in wayward thoughts about such an *un*suitable man.

As for where it had come from, perhaps it was simply FOMO. Was she missing out on discovering that sex could be like it was in the movies or the books she had secretly devoured as a teenager? That – if she was daring enough – she might be able to exorcise the vaguely distasteful and definitely disappointing experiences she had had so far in her life?

It was exactly what she was doing in a way, wasn't it? Allowing herself a fantasy because it was safe. It wasn't as though this was ever going to be more than a long-distance flirtation disguised as a business relationship. The house would get sold and she'd never see or hear from Monsieur Dufour again. This tiny seed of rebellion against the firm rules that Laura lived her life by was only temporary, so it couldn't do any real harm.

And it was undeniably irresistible...

* * *

The messages between Laura and Noah were getting steadily less businesslike.

So was the time that they were being exchanged. A line was definitely crossed when Laura received a message late enough for her to be in bed.

This felt... intimate.

Private.

Maybe he was in bed, too? Thinking about her?

> What is your absolutely favourite food, Laura?

Maybe she wanted to shock him. She shocked herself by confessing it.

> Hamburgers. And fries...

He could have sent back a horrified face emoji. Or a laughing face. Instead he sent the one that was licking their lips, after the words, *moi aussi.*

> And what is your favourite passe-temps? Your hobby?

Laura had to think about that one. Hobbies implied pleasure. Playtime. And she didn't do playtime. She couldn't even remember playing as a child. She'd watch her sisters playing. She'd join in sometimes but she could never lose herself in a game. She always had to watch and listen for the moment the fun had to stop.

When real life would take over.

When she might have to try and protect her mother and her sisters.

I don't have time for hobbies.

A beat later, she felt the need to soften her sharp response.

What's yours?

She was almost asleep when the response finally came. It was a voice note – a recording of someone playing a guitar, delicately picking the separate notes of a melancholy but beautiful tune that Laura recognised but couldn't instantly place. It sounded professional.

Exquisite.

Utterly romantic.

She had to ask.

What is it?

Eric Clapton. Wonderful Tonight. Bonne nuit, Laura.

But who's playing it?

C'est moi. It's one of my passe-temps. Did you like it?

Perhaps if Laura wasn't in her own bed and on the verge of falling asleep, or maybe if she hadn't been totally disarmed by the revelation that Noah was a talented musician, she would never have done what she did next.

For the first time in her life, Laura sent nothing but emojis.

A whole shower of red hearts.

4

Laura didn't eat any lunch the next day but it wasn't because she was too bored with quinoa salad. Her appetite had been killed by irritation.

Weirdly, there was only one person she thought she could vent to who would understand.

Why is it that some photographers want to take pictures on strange angles? Or use a fisheye lens??

You should take your own photos for the properties you sell. I do.

You do?

Oui. Photography could be a perfect hobby for you. Useful as well as relaxing.

You do take good photographs.

Laura felt qualified to judge. She had dozens of them in her phone and email records and she'd looked at them all many times.

It's not difficult.

What sort of camera do you use?

A Leica. Only the best.

Is it hard to learn to use?

Pas de tout. I could teach you.

I'm sure you could.

Laura added an eye-rolling emoji but she found she was smiling. She wasn't feeling remotely irritated now.

She had to end the text conversation, however. Even the idea of Noah showing her how to hold a camera was enough to distract her completely from what she was supposed to be doing. Would he stand behind her? Put his hands over hers as he showed her how to hold it and which controls to adjust?

The notion was as distracting as it had been to imagine being the pillion passenger on his motorbike.

But it added another reason to make that booking to go back to France for a weekend. A professional reason that made it an opportunity she would be foolish to pass up.

She'd told Ellie that she would be happy to sleep on the couch if she came, but it occurred to Laura now that she could go back to that little hotel in Vence instead.

If nothing else, it was fodder for a whole new fantasy that she could add to the motorbike ride and the photography lesson. One where she not only went out to dinner with Noah Dufour but they ended up back in her – private – hotel room.

And why not?

If the fantasy couldn't last, she may as well make the most of it while she could.

* * *

Ellie video called Laura to offer to pick her up at the airport when she arrived for the photo shoot visit. Finding the vintage 2CV in the garage of La Maisonette had been one of the unexpected recent developments in the restoration project. That Ellie had found the courage to start driving it when she'd been so nervous of driving on the other side of the road had been even more unexpected. Chiding her sister for the silliness of giving the car a name – Margot – had only been an attempt to put off the inevitable.

Having to confess that arrangements had already been made.

That Noah was picking her up.

On his motorbike.

Laura deliberately froze her expression so there would no chance of her sister guessing even a hint of the fantasy that had become an increasingly dominant feature of her life. Fortunately, Ellie seemed diverted by something far more practical.

'What about your suitcase?'

'I'm only coming for a couple of days. I could put my toothbrush and some clean knickers in my handbag if I need to.'

The silence from Ellie had been eloquent. The idea of Laura doing something so wild and irresponsible was so far out of character, it was disturbing. But Laura made light of it. Noah was being helpful, that was all. He was going to show her some of the area's features that were worthy of mention in the brochure and... that included him taking her out to dinner.

Perhaps they'd go to one of the local restaurants, like the Colombe d'Or. Or La Farigoule.

She'd found she could actually hear his voice instead of seeing the words as she remembered the text he'd sent the night of the awards dinner.

Notre table, Laura. Une coupe de champagne pour toi, peut-être?

Or maybe he'd take her to the one he'd told her about in St Paul de Vence that was as much an art gallery as a famous restaurant?

'He's taking you out to dinner?' Ellie had sounded shocked. *'Have you been online dating without telling me?'*

It was exactly what Laura had been doing but she wouldn't have admitted that to anyone. Including herself? She'd laughed off the suggestion. Did Ellie really think she'd be interested in someone like him?

Her sister's echo of her laughter had held a note of relief. *Not in a million years...*

And maybe that had been the tipping point, knowing that Ellie thought she could never be daring enough to go near a bad boy like Noah Dufour.

How shocked would her baby sister be if she knew the kind of things she was thinking about doing with him? Things that took her back to her teenage years when she'd read those steamy romance novels by torchlight under the covers of her bed.

But all that had been promised was a purely professional list of excursions and experiences. Impersonal enough to be able to tell Ellie about them and sound completely innocent. Imagining being on the back of his motorbike, however, when Noah had offered to pick her up at the airport, had been vivid enough to have almost scared Laura off the entire idea. Had he picked up on her second thoughts when he'd called to confirm her flight details?

Was that why he'd offered reassurance along with a final promise?

'You need to live a little, ma puce. *It's a couple of days you'll never have again. Something very French to remember. You'll love it... I promise.'*

Laura thought again of the way Ellie had laughed at the idea of her with a man like Noah.

The echo of the way that had made her feel – almost ashamed of not having the courage to do something so outside of her comfort zone – morphed with the knowledge that this *was* only a blip of a couple of days in her lifetime. One night. It was also an opportunity she was highly unlikely to ever be offered again.

Did she want to spend the rest of her life wondering what might have happened if she'd thrown caution to the wind, just for a day or two?

What it might have been like to be with a man like Noah?

No.

Dammit, Laura was going to do it.

Nobody else had to know the truth. Not her mother or Ellie. Not even Noah.

If it did turn out that fantasies could come true, it would be entirely *her* secret. And that – almost – made it feel safe.

PART II

5

Laura Gilchrist was a perfectionist. Given enough time, she had the ability to find something that was less than perfect in anything, including the things she put the most effort into herself. Maybe especially those things.

She'd learned long ago that it was all about control. The more you could notice details and keep things perfect, the less likely it was that your world could be tipped upside down and shaken to pieces.

But it seemed like her first breath of French air in months, as Laura walked outside the terminal building at Nice airport, was nothing less than perfect. Maybe that had something to do with the warmth of the sunshine or the feeling of suddenly being on holiday from real life. More likely, it had everything to do with the tall man in the leather jacket, standing beside his huge motorbike, watching her with an intensity that made her feel... good grief... as if he could see straight through her clothes and that he thoroughly approved of what he could see.

It wasn't shocking, though.

It was more like... deliciously exciting...

He was exactly the same laid-back, rather shockingly disreputable-looking managing director of a successful French estate agency that she'd met when she'd come over with Ellie to inspect their inheritance. But this wasn't a first meeting, and there was a sense of familiarity that made it far less shocking that Noah leaned in to give her a kiss on each cheek after greeting her. The touch of his lips on her skin started a strange melting sensation for Laura – one that seemed to start low down in her belly and reach as far as her knees, which actually felt wobbly for a heartbeat, just like one of the heroines in those old romance novels.

This wasn't entirely unexpected, mind you.

Because she was stepping into a fantasy she'd been creating for weeks now.

It felt like months.

Her whole adult life, perhaps?

What Laura hadn't bargained on, however, was how it felt to be on the back of Noah's motorbike a short time later. Her imagination hadn't been completely off point, it had just been lacking an extra few notches on whatever scale she'd been using to measure the projected level of physical response to a person or situation. Or was there a whole dimension of sensation she'd never known existed?

The power and noise of the engine beneath her. The solidity of Noah's body wrapped in her arms. The wind rushing at them. Or maybe it was simply the danger, not just of feeling so unprotected amongst cars and buses that could squish her with no more than a nudge, but of how reckless she was being – albeit very temporarily – by abdicating the kind of control she would normally keep over every situation she found herself in.

It took a little more than twenty minutes to get up into the hills and arrive outside La Maisonette. Long enough for Laura to have regained at least a sense of being in control. There were good reasons for her to be here, after all, and it had been entirely her choice to make the trip. If she wanted to, she could also choose to keep her time with Noah Dufour purely professional, and while they were here at the property to start their joint marketing campaign, that was exactly what was needed.

Ellie's fierce hug, as soon as Laura had pulled her helmet off and handed it to Noah, was filled with notes of both joy and homesickness.

'It's *so* good to see you, Laura. I can't wait to show you *everything...*'

It was suddenly easy to focus – and to bury her fantasy deep enough to forget about it herself for now, let alone let her sister guess. She could sense Noah coming closer. Too close...

He handed her the large, suede shoulder bag he had stored in the motorbike's pannier for travel. He had a smaller, square bag hanging over his own shoulder.

'My camera,' he said, noticing her glance. 'I'm going to give you your first photography lesson, yes?'

Laura made a vague sound of agreement but turned away as a flash of her imagined photography lesson surfaced. Maybe she needed to bury that a little bit deeper? She walked towards the wrought-iron gate.

'Do you remember when we got here?' she asked Ellie. 'When I couldn't believe this was the right address?'

'You were hoping it wasn't.' Ellie smiled. 'I think you were horrified when I found the old ceramic tile under the ivy.' Her smile widened. 'Look at it now.'

'You've repainted it.' Laura touched the tile with the fresh lettering of *La Maisonette*. 'And is that a bunch of lemons in the corner? Clever.'

She looked at Noah who had opened his bag on top of the stone wall and was taking out a very professional looking camera. 'Maybe this is the theme we've been looking for to weave through all our advertising? The USP?'

'*Oo-es-pay*?'

'Unique selling point. The lemon orchard here. Everything about lemons suggests something fresh and colourful and... and delicious.'

'Ah, *d'accord*.' Noah was smiling, his eyes crinkling at the corners. 'Do you want to take a picture?'

'Yes, please.'

He didn't come and stand behind her or guide her hands to adjust anything. He simply pointed out the button she needed to push and handed her his probably hugely expensive camera.

'That lens is fine for now,' he told her. 'I'll use the wide-angle one for the rooms inside.' He gave her the ghost of a wink. 'Not a fisheye.'

'What I really want is to capture the ambience,' said Laura. The shutter of the camera clicked softly as she took pictures of the ceramic tile. 'Like this. And that...' She straightened and stepped away from the gate to look at the open door of the garage where the little red car could be seen, its headlights peeping out like surprised eyes.

'What was that name you gave the car?'

'Margot.'

'Short for Marguerite,' Noah said helpfully. 'I believe it's Margaret in English.'

'It's quintessential French flavour, that's what it is,' Laura said. The camera whirred as she took some rapid shots. 'Such a bonus to have found it in the garage, Ellie. Well done. We need some photos with... erm...' Laura cleared her throat.

She'd never named a car in her life so this felt rather silly. '... Maggie parked on the road, here in front of the house, don't you think, Noah?'

Ellie didn't give him a chance to answer. 'Her name's Margot,' she said firmly. 'Margot the escargot. Because these cars used to be called tin snails in England.'

Noah's laugh was a deep rumble that Laura realised she'd never heard before. A delicious sound that went into her ears but managed to travel all the way down to her toes. It would be so easy to sink into a sensation like that and let the rest of the world fade into irrelevance.

'I've also heard them called "umbrellas with wheels",' Noah said, still amused. 'Me, I prefer two wheels. Do you want me to shift the bike so you can take some photos, Laura?'

Oh... was that sexy growl at the end of her name when he pronounced the *r* always going to create a visceral effect like his laughter just had?

'Not now.' Laura's tone was crisper than she had intended it to be. She wasn't ready to dismiss the rest of the world just yet. She wasn't completely sure she was ready to do that at all, to be honest. 'I want to see the rest of what Ellie's done to the house.'

Laura stooped to pat the scruffy little dog with the floppy ear who was staying very close to Ellie.

'Hullo, Pascal,' she said. 'It's very nice to be able to meet you properly instead of just seeing you on the phone.'

She walked ahead down the cobbled path between lavender plants that had been trimmed into a neat hedge.

'We could barely get down this path that first day. Or see the front door thanks to that monster rose bush on the stone archway.'

'It's a Banksia rose,' Ellie told her. 'I sent a photo to ask

Mam what it was when the first flowers came back after I'd pruned it.'

There were quite a few of the old-fashioned frilly-petalled, pale-yellow blooms adorning the thick, gnarled branches but Laura was looking at the solid wooden door to the little house, with its carved four-petalled flowers, which was open just enough to get a glimpse inside. She could see the living area with the stone walls now free of the crumbling plasterwork, and the rich ochre tones of the *tomettes* adding their solid depth and warmth. The doors from the kitchen to the terrace were also open so the invitation of that shaded courtyard, where a glimpse of the view could be seen even before you set foot in the house, was impossible to resist.

But Laura still paused to lift the camera again to take a picture of the brass door knocker on the centre panel, shaped like a delicate female hand holding an apple. It was shiny enough to look newly gilded.

'This is so lovely,' she murmured. 'I never noticed it last time I was here. Is it new?'

'It just needed a bit of love,' Ellie said. 'Like we all do,' she added softly, stooping to pick Pascal up in her arms.

Laura could hear a note in Ellie's voice that she'd never heard before. Her baby sister was older and wiser now, wasn't she? And... happier?

Oh, she hoped so...

Going inside, Laura took snaps of the stonework on the walls and the pots by the fireplace.

'These pots remind me of something... I just can't think what it is.'

'Imagine them without those little handles,' Noah suggested. 'And full of... *tournesols*. I forget the English name. The flowers of the sun?'

'Sunflowers,' Laura said. And then, 'Oh, my goodness... Van Gogh... of course. I wonder if we can find some sunflowers to put in them.'

'Perhaps they're perfect the way they are.' Noah's tone was a gentle admonition. 'They're a bit of Provençal history just like that.'

'So they're old?'

'*Ouais*. Probably mid-nineteenth century. They're confit pots and they were the first form of refrigeration.'

Something in Noah's voice suggested that this was a subject he was passionate about.

'They would cook the duck in its own fat and then put the meat in the pots and cover it with a layer of the fat. They put a cloth over the top and took it down to the cellar beneath the house where the ground stays cold, and the pots would be half-buried. That's why they're only glazed on the top because that's the line to bury them up to. The cold ground helped to preserve the meat.'

It was antique pottery Noah was telling her about, but it could have been the history of Provence or perhaps art or even Harley-Davidson motorbikes. It didn't matter. It was the passion that was captivating.

It was very, very attractive.

Because if a man could show his passion about something in public, how much might he be capable of showing in private? By using communication that needed no words at all...

Laura was hearing Noah's voice more than taking in the information. The deep timbre of it. That gorgeous accent. It occurred to her that it was a voice she would never tire of listening to, which was a shame because she'd probably never hear it again after this property sale went through. Ah, well... she just needed to make the most of it, then, didn't she?

Noah stayed downstairs to take a phone call as Laura followed Ellie to the bedrooms. She was dreading seeing the state of the room that had housed the bats because she had promised Ellie she would do whatever needed to be done in this particular room to get it ready for viewing. She wished she'd done it before she'd left Ellie to live in this little house, in fact. She'd been aware of how fragile her sister's mental health was but had not given enough thought to how hard it would be for her to have a baby's cot in the bedroom next to her own.

Had she become so good at closing down her own emotions that she could ignore how the people she cared about were feeling?

There was something shameful about that.

Laura's hand was on the door handle of the second bedroom when she hesitated. There was something in Ellie's gaze that made her catch her breath.

'Go on,' she said, with a tiny wobble in her voice. 'Have a look.'

So Laura opened the door. She gasped, pressing her fingers to her mouth and then she simply stood for the longest moment, taking it all in: a picture-perfect child's room, complete with the fantasy garden painting on the wall. Dark green ivy scrambled along the walls, low enough for a child to reach up and touch, and dotted amongst the leaves were bright white daisies and scarlet poppies and droopy purple spears of lavender.

It was gorgeous, but that didn't explain the sudden prickle of gathering tears that made Laura pinch the bridge of her nose to make sure they couldn't finish forming.

'You did this,' she whispered. 'Oh, Ellie... it's just... perfect.'

And it was. For more than just its contribution to the renovation of this ancient cottage and the unique element it added to its marketing potential. This was tangible evidence of Ellie beginning to heal after the tragedy of losing her baby. It was confirmation that the time she had spent here in this beautiful part of France was already changing her life. Giving her back a future.

Laura was just so damn proud of her sister in this moment. The amount of love filling her heart was making it feel like it might burst. It was definitely making it hurt.

As Noah came upstairs, he probably assumed that the tight hug the sisters shared in that moment was in appreciation for all the work Ellie had done to La Maisonette to get the property ready to sell. When it went on a little too long, he looked at his watch.

'I have to go, Laura. I have an appointment to show people an apartment for sale in Cannes. I will be back to collect you later, yes? *Quatorze heures*?'

'Ah... Two o'clock, yes? Do you need to take your camera?'

'No. You may find more things to use for... how do you say it? For *l'ambience*?' That charming, lazy smile was growing as he held eye contact with her. 'The *oo-es-pay*?'

Laura was shaking her head again but this time she really was smiling. He knew perfectly well that she was enjoying his accent. This was no more than thinly disguised flirting.

'Ambience is the same word in English,' she told him. 'We'll work on your USP pronunciation later.'

* * *

There were many things that caught Laura's eye as Ellie showed her around outside. She snapped a close-up of some lavender flowers and a bunch of lemons and then glimpses of the view, framed by the glossy foliage of the lemon trees. The donkeys were snoozing under the shade of olive trees and Laura made an approving sound as she took more photographs.

'They look... different to how I remember them.'

'You didn't get that close, remember? When you got a lemon stuck on the heel of your shoe, you didn't want to go any further into the orchard. But they are cleaner. We gave them a bath.'

'*We*?'

'Julien helped. He's the neighbour. I'm sure I told you about him. He's a single dad who lives there with his mother and he's got a little boy called Theo who's very fond of the donkeys. They've been looking after them ever since they moved in because they've never seen anyone else coming here to care for them. He's been very helpful. It was Julien who gave me the driving lessons in Margot.'

She sounded offhand. So casual, in fact, that it made Laura give her a second glance, but she couldn't ask whether 'being helpful' was a euphemism for something more going on. What if she inadvertently revealed the secret behind why she'd been so willing to come back to France for a quick visit? If Ellie wanted to tell her that she was having a bit of a fling with the single dad next door, that was fine. If she didn't, it meant that it was none of Laura's business. It might be a secret for Ellie and possibly an important part of why she seemed to be embracing life again finally. Who knew?

Fortunately, Ellie hadn't noticed her curious glance. She was reaching out to the donkey who had woken up and come to the fence. It dropped that huge head far enough to press its forehead against Ellie's arm, and the way she began rubbing the bottom of one of those extraordinary ears looked like a well-practised routine. The donkey clearly loved it, leaning even further over the fence and making Ellie laugh as she had to push back to keep her balance.

It was, Laura realised, the first time she had heard Ellie laugh like that in a very long time.

'Marguerite,' Ellie protested. 'Stop...'

'Marguerite? You've given her the same name as the car?'

'I didn't name them. Julien and Theo did – after the flowers that grow wild amongst the grass here. A marguerite is a daisy. And that's Coquelicot coming over to say hullo to you. That's a poppy.'

Laura took a step backwards. She'd never been particularly drawn to people's pets. Especially one this large. 'What on earth will we do with these donkeys when the place is sold?'

'Fi was going to look into a rescue organisation that might take them,' Ellie said.

'Maybe we could offer them to the new owners. Some people really love donkeys.'

'Mmm.' Belatedly, Ellie responded to Laura's observation. She bent her head to plant a kiss on Marguerite's nose and moved to give Coquelicot some love. 'I was hoping Fi might come over for a weekend,' she added, 'but I haven't heard from her for ages. Have you?'

'I never hear from her. She called Mam to talk about the donkeys and I think she said something about coming over to look at their feet.' Laura turned back towards the lemon orchard. She wanted to get some photos of the house framed by a branch of one of the lemon trees with fruit on it. 'You should ask her again. Otherwise you might find yourself back in Scotland before she can organise any time off.'

She could feel the donkeys watching them as they walked away. Ellie was beside her, so quiet it made Laura wonder if she'd said something wrong. Or was she thinking about their missing sister?

'What was it, do you think?' Laura asked. 'That made Fi change so much when she went to university?'

'I don't know.'

'Do you think she's gay but doesn't think we'd be okay with that? Or that she's had a traumatic breakup that she can't talk about because that would mean coming out? Has she ever talked to you about things like that?'

'We haven't talked about anything really personal in years,' Ellie said. 'It got worse after I met Liam.'

'Hmm...' Ellie's choice of life partner had been a rather pretentious fellow student on her fine arts course. Laura didn't want to open that can of worms. It would just be rubbing salt into a wound that was only now beginning to noticeably heal.

Laura found the perfect lemon tree branch and lifted Noah's camera to take some shots of the house.

Ellie led them back to the house. 'I'll make us some lunch,' she said, her voice sounding a little too bright, as if she was determined to change the subject. 'Wait till you taste the baguettes from our local shop with ham and mustard and cheese. It was the first meal I had in this house and it never gets old.'

They chatted as they ate and Ellie asked where Noah was taking Laura that afternoon.

'We're going to the Fondation Maeght first. When he takes me to Vence to check into the hotel, he thinks I should see the cathedral and the Chagall mosaic there. If there's time, we can go to the Matisse chapel and the cemetery where D. H. Lawrence is buried. Well, not buried there any longer, but that's a whole other story he hasn't told me yet. There's still a plaque.'

Ellie's eyes had widened. 'You and Noah have been doing far more talking to each other than I would have expected. Why do I get the impression that you really like him?'

Laura kept her shrug offhand. 'He's all right,' she said. 'As you said yourself, I was probably a bit judgy when I first saw him.'

Ellie said nothing, but her silence was meaningful enough for Laura to narrow her eyes.

'Just to be clear,' Laura said, 'I'm never getting married. I'm never going to allow even a relationship with a man to control any part of my life. Because I'm going to avoid the kind of catastrophe it can become – like what happened to our parents.'

Like what had happened to Ellie? Laura didn't say it aloud but the implication was there.

'Call me later,' Ellie said as she watched Laura freshen up her lipstick. 'I want to hear about that restaurant in St Paul de Vence, too. I've walked past it a few times now but you can't really see anything from outside.'

'It might be a bit late by the time I get back to the hotel, but I'll tell you all about it tomorrow. I'm not sure about what time that will be, either. I'm going to ask Noah if it might be possible to go and see the lavender fields. They're quite a long way away but we could get up at first light and go. I might never get another chance to see them, and it could be another lovely photo for the brochure. It's a shame we'd be going on a motorbike or you could have come, too.'

The look her sister gave her suggested that Ellie had seen right through that excuse. She might not be going to say anything, but she knew perfectly well that Laura wanted Noah all to herself.

6

Noah Dufour was intrigued.

And he was enjoying this rather unfamiliar feeling, probably because he was too used to being able to predict exactly what it would take to charm a woman he desired into his bed.

He hadn't expected this, however. To sense something so different about Laura Gilchrist from the moment he'd seen her walking out of Nice airport a few hours ago. This was a very different version of the beautiful but disapproving woman that he'd been so instantly smitten with when she'd walked into his office in that elegant, pale-green dress. Today she was wearing blue jeans and a soft-looking white shirt that had the sleeves rolled up and fastened with a little tab and button. There were delicate sandals on her feet, sunglasses perched on that stunning rose-gold hair and a large soft leather bag slung over one shoulder.

She looked like a woman who had, at least temporarily, walked away from whatever responsibilities she had in her life.

Someone who was ready to play?

Someone who was determined to play, even?

Someone who might, in fact, want to be in charge of the rules of this game?

Noah wasn't about to argue the toss. The flirting via text messages and email over so many weeks had built anticipation to an unprecedented level and the idea that there could be something even more surprising waiting in the wings was... well, it was the most exciting thing that had happened to him in a very long time.

Possibly the most exciting thing ever.

He could hear echoes of his own voice when he'd sensed that she might be talking herself out of coming back to France.

'You need to live a little, ma puce... *You'll love it... I promise.'*

It seemed as if she had taken his words to heart. And Noah had the feeling that they were both going to love it.

Not that he was about to rush anything.

Because he was intrigued.

If it was what she wanted, he was going to give Laura every opportunity to take charge.

He might even tease her a little and make this seem like business, with a visit to his office before he took her to the nearby gallery to start her tour of local features. He could suggest that they needed to discuss La Maisonette's marketing brochure, even though it was so close to being finished it really only needed suitable photographs.

* * *

Oh...

Laura hadn't expected this.

This... was it playfulness? Was it her imagination, or was he *teasing* her?

Laura was even more unfamiliar with teasing than she was

with playing. She'd been the eldest sibling. Too serious about life to tease her younger sisters, and they had probably been too intimidated to try teasing her. It was a form of banter that she didn't really understand, to be honest.

The somewhat intimidating receptionist and assistant, Blandine, was not in the agency office. No one else was there. Noah could have taken Laura into his office with those masculine aromas of leather and tobacco and red wine and... could have had his wicked way with her on top of the magnificent antique desk Laura remembered dominating that private space.

Laura had a feeling that she wouldn't have mustered much of a protest. Her breath caught in her throat when Noah stepped in the direction of his office but then, with a glance that crinkled the corners of his eyes – like a smile that his lips hadn't been invited to – did a U-turn and passed so close to her she could feel a wash of warmth from his skin.

Was he going to lock the door?

No...

She let out her breath in something too close to a sigh of disappointment as he merely reached up to remove a couple of laminated window display advertisements and put them on the reception desk for her to peruse.

Were they not even going to go into his office, away from where they could be seen by any passers-by? Frustration added a new note that, unexpectedly, intensified the heat that Laura could feel simmering deep in her belly.

She'd never felt this level of physical attraction before.

She had vague memories of science lessons at school that she hadn't been particularly interested in. She had doodled on the edges of her notepad while the teacher talked about cells and atoms and spinning electrons. About positive and negative electrical charges and magnetic fields. Not that she'd be able to explain it coherently to anyone else now, but it felt like she could actually *feel* it happening in her own body. As if something on a cellular level was responding to the force that was coming from Noah's body.

A case of opposites attracting, creating an irresistible magnetic field that she had no control over?

No...

Of course she could control this.

If she wanted to.

Or if Noah intended to. She suspected he could feel that hum in the air between them as clearly as she could.

He might not be creating it on purpose but he was definitely playing with it. Intensifying it. That had to be why his hand brushed hers with a whisper of skin contact as he showed her the examples of advertising he could put in the window of the agency for La Maisonette. Was he simply enjoying the sensation himself, or was he trying to push it towards a point where it simply couldn't be restrained any longer? Laura felt too shy to make the eye contact that might have answered that question.

Maybe she wasn't quite ready to find out.

The twinges of this attraction might be powerful enough to border the realm of physical pain but, oddly, she didn't want them to stop. It was a welcome reprieve, however, when they left the office and were in an open space that seemed to dissipate the effects of being close to Noah instead of bouncing them back. Laura was more than happy to be distracted. Especially since a new fear was starting to form, like a rock that had the potential to interfere with the swift flow of these unprecedented and undeniably delicious sensations.

The fear that real sex with Noah Dufour, instead of fantasy

sex, might turn out to be just as disappointing as it had always been with the more suitable men she had chosen in the past.

They left the motorbike where it was and walked further up the hill. The road kept climbing as they went through a stand of pine trees that hid the beautifully manicured lawns on this side of the Fondation Maeght's buildings – a lush surface for artfully placed sculptures that led them into the gallery's reception area.

The first surprise was that someone greeted Noah by name and he walked straight past the queue of people waiting to pay the entrance fee.

Noah noticed her startled glance.

'I've been coming here all my life,' he explained. 'My parents were patrons of the arts and some of the first members of the *Société des Amis* of the *fondation*.'

The second surprise, as they walked into the large internal gallery, was that there were children everywhere she looked: in paintings, photographs and sculptures. She could see stiff, unsmiling family portraits from centuries past on a nearby wall, images of children playing and mothers with babies in their arms. There were far more recent photographs and artworks, and in the centre of the gallery space was a charming, life-sized circle of children cast in bronze, holding hands and dancing.

Forever Young, the exhibition was titled. *Representations of Children in Art Through the Ages.*

A large oil painting in an ornate, gilded frame drew Laura irresistibly forward the moment they entered the room. She barely registered that Noah was following her.

The date of 1782 as part of the work's title caught her peripheral vision but there was nothing stiff about this painting. Laura had no interest in reading the fine print and finding out who this aristocratic woman – with her impossibly small, corseted waist and elaborately curled, grey wig – might be. Or who the artist was, even. She was caught by what she could see that was bigger than any frame could enclose.

The woman was holding a baby on her silk-covered lap with one arm, holding her other hand up as if she was waving. The baby looked to be about six months old, the age Jack had been when he died, and could well be a boy despite small, bare feet peeping out from beneath a long dress. Chubby arms with perfect little starfish hands were thrown up in the air, mirroring the action of the mother.

But what was hitting Laura with all the force of a punch in her gut was the way the baby and mother were looking at each other. Holding direct eye contact. This unknown artist had, somehow, managed to completely capture the strongest bond ever: that link between mother and child.

And, to her absolute horror, Laura found her eyes filling with tears that felt hot enough to burn. She fought the urge to blink because that would make them fall and everybody would see that she was crying.

Noah would see.

But maybe he had already? Or could he feel her distress as he stood beside her? She felt a feather-light touch on her arm.

'Come,' was all he said. So softly that only she could hear. His hand slid down her arm until his fingers found hers and then cupped her hand.

Blinded by tears that she could now feel on her cheeks as well, Laura let herself be led away from the painting. Out of the gallery, past the reception desk and then through an external door into a courtyard that filled the space between two wings of the building. The time it took to walk to a bench was enough for Laura to find she could breathe again without fear of emitting even a hint of a sob. She sat down, brushed the moisture from her face and then rummaged through her shoulder bag in search of a tissue so that she could blow her nose.

'I'm sorry,' she said quietly. 'I never cry. It's just...'

Noah didn't say anything but his silence didn't seem to suggest a lack of interest. Or lack of concern. Quite the opposite, in fact. He was waiting.

Listening.

'It was the way that baby and his mother were looking at each other,' Laura whispered. 'It made me think of Jack... Ellie's baby.'

Noah's tone was surprised. Wary, even. 'Ellie has a baby?'

'*Had*,' Laura corrected. She gave up on trying to find the tissue she knew was in the depths of her overfilled bag somewhere and sniffed, inelegantly, instead. 'He died when he was six months old – about the same age as the baby in that painting.'

'Oh, *mon Dieu*...' Noah sounded horrified now. 'I'm so sorry. I had no idea.'

'Of course you didn't. There's no need to apologise.'

Laura had received sympathy from many people at that dreadful time, even colleagues she barely knew. Everybody had been so shocked. They'd all said how sorry they were, but hearing Noah say the same words felt different somehow. Was it because the reaction was in response to her offering the information instead of having sympathy thrown at her like salt being sprinkled into an unbearably raw wound?

Maybe it was the sincerity she could hear in his tone. The gentle note. The respect with which he encouraged to her to say more.

'Can I ask... what happened?'

Laura hesitated. This was a subject that she never talked about. Ever. To anyone outside the family. It didn't make sense that she suddenly wanted to – so much that it felt that she couldn't stop herself. Had it been bottled up for too long? Did it feel safe to tell Noah because he was almost a complete stranger and, after her visit to France, they would probably never see each other again? Was this how someone might feel if they were in a strange country and went to find a priest to make a confession? Stifling the weird desire to bare her soul and tell him every shameful secret she'd collected in her life made it easy to open a smaller window to her personal life.

She shook her head. 'Nobody knows. He just died in his sleep. They used to call it a cot death but now it's called SIDS. Sudden Infant Death Syndrome.' She let out a shaky breath. 'That was why Ellie was with me when we came to your office the day I met you. It was six months after Jack had died but it felt like Ellie was sinking into a hole she was never going to be able to climb out of. We were all worried about her, and our mother thought that it would be a good idea to bring her to France with me for... you know... a change of scene.'

'Your mother sounds like a wise woman. This *is* a good place to be.'

They sat in silence for a long moment and Laura finally looked around the courtyard that was, she discovered, populated with sculpted figures. Very tall, thin and knobbly people, single people and groups standing sentinel, others looking as if they were walking to a new position. She could imagine that one was walking towards her. To protect someone vulnerable who had entered their community? A flight of fancy, of course, but it added to the feeling of safety that surrounded her like a heartfelt sigh.

'I *love* these sculptures,' she said.

'They're beautiful,' Noah agreed. 'Do you know the sculptor? Alberto Giacometti?'

'No.' Laura bit her lip. 'I'm ashamed to admit that I'm a bit ignorant about art.'

Noah's lips curved with just a hint of a smile. 'I envy you,' he said. 'I have been here so many times, the pieces in the permanent collection are like close friends. You will get the... *émerveillement* for the first time. Come...' His smile grew. 'There is so much to see. Come with me into the labyrinth.'

He held out his hand and it felt the most natural thing in the world to take hold of it, but Laura felt a little shy. She distracted herself by trying, and failing, to remember what the French word Noah had just used meant.

'*Qu'est-ce que c'est l'émerveillement*?' she asked, finally, as they left the courtyard.

'It means...' Noah frowned. 'The surprise, I think. But also the joy and... something being so wonderful it's hard to believe.'

Laura was nodding slowly as she took in the fantastically shaped marble sculpture beside them, with the shiny patches where countless people had touched the creature. 'I think I have some of that *émerveillement* right now. And... ohh...'

She had turned her head and then drew Noah further along the path to get closer to what had elicited the exact sound that word embodied – that moment of being captured by something that, for whatever reason, touched a part of your soul.

On top of a stone wall ahead of them was a metal sculpture, dramatically dark against the endless forest and bright blues of the sky and sea beyond it. A cone-shaped base supported a triangle with a circular hole in it, and balanced on the sharp tip of the triangle was a huge pitchfork.

'This piece is called *La Fourche*,' he told Laura. 'It's one of many works by Joan Miró here and one of my favourites. They suggest it's like a bird. The circle is the eye and the teeth of the fork are... plumes. No... feathers. Sometimes I forget my English.'

'Your English is perfect. But what I'm forgetting is to take some photos.' She let go of his hand to take the camera from the bag he had over his shoulder, and the sound she made now was one of bemusement, as if she couldn't understand how she could have been so distracted. 'And that's what we came here for, isn't it?'

* * *

Noah smiled but said nothing.

A brochure for a house that was about to go on the market was the last thing he was thinking about right now.

He'd known there was something different about her when they'd met face to face for the second time, but it wasn't what he'd thought – that she was a woman with a couple of days off from her normal life who was determined to have fun. Well, that was part of it, perhaps, but there was something else there.

And now he thought he knew what it was.

Laura wasn't going to be making up rules to enhance the pleasure they could have together. Any rules she imposed would be to protect herself.

Beneath that confidence and the beauty and distance that had made her seem such a goddess, she was – unexpectedly – vulnerable.

Lost, even...?

To see those amazing eyes fill with tears like that had

shocked him. So had hearing the bare bones of a story that he knew had scarcely touched the world of pain buried between its lines.

Curiously, what he'd just learned about her was pulling him closer when it would normally have sounded an alarm for him to retreat – politely, but swiftly. Noah avoided any significant emotional involvement with the women he invited into his bed. With anyone in his life, in fact.

But there was something about Laura Gilchrist. Something he understood all too well. He knew what it was like to feel lost. To be unable to let anyone too close. How hard it was to learn to cover it up with things like confidence and success.

There was only one way to *not* feel lost.

And that was to not feel alone in that dark, empty place.

Noah wanted to take hold of Laura's hand again. He wanted to let her know that he understood.

That, in this moment, she really wasn't alone.

He wanted it so much it should have been another warning, but it was easy to dismiss because it wasn't actually possible. Both of Laura's hands were occupied with the camera, taking pictures of *La Fourche*. She was moving on from the pull back into her past that had left her in tears and that was a good thing.

But Noah couldn't let go of the thread that he could feel connecting them on a level quite unlike anything he'd ever experienced, and he felt it was important that Laura knew it was there. Physical contact had been the obvious way to try and communicate that sense of connecting without giving it too much significance, but it wasn't the only way, was it?

Words might be a clumsier pathway, especially in a language that wasn't his by birth, but it might be safer. He could take the first steps on what was a more circuitous route and turn around to escape if it felt like he was treading on dangerous ground.

They walked further into the labyrinth. There were other people nearby but it was quiet in the summer heat of the afternoon. Even the cicadas sounded as if it was too much of an effort trying to attract a mate. Laura was, again, drawn to one of Miró's works, this time the mammoth egg, reflecting its mysterious engravings on the still surface of the shallow basin of water that surrounded it.

'I love this, too,' she said quietly. 'I love everything about this garden. Thank you so much for bringing me here, Noah. There's... something magical about it.'

'Perhaps you are one of the guests who are able to sense what went into its creation,' Noah said. 'Some would argue that's a curse rather than a privilege, I think.'

Laura's brow creased, making lines that Noah was tempted to smooth away with a fingertip. 'I don't understand,' she said.

'This is La Fondation Maeght. Aimé and Marguerite Maeght had a successful art gallery in Paris but they moved to the French Riviera in the 1950s because they thought the climate would help their young son who was very ill. With *leucémie*. A blood cancer?'

Laura nodded. 'Leukaemia.'

'*Oui, c'est ça*. The son, Bernard, sadly died and the Maeghts were in despair. It was some of their artist friends who suggested the project of building a place like no other. A place that was built with the sole purpose of being perfect to exhibit paintings and sculpture. I expect they were trying to give them a reason to live again.'

Laura's face had gone very still. 'Like Ellie and that house,' she whispered. 'It's brought her back to life.'

There was a shine to her eyes that suggested more tears

weren't far away and Noah felt that he was seeing, for the first time, a small window in the walls he had constructed so carefully around his heart.

He opened it. Cautiously. Just a crack.

'That was why my parents became involved. They also knew the pain of losing a child. My sister, Elise.'

Noah could actually feel Laura picking up the other end of that thread of connection. Holding it as she pushed that window open a little further.

Her voice was as soft as the warm air around them. 'How old was she?'

'Only seven. She had been unwell with brain cancer for several years.'

'How old were *you*?'

Noah shrugged. 'Twelve. More than a child but too far away from being old enough...'

Laura's hand moved, as if she wanted to make physical contact, but something made her change her mind so it was only her gaze that held his. But it felt like a physical contact.

'You can never be old enough for something that changes your life so unfairly,' she said.

'No...'

They held that eye contact for a heartbeat longer. A space of time that crossed the barrier of acceptable closeness between friends and became a foray into a more intimate arena. Not that it was acknowledged by either of them. By tacit consent, a long moment later, they walked on through the labyrinth, visited the chapel and revisited the sculpture garden that led back to the pine forest.

Neither of them said anything for stretches of time but the silence wasn't awkward. It felt as though they were both feeling that invisible thread between their fingers and trying to define its strength or significance.

They paused for a final time as Laura took a photograph looking past the trunks of pine trees to a huge, spiky, sheet-metal sculpture with the gallery buildings behind it. Watching her intent expression as she focussed on getting the perfect shot gave Noah a moment of clarity.

He didn't want Laura making up any rules.

He wanted to teach her how to throw her rule book away.

He could give Laura far more than he'd planned for this time, which had been no more than *une liaison sans lendemain.* A brief affair that might well be memorable for the sex as well as experiencing some of the delights of the South of France, but nothing that would actually change her life for the better.

Noah knew exactly what it was like to be inside walls that were built for self-protection. He knew how lonely it could be, but he also knew what had helped him survive. Techniques that made life something to be celebrated and not simply coped with.

He knew how to focus on what was in the moment, not in the past or the future. How to make the most of the best that life had to offer.

Did Laura know how to do that?

Now seemed as good a time as any to find out. Here, in the shade of the pine trees, with their scent heavy in the air around them and the sound of cicadas providing the music of summer. It seemed inevitable, in fact, when Laura came close to put the camera back in the case that was still hanging from his shoulder.

Perhaps she could feel the intensity of his thoughts, because she went very still, slowly lifting her chin until her gaze met his. The question he was asking received a response so clear that it felt as if this conversation couldn't possibly be as silent as it was.

Laura wanted this.

As much as he did.

Noah lifted his hand to brush one perfect strand of fiery gold hair away from her face. Then he traced the line of her jaw, very lightly, until he reached her chin. He left it there, tilting it just a little, so it was at the perfect angle when he lowered his mouth to touch hers. A gentle kiss, to seal the connection they had found. A connection that they could both trust more than well enough for the short time it was going to exist. A time where they could be together and neither of them would feel alone.

This was where it would begin.

With this kiss...

7

That first kiss had flavour notes of coffee and cigarettes and... the spice of something else that was purely Noah's and could possibly be the smokiness of slightly scandalous pleasure. It marked the moment Laura could feel real life begin to slip away as she stepped into the fantasy that had been forming and growing in the most private parts of her brain – and her body – for long enough to feel... what was it, exactly?

Legitimate?

Safe...?

Yes. She knew the beginning, the middle and most importantly, the end of the fairy-tale affair she had created that was now coming to life.

Okay... she hadn't allowed for the extra dimension of there being another human involved here and not simply a clichéd example of a type of man Laura had never considered suitable. Who would have thought that a sinfully gorgeous bad boy who ignored any rules that would stop him doing exactly what he wanted to do would be so attuned to someone else's emotional struggles?

So attuned that he had felt her falling apart before she'd shed a single tear. Who had taken control and rescued her so smoothly and casually that she doubted anyone else had seen that she was falling apart. With just the touch of his hand taking hers and merely a single word.

'Come.'

Noah Dufour might ride a motorbike in lieu of a horse but that didn't make him any less of a knight in shining armour. That, on its own, was enough to take her fantasy to new, unexpected heights and, because it was a fantasy and Laura knew exactly when it was going to end, she could let herself fall just a little bit in love with him.

Well... what woman wouldn't fall for someone who could make them believe that how they felt mattered enough – that *they* mattered enough – to deserve comfort? Being rescued in a way that kept dignity intact suggested a sensitivity Laura hadn't factored into her fantasy.

Learning that Noah had experienced the tragedy of losing a young and precious life had given her a disconcerting feeling of connection. To know that he'd been dealing with that grief at almost the same age she'd been when her father had walked out, when life had changed forever for the Gilchrist family, had been disturbing enough to make her think that it might be safer to walk away before she got any closer to this man.

But then he'd kissed her.

It hadn't even been about sex. Not to start with, anyway. It had been such a gentle kiss that it felt like simply a more intimate touch in the same spectrum as holding her hand. But, in the same way that their eye contact could be a conversation in itself, the touch of his lips against hers had ignited the flicker of something much, much more exciting than holding hands. It was a promise of things to come.

And, beneath that layer, there was another promise. That Noah would keep her safe.

It was in that moment that Laura had given up trying to ensure that the fantasy stayed within the boundaries she'd imagined. Or to worry about any repercussions when it came time to walk away. Because the time when it would end was too close already and, if she didn't surrender, she was never going to know how exciting it might be to ignore the boundaries of reality.

This was why she had come here and precisely what she'd been hoping would happen. She would never have this chance again.

She wasn't going to throw away even the tiniest part of it.

* * *

The hotel Laura was staying in was near the centre of the historic part of Vence, in a narrow street near the Grand Jardin. Noah parked in the designated area for motorbikes between the central square, which housed the markets, and the restaurants on the other side of the road.

'We can walk everywhere we want to go from here,' he said. 'It's not as if you have a suitcase to carry.'

Laura smiled. 'I've never travelled this light before but I have everything I need. Even a dress.'

'A dress?' Noah raised an eyebrow as he looked at her shoulder bag. His smile was lazy. 'A very short dress?'

'No.' Laura's tone was prim. 'I wanted something to wear when you took me out to dinner tonight, and this one rolled up surprisingly well. I've even got a pair of sandals in the bottom of my bag to go with it.' Her glance was speculative. 'You haven't told me where we're going yet. Are you taking me to La Farigoule, or the restaurant in St Paul de Vence where all the artists used to go? I've forgotten the name.'

'La Colombe d'Or.' He was still smiling. 'I haven't decided yet. Luckily I have friends everywhere and a table can almost always be found.'

If he wanted to impress her, he would choose La Colombe d'Or with its wonderful history, he thought. But it was tempting to take her to La Farigoule because that had been where he'd started flirting with her via text messages. Where he'd photographed the most romantic table in the establishment and had taken the risk of stepping well outside of any purely professional exchange.

Notre table, Laura. Une coupe de champagne pour toi, peut-être?

Another thought struck him then.

'*Oh, là là,*' he murmured. 'Is it *the* dress? The black one?'

'Yes.' Laura wasn't looking at him and she sounded slightly defensive. Was she embarrassed? 'You do realise I sent you that photograph by accident, don't you?'

'*C'était le destin.*'

She looked up then, and Noah resisted the urge to kiss her again and, instead, simply held her gaze long enough to let her know he was more than happy with what fate had delivered. It wasn't only because he had a feeling she would not appreciate being kissed with this lack of privacy. Something was warning him to be careful. To take this slowly so that Laura would not duck back into safety. And hide.

This was about more than anything physical, although he was confident that not rushing anything would make it worth the wait – for both of them.

There was an unusual extra dimension to this *brève affaire* now, however. Noah was genuinely curious about who the real

Laura was. And whether she, herself, had ever truly acknowledged the existence of that person.

They walked to the hotel, a three-hundred-year-old stone building that Noah discovered had been where the two Gilchrist sisters had stayed on their first trip to France. He listened to Laura's somewhat shy, but definitely adorable, efforts to speak in French as she responded to the welcome from the receptionist, who had recognised her, and completed the formalities to check in and get the key to her room on the first floor.

'*Montez les escaliers*,' he heard the receptionist say as she handed over the key. '*Allez tout droit et c'est la première pièce à gauche.*'

'I hope I remember those directions,' Laura said, as they went back into the street. 'My French is so rusty.'

'*Pas de problème*,' Noah responded. It wouldn't be a problem. Not if he was there. 'Now... where would you like to go first? The cathedral? The famous tree? The most beautiful street?'

'Everywhere.' Laura smiled. 'But... can I ask something else?'

'*Bien sûr, ma chérie.*'

'Would it be possible to go to see the lavender fields tomorrow? It's the right time of year, isn't it?' She caught her bottom lip between her teeth. 'I know we could just use a picture someone else had taken for the brochure but... I'd love to walk amongst the flowers in the sunshine and smell the blooms. It's...' She sounded even more shy than when she'd been speaking in an unfamiliar language – as though this was a confession she shouldn't be making? 'It's always been a dream for me to do that.'

There was a plea in her eyes that no man could have

resisted. She was asking *him* to make a dream come true for her.

That was when Noah knew exactly what he wanted to do for this astonishing woman who would only be in his life for such a short time. He would make her dream come true. He would, as far as possible, make everything as perfect as any dream could be.

He wasn't going to take her to either of the places she'd expected to go for dinner this evening, either.

He had something rather more fantastical in mind now. Something that would capture as many of her senses as possible. That would make her feel like she was walking right into the middle of one of her dreams.

The opportunity to make a couple of private phone calls came when he took Laura to one of the outdoor bars flanking the Grand Jardin. He ordered a flute of champagne and then snapped his fingers as if he'd just remembered something important.

'The camera,' he said. 'I left it in the pannier. Stay here and guard the champagne – I'll be back in... what's the expression? The shutting of one eye?'

'You were very close.' It was just a hint of a smile but it managed to reach all the way to Laura's eyes. 'It's the blink of an eye.'

Noah blinked just one eye at her. He already had his phone out as he walked to where he'd parked the bike and, when he returned, he was the one with a small smile playing with the corner of his mouth.

Noah was quietly confident that Laura would still be thinking about this evening when she was walking amongst the lavender tomorrow morning.

* * *

Laura wasn't much of a drinker.

It was a wonder she wasn't teetotal, really, given that she'd been so aware of the damage caused by drinking too much, but there was something about champagne that made it acceptable in moderation. For celebrations.

And this was a celebration.

Or had she taken that first, rather large, sip as she watched Noah walk away because she was trying to dampen the flicker of heat she could feel low down in her body?

The flicker had started with that wicked wink and had only intensified at the view she was getting now of the dark waves of hair that were long enough to cover the collar of a clearly beloved leather jacket. And those faded denim jeans that clung closely enough to define rather than hide muscles.

Oh, là là...

Maybe it was a tingle rather than a flicker. Not unlike the tingle from the bubbles dancing across her tongue.

She was halfway through her drink by the time Noah came back from fetching his camera, but he had easily caught up with her by the time she finished the champagne that was so deliciously dry she suspected it was a rather expensive variety.

With her head spinning ever so slightly and by no means unpleasantly, she let Noah take her hand and they walked around the corner of a large, ancient building to see a massive tree trunk in a circular garden, surrounded by paving. Its branches seemed to have been carefully pruned, the leafy shape much smaller than she would have expected for the size of the trunk.

'This is the Place du Frêne,' Noah said. 'And that is the

famous tree. They say it's five hundred years old, planted by King François I to mark a visit he made to Nice.'

Laura was scrolling her phone. 'Ah... a *frêne* is an ash tree. I was thinking that meant oak but I could see the leaves were different.'

'You were very close.' Noah's smile told her that he was deliberately echoing her words to him. That this was a phrase he might associate with her in future. The kind of phrase that became part of a private language for couples because it could bring back a special memory.

Like a wink...?

'An oak tree is *chêne*,' he added. 'Shall I take a photo of you looking at the tree?'

'No, thank you...' Laura was staring past the tree now, to where the street ended with a low stone wall. 'What's everyone looking at there?'

'Come and see. It's a lovely view of the valley of the Lubiane River. And the *baous*, of course.'

'*Baous*?'

'The mountains.'

Noah stood behind her as she stood by the wall and admired the view. So close that Laura thought she could feel the heat of his body and she found herself leaning back. Or was he leaning forward as he reached to point out a landmark? It didn't matter. Laura was quite happy to feel a frisson of physical touch. She was getting used to those flickers of heat. That tingle...

'*Baou* is an old Provençal word, I believe. I think the closest translation might be "barrier"? They are the first layer of the mountains. Behind them are the Mercantours and then the Alps. Vence sits just under the Baou des Blancs. There's a huge star near the top that lights up in December for the *la saison de Noël*.'

'Really? I'd love to see that.'

But they both knew she wouldn't be here at Christmas time.

Noah broke the silence before it could become awkward. 'The most well recognised is the third one, the Baou de Saint-Jeannet – the biggest and most dramatic of the four. I love to see it when I'm flying into Nice. It feels like I'm already home. Anyway... come... I have so much to show you.'

He took her to the most photographed street in Vence, narrow and notable for the plants and vines adorning the typical old stone houses. He showed her a tiny and pretty space between houses off another street, called the Place Vielle, that was apparently famous for being the smallest square in France. They went past the cathedral but didn't go inside to see the mosaic because too many tourists were blocking the doors. And, by then, it was getting late.

'I will take you back to your hotel,' Noah said. 'I will be back later to collect you for dinner.'

'Have you decided where you're taking me?'

'I have.'

'Are you going to tell me?'

Noah's smile was wicked. '*Non*,' he said, leaning in to place a soft kiss on her lips. 'You will love it, I promise.'

* * *

The nerves kicked in about the time Laura got out of her shower and looked at the black dress she'd hung in the bathroom so that the steam would remove any creases.

How on earth was it going to work, climbing onto the back

of a motorbike in a figure-hugging dress like this? Would she need to hike up her dress and bare far too much leg?

She couldn't wear her jeans, though. She'd already rinsed out her white shirt so it could dry in time to wear again tomorrow. Besides, she was quite sure that Noah was planning to take her somewhere very French. And very classy, like the famous restaurant in St Paul de Vence.

Maybe he'd chosen that restaurant here in Vence and it would be within walking distance?

Otherwise, she could suggest they took a taxi.

Or... she could trust that Noah would have already thought of that. He had, after all, promised that she was going to love whatever he had decided to do with her this evening.

Oh... Laura pressed her face into the soft folds of the towel while she took a very deep breath. Yes... that was what she was going to do. Because hadn't she already decided that Noah Dufour could do anything he liked with her this evening?

* * *

They had arranged to meet in the foyer of her hotel and, as Laura arrived at exactly the appointed time, Noah was already there, sitting in an armchair, his legs crossed. Waiting for her.

Looking impossibly gorgeous. In black-tie attire, but without the tie. He was wearing black trousers and a classic tuxedo that fitted so beautifully it looked like it had been designed especially for him. The jacket was unbuttoned. The white dress shirt also had a couple of buttons undone below the collar. He looked sophisticated but oh-so casual at the same time. Letting life wash over him but giving the impression he could take complete control in a heartbeat. He was the sexiest man Laura had ever seen but what was utterly enchanting was the way he was looking at her – as if *she* were the dream come true.

She was so happy she'd thought to bring this dress, and so pleased that she'd made the effort to do her hair and make-up as perfectly as possible.

Noah got to his feet and dropped a whisper of a kiss on both her cheeks.

'You look... beautiful,' he said.

'So do you.' Laura felt suddenly shy. 'But you don't look as if you came here on your motorbike.'

'I arranged a car for us.'

It wasn't just any car. It was a sleek black Mercedes sedan with tinted windows, leather seats and a chauffeur. Laura decided that Noah was taking her somewhere in Nice when she saw they were passing the airport, but they bypassed the city and headed up into the mountains again.

Sunset was still well over an hour away, but the light had softened noticeably by the time they turned off the main road into a town with a jumble of buildings on top of a hill that was a quintessential, centuries-old, French village.

'Where are we?' Laura asked.

'Èze. One of the most famous medieval villages in the South of France.'

'Like St Paul de Vence?'

'*Oui*. But the view from the top of the old town here is better. Also, my favourite restaurant is here.'

'Is it as famous as the Colombe d'Or?'

'The Château de la Chèvre d'Or is much more spectacular. And the food is...' Seemingly lost for words, Noah gave a chef's kiss.

Laura's stomach did an odd little somersault as she watched him.

'Did you bring your camera?'

'*Non*. Tonight is not about the brochure.' Noah leaned forward to speak to the driver in French that was too rapid for Laura to follow. As the car slowed to stop under the towering ramparts of the ancient city, Noah turned back to her.

'Tonight is about *you, ma chérie. Seulement toi.*'

Noah got out of the car and extended his hand to help Laura as she slid across the leather seat.

'We have to walk from here,' he said.

He didn't let go of her hand as they walked. The magic of stepping back in time folded itself around them as soon as they walked through the first arched gateway. It only grew stronger as they followed cobbled streets that had smooth terracotta tiles between rough-hewn stone borders and were steep enough to need low steps. As they got higher, they were looking down on the crowded, stone-built dwellings. The patchwork of roofs on different levels, with chimney pots like tiny houses on top of the curved tiles, made it feel like a town from a long-forgotten fairy tale. The rocks of ancient walls had the contrast of fresh greenery and splashes of colour from pale roses and sky-blue plumbago. Lush, mossy fountains had cool streams of water coming from pipes hidden within faces or creatures carved into the stone.

There were tantalising glimpses of the sea so far below on the way up the hill, but the uninterrupted view from the summit was enough to take Laura's breath away completely.

The sun was low enough in the sky now to light up the gleaming superyachts that looked no bigger than toys in the inky-blue scoop of the Mediterranean.

'Is that Saint-Jean-Cap-Ferrat?' Laura pointed to the finger of land in the distance.

'It is.'

'So, behind that hill are the *baous*?'

'*Exactement*.'

Laura soaked it all in for another long, glorious minute. 'It's gorgeous,' she murmured. 'Paradise.'

The sun was even lower when they made their way back down the hill, past restaurants with people sitting at candlelit tables. Their chatter and laughter, punctuated by the clink of glassware and cutlery, followed them around corners and the aroma of their food caught Laura's nostrils and made her mouth water.

'Here we are.' Noah was smiling as he guided Laura onto a new pathway. '*Bienvenue au Château de la Chèvre d'Or*.'

* * *

This had been a good choice.

The luxury hotel, with its complex of pathways, buildings and gardens, felt as if it had been clinging to the sides of this special hill long enough to earn its status as a jewel in the crown of the famous destination.

Watching Laura seeing it all for the first time made it fresh in Noah's eyes and sharpened his senses. He loved the *émerveillement* he could see on her face. He could feel her surprise at the tantalising glimpses of the terraced château gardens below the path with their remarkable, life-sized bronze animals standing on grassy ledges: a mother elephant and her calves, a horse, a giraffe. He could hear sounds that he might not have noticed normally, like the trickle of water from fountains crafted from the same rough stone that formed the pathways, nestled amongst trees and carefully clipped shrubs. He could feel the almost childlike pleasure of finding that one of the fountains had an elegant frog standing behind the stream of water, holding a lily leaf as an umbrella.

He loved the tiny, incredulous gasp she made when she realised they were being taken to the best table in the restaurant, right by the window that commanded the same extraordinary view they'd seen from the hilltop. It also looked out on the symbol the château was named for: the statue of a goat that looked as if it had been made of pure molten gold, standing on a pile of rocks so it gave the impression of climbing up to get the best view of his Mediterranean home as the sun completed its slow descent to the horizon.

Course after course was served and every plate of food was a work of art, with tiny edible flowers, colourful sauces and unexpected taste combinations to enhance the precise placement of every morsel. And Laura was clearly loving every bite. There were tiny versions of pissaladière – the local speciality, onion tart – a watermelon soup, a plate that simply had three spears of asparagus with a shower of freshly ground black pepper and a drizzle of sauce. There was a forest of mushrooms, prawns that were emerging from small puddles of yet another sauce that captivated the taste buds, and fish that had no skin but had been scored and sprinkled with flavourings to look like geometric scales.

Noah had eaten here many times before but, somehow, the food looked more impressive this time and the taste and textures of everything seemed enhanced. The wines that were paired with every course even more perfect.

'This is *so* good,' Laura declared, as champagne was served to signal the transition to dessert. 'It's to die for.'

'We say that in French, also,' he told her. '*C'est une tuerie*. Or *c'est à tomber*.'

The top of the list, as a *tuerie,* for Laura was the final dessert course.

It was a dessert that was a speciality of this restaurant. A lemon shaped from a shell of thin chocolate, coloured yellow and green. Noah knew that when you cracked it open you would find lemon cake and mousse inside. It would be delicious and it would be the end of this memorable meal.

But not the end of this perfect evening.

The car was waiting for them and he would take Laura back to her hotel very soon. Perhaps the pleasures of this astonishing day were not anywhere near over.

Noah had the feeling that the best was yet to come.

For both of them.

* * *

Une tuerie...

Something so good, it was to die for.

That could have been many things that day for Laura.

That first sight of Noah at the airport, lounging beside his bike. Waiting. For *her*.

That whisper of touch in his office when he was teasing her.

It was definitely that first kiss...

And every bite of that astonishing dinner had to be included.

But the absolute winner came much later.

When Noah hadn't let go of her hand until he'd pushed the door closed behind them with his foot. When they were behind the locked door of her gorgeous hotel room with only the soft light from a lamp on a dresser, long, delicate curtains rippling in the breeze from open windows, and a bed that had been turned down to reveal a cloud of pure white linen.

When Noah had lifted his hand with what felt like reverence and watched his own fingers as they traced her collarbone, from her shoulder to her neck, leaving a trail of fire behind them.

She could feel the pulse in her neck beating against his fingers as his gaze lifted to meet hers.

'I knew it would be this good,' he said, so softly she barely heard the words.

Not that she needed to reply.

How could she when his lips were already on hers?

Any fear that sex with Noah Dufour would not live up to the fantasy had already vaporised. When he slid the zip at the back of her dress open, moments later, and she felt his hands slide against her skin, effortlessly starting an ambush on every one of her senses, Laura realised that her fantasy had, in fact, been way off the mark.

But how could she have possibly known how this would *feel*?

Every touch of his fingers, his tongue and his body. The sound of the murmured words in his own language. The look in his eyes when she was bold enough to meet them. The scent of him. Oh God... the *taste* of him...

The way it was stealing not only her breath and her mind but her heart as well made it truly feel like something Laura *could* actually die for.

How extraordinary was it that, at exactly the same time, it could make her want to live forever?

So that this would never have to end...

8

Dawn hadn't quite broken when Noah returned the next morning.

On his bike, again. With another leather jacket for Laura.

'It's the one I used to wear many years ago when I had my very first bike,' he told her, as he held it out for her to put on. 'But it's warm and you'll need it. We have a long ride ahead of us, *ma puce*. All the way to *le plateau de Valensole*.'

How could she feel this awake? Laura wondered, as she slipped her arms into the sleeves and pulled the jacket around her. This *alive*?

She doubted she'd had more than an hour or two of sleep.

Noah gently eased the helmet onto her head. She tilted her chin and closed her eyes, not just to make it easier for him to fasten the chin strap, or even to focus on the touch of his fingers. She knew that Noah was thinking about kissing her and this would be her invitation. His acceptance was palpable even before his lips settled gently against hers for a heartbeat and then again, longer this time.

Who knew that it was possible to develop a silent means of

such intimate communication with someone when you'd been in their company for less than a single day?

Magic, that's what it was, and this was definitely not the time to try and analyse it, when being on the back of this bike again was a part of that magic, with her arms around Noah and the feel of his body against hers. When she could so easily imagine that she could still smell the scent of him. When she could feel the warmth of his skin seeping into her own body through the lining of the old jacket he used to wear when he was probably still a teenager.

They might be both fully clothed and hurtling through time and space but part of Laura was still in the rumpled sheets of her hotel bed, because those hours would always be the core of this fantasy that she was living. And for this part of the new day, at least, she could pretend that it was never going to end.

That she was going to live happily ever after inside a fairy tale in which all her dreams would come true. This was a game that Laura was giving herself permission to play because another part of her was all too aware that the clock was ticking and it would have to end very soon.

In the meantime, however, she could be in love with her prince. Flying on a magic carpet that was taking her to make a dream come true. In a couple of hours, with the sun far enough over the distant mountains to make this summer's day perfect, she would be walking in the purple sea of the lavender fields.

They stopped in a small village for a strong cup of coffee and a croissant. Except that it wasn't the plain croissant that she thought Noah was ordering for her that arrived at their pavement table. It was a pain au chocolat. Something so rich and so decadent it hadn't even occurred to Laura to ask for it.

But it was as perfect as everything else today.

Noah had known it would be. A quirk of his eyebrow and the glow of amusement in those golden-brown eyes told her to simply forget any rules she had about her diet and enjoy the treat.

She had to close her eyes as she felt the warm, flaky layers of pastry in her mouth melt away to reveal the velvety chocolate hidden between them. She had to lick away a smear of chocolate on her lips and, as she did so, she opened her eyes to find Noah watching her. He held a small cup of espresso in his hand, poised in mid-air as he gave her one of those slow, lazy smiles.

He knew exactly how much she was enjoying this mouthful of food, in the same way he'd known exactly how to touch her last night. And exactly how much time and confidence she'd needed to allow herself to experience what she'd believed only existed in the movies or the pages of a steamy romance novel.

Oh, *help*... the look in Noah's eyes now made her think he could guess what she was thinking about. She had to break that eye contact and try, desperately, not to let the heat of a blush staining her neck reach her face.

But she could feel herself smiling and her gaze met Noah's again.

'*Ce pain au chocolat?*'

'*Oui?*'

'*C'est une tuerie.*'

Noah's smile widened. '*Ouais. Profite, mon coeur*. Enjoy...'

* * *

Noah sipped his coffee. He hadn't expected Laura to be okay with him lighting a cigarette, but she gave her permission with a tiny shrug that made him instantly remember she had French heritage.

Maybe it shouldn't have surprised him this much.

Laura looked different today.

No, that wasn't true. She'd looked different at the airport yesterday because her clothes and her attitude had been a revelation.

But… she *was* different today.

She looked…

Noah hid his smile by pulling smoke into his mouth and releasing some of it in a perfect ring, watching it expand as it rose.

She looked like a woman who'd recently been made love to and loved it.

He'd known he needed to take it slowly with Laura. Right from when he'd met her he'd sensed a wariness that wasn't dissimilar to a wild creature that could flee and run at any moment. That was what had intrigued him all along, was it not?

To be as stunningly beautiful as she was and to be so… restrained, was that the word?

Controlled. Almost afraid to surrender to her senses, even for a moment.

But she'd surrendered last night. Strangely, it had felt as if this was her first time. Not for sex, of course, but for that level of satisfaction – the pleasure that was so intense it was almost pain.

Even more strangely, given that Noah had long ago lost count of how many women he'd taken to his bed, it had felt the same for him.

Because it had been so different.

The real Laura he could see beside him today was so different.

So compelling, but it was a warning that Noah could dismiss as easily as he stubbed out his cigarette. They only had a few more hours to be together. This was simply one of life's temporary pleasures.

Like a pain au chocolat.

Only much, much more delicious.

* * *

A rainbow-striped hot air balloon hung in the distance, between the purple smudge of the endless rows of lavender and the misty mountains far away. Closer, right amongst the lavender, were the ruins of an ancient stone building, with just enough of the walls remaining to show the peaks that had once held a roof and the spaces where windows and a door had made this a dwelling.

'*Parfait*,' Noah declared, using his camera himself this morning as he snapped photo after photo. 'Go into the field, Laura. I need a picture of you.'

'Are we allowed to do that?'

'There will be hundreds of people here doing that very soon. We're lucky we're early. See?' Noah pointed at the sign near where he'd parked the bike.

'"*Propriété privée*",' Laura read aloud. '"*Ne pas couper la lavande*".' She shook her head. 'People wouldn't really do that, would they? Pick the lavender?'

'*Pfft...*'

The sound suggested that there were things tourists could do that would horrify her. It made Laura laugh. Noah lifted his camera but she turned away before she heard the click of the shutter. She wanted to remember this moment forever, but a camera could never truly capture what she was feeling and she didn't want to remember anything less.

The earth between the rows of lavender looked recently tilled – a fine, dry mix of stones and dirt. Some of the lavender flowers almost reached the waistband of Laura's jeans. She stopped for a moment to inhale the scent, tilting her head back and holding out her arms, filling her nose and mouth and throat with the gorgeous herbal, floral, smoky aroma. She could taste it as much as smell it. She reached to lift the drooping head of the nearest flower to admire the tiny, individual blooms that made up the spear, and then let it drop to merge with so many others that it became a purple cloud over the straight green hedges beneath.

The only sound she could hear was the soft buzzing of what had to be a million bees getting on with their work. She knew Noah would be taking a photograph of this but that was okay. If her face was hidden, the memory that the image would evoke would be the one imprinted on her heart right now.

And in her soul.

She didn't want to be anywhere else in the world.

Or *with* anyone else.

She'd never been this happy in her entire life. So happy, she could feel the prick of tears behind her eyes for the *third* time since she'd returned to France. Why was she so emotional when she probably couldn't even remember the last time she'd cried as a child?

She blinked hard to crush the prickling sensation as she heard the crunch of Noah's boots on the stony earth. By the time he was beside her she was smiling. It didn't matter that it was a misty smile because she knew that he would understand.

This was a dream coming true for her.

It was huge.

If she hadn't already told him how much she'd wanted this, he would surely have known by the glitter of tears in her eyes because he knew that she would never normally lose control enough for tears to even form.

He knew *her*.

Better than she knew herself?

This alchemy had started to simmer when they'd first started messaging each other, but what was happening between them now – this ability to communicate with no more than eye contact – was not simply due to the words or images they'd shared. She hadn't realised how close they'd come to each other through the invisible dance of navigating what lay between the lines, the stories behind the images, or... the emotion behind the music.

Becoming close enough to build trust, on Laura's part at least, had only been possible by playing with time and taking as long as she'd needed to absorb every response. Persuading herself that it was still safe. Letting herself peep through a gap in her defences.

Letting herself live a little?

Because it had been with this man. This extraordinary man who was the opposite of everything Laura had always imagined she wanted but was actually exactly what she'd needed. He'd stepped into the most private space she had by sharing the grief of losing his sister – at the same age that her own life had changed forever when her father had vanished. That had taken their connection to a completely new – albeit sombre and slightly disturbing – level.

But Noah had balanced it perfectly.

With an evening out fit for a princess.

By making love to her as if she was the only woman in the world he could ever want to be with.

By making her dream of walking through a lavender field a reality.

'*Merci*.' Laura's whispered word faltered just a little. '*Merci infiniment*, Noah.' She searched for something more to convey how much this meant. '*C'est inoubliable*.'

This *was* unforgettable.

Not just the lavender fields.

Everything.

The corners of Noah's eyes crinkled but the smile didn't reach his mouth, which made it, somehow, even more genuine.

He touched her cheek and, as Laura's lips parted to take in another wonderful breath of the scented air around them, he let his fingers drift slowly down to lift her chin.

He kissed her then. Slowly. Deliciously. And Laura knew that she would never again catch even a whiff of lavender that wouldn't bring her back to this place and this moment in time.

Laura had never got this close before, and maybe it was only because this was such a fantasy, but she also knew, beyond any shadow of doubt, that this was what it felt like to fall in love.

9

Finally...

Noah could see the real Laura Gilchrist and she was even more beautiful than he could have guessed.

She was vulnerable and sensitive. A dreamer. Someone who could totally understand and appreciate the simple things in life – like the scent of lavender or the softest touch on her skin. Someone who had so much love to give but had, somehow, been so badly hurt that she had built walls to make sure that didn't happen.

She'd had her own share of grief, with the death of her sister's baby, but whatever had made Laura the way she was had happened long before that. Noah didn't need to know how.

He didn't want to know.

The sense of connection between them was getting too real. They were getting too close to dangerous territory. Noah knew when it was time to back away. Politely, of course. With charm, in fact. He'd had plenty of practice, after all.

Fate stepped in as he was kissing Laura in the lavender

field – a gentle nudge in the right direction. A tourist bus parked just behind his motorbike and dozens of people emerged with cries of delight to walk amongst the flowers. The women were dressed for the occasion in floaty white dresses and classic sunhats. One was even wearing a set of monarch butterfly wings attached to her back and arms. Their voices had already broken the silence, but a man who looked like a professional photographer was setting up to fly a drone and Laura's eyes were widening in shock.

The bubble of her dream had been burst. Noah took hold of her hand.

'Time to go,' he said. '*C'est parti, mon kiki*.'

He got her away from the tourist invasion before the echoes of the dream she'd experienced could evaporate completely. He took them down a side road, and when they found a field of sunflowers right beside another lavender field, separated by a city of beehives, Laura's smile finally returned with enough strength to light up those gloriously soft brown eyes.

They stopped to watch a lavender field being harvested. A tractor pulling an enormous high-sided trailer was keeping pace with the harvester, and lavender was pouring through a chute to fill the trailer. The field to one side of the vehicles was still a purple haze but on the other side it was no more than green stubble.

Noah didn't want the reminder that nothing lasted forever to be Laura's final memory of her visit to the lavender fields.

'What time do you need to be back to help Ellie?'

'We didn't make a particular time. I just said that it would be this afternoon.'

Noah nodded. '*C'est bien*. We have enough time, then.'

'For going over the photos? Choosing the ones we want for our brochure?'

'We can do that, too. While we have lunch.'

'Will we go back to Vence for lunch?'

'Why would we do that, when we have one of the most beautiful villages in France only a few miles away?'

The way Laura's eyes were widening this time was because of anticipation, not shock. It was so easy to bring joy into this woman's life, he thought. He could imagine a very young Laura looking like this when she woke up on Christmas Day and it made him curiously proud to be the person who was creating such happiness.

'Moustiers-Sainte-Marie,' he said. 'Famous for its *chapelle* on the cliff, its waterfall and its *faïence*.'

'*Faïence?*' Laura was pushing her arms into the sleeves of his old leather jacket and it gave Noah an odd sideways slip in time.

Was that why he'd always kept this the jacket he'd bought when he was sixteen, along with his first ever motorbike? Because he might have imagined his baby sister wearing it when she came for a ride on the back of his bike? Because it would have been a priority to keep someone he loved that much as safe as humanly possible?

He'd never let anyone borrow it before now. He doubted that he ever would again. He kicked his bike into life and revved it enough to drown any inclination to wonder why that might be.

'It's a kind of pottery.'

* * *

Moustiers was tucked into the base of two massive limestone cliffs and was divided by a small ravine with a river rushing along its base. There was a space to park the bike right beside the main entrance into the village – a bridge decorated with hanging baskets of brightly coloured flowers. The splash of the nearby waterfall was clearly audible and Laura could also hear the joyful tolling of church bells, but Noah wasn't taking her directly into the centre of the village.

The first narrow, cobbled street they followed had attractive shops and galleries, and one they walked past had a window filled with the kind of pottery Noah had told her about: gorgeous plates and bowls that were painted with bright red poppies and delicate stalks and leaves.

'I should get something there as a gift for Ellie.'

'We'll stop on the way back,' Noah promised. 'There's something I want to show you before it gets too hot.'

'Don't let me forget. She's got a thing for poppies now. And daisies. Because of the donkeys.'

'Oh?' Noah seemed to be heading away from the village. There were more houses than shops, their pale green, blue and grey shutters already protecting them from the increasing heat of the summer sun.

'That's what they're called. The names of the flowers. Marguerite and... oh, what's the French word for poppies?'

'*Coquelicots.*'

'That's it. The other one is called Coquelicot.' Laura pulled in a new breath as the street became steeper.

'I saw the *coquelicots* in London on a visit. The ones that were put into the moat at the Tower of London?' Noah didn't sound out of breath at all. 'To represent all the soldiers who died in the war? It was... *magnifique*.'

'It's the flower of remembrance. And it's the colour of blood, which makes it perfect to remember fallen heroes.'

'Not in France. We use the *bleuet*.'

'I don't know what that is.' Laura was shading her eyes, looking at the steps that lay ahead of them, leading up the side of the cliff. Hundreds of steps. Well above them she could see the turret of what had to be the famous chapel, the colour of its stone blending with the walls of the cliff around it.

'A little blue flower. I don't know the name in English. It grows wild in the fields. Like poppies.'

'A cornflower?'

'*Peut-être*.' But Noah's sideways look suggested he wasn't thinking about the names of flowers any longer. 'It's not as steep as it looks,' he said. 'And the view is worth it.'

He held out his hand and Laura smiled as she took it. She didn't care how steep this path was. The way Noah was looking at her right now, she would have followed him to the ends of the earth, even if it killed her.

It *was* worth the climb. The small chapel was guarded by elegant, pointy cypress trees. The final steps took them through an ornately carved wooden door and into the coolness of the interior with its vaulted ceiling, beautiful stained-glass windows and a gilded altar that featured the statues of the Madonna and child. Still holding hands, they stood in silence at the railing that protected the sanctuary, taking it all in, but then Noah let go of Laura's hand.

He took some coins from his pocket and put them into a collection box beside the stand where dozens of small candles were burning in layers of glass holders. He picked up two candles and offered one to Laura. Still in silence, they each placed a candle into an empty holder. Noah picked up a match, lit it from an already burning candle and held it out for

Laura. She waited for a moment so that he could light another match and then they both lit their candles at the same time. The spent matches went into a small bowl and, for another long moment, they both stood there, watching the flicker of the flames. It felt right that their hands found each other's as they honoured the people they'd lost in their lives.

It also felt like Laura had never been this close to another person – not even her mother or her sisters.

They stopped to take in the gorgeous view across the Valensole plateau, and by the time they were retracing their steps down the cliffside and could hear the church bells ringing again in the village, any sombreness from that moment in the chapel had dissipated.

'Look... that's why the bells keep ringing. There's a wedding happening in the village.'

They could see a small patch of the square beside the bell tower of the church and the froth of a gorgeous white dress as the bride and her groom were showered with flower petals or confetti by the waiting guests. Even from this distance, Laura could see the joy on the bride's face as she looked up at her new husband.

The sound Noah made suggested he might not share Laura's appreciation of the spectacle. She glanced up at him.

'You don't like weddings?'

'I adore weddings,' he said. His face was absolutely still, until an eyebrow quirked. 'As long as they're not mine.'

'Have you ever *been* married?'

'*Non.*' The word could not have been any more definite. 'And I never will be. The happiness people believe it brings is nothing more than a fantasy. It's not something I want, any more than having a child.' His glance was enough to tell Laura that she already knew why that was a given.

And she did. Of course she did. She'd felt the pain of his loss every second they'd been standing in front of those tiny candles together. The pain of losing his sister had been unbearable. The potential pain of losing a child would be unthinkable.

Was it also a plea not to talk about it again?

Fair enough. Laura didn't particularly want to discuss her own status as a single woman of her age. Why she'd preferred not to marry because she knew, too well, the disaster a bad marriage could become to everyone involved, including innocent children.

She was well aware, however, that many people assumed it was because no one had wanted to marry *her*.

So why would she want to even broach the subject with Noah, when she'd been able to believe that, for this blink of time in their lives, he thought she was perfect?

Instead, she gave him a look she could only hope he understood. One that said he knew all he needed to know about her. Why spoil it?

'Can we go back to the shop with the poppies? And then have lunch? Breakfast feels like forever ago.'

Noah laughed, and any threat of heavy conversations evaporated.

'*Tu a une faim de loup*,' he suggested. 'You are as hungry as a wolf?'

'*Oui*.' Laura smiled back at him. '*C'est ça*.'

'*Moi, aussi*.'

She watched as he turned away to continue their descent into the village. Yes... she could see him as a wolf.

A lone wolf.

Which fitted perfectly with everything that was so attractive about Noah Dufour.

He was alone but not lonely.

It was simply the way he preferred to be.

* * *

They ate lunch on the terrace of a restaurant built onto the side of the ravine right beside the waterfall, and the audible tumble of the water was as delightful as every course of their meal.

The food was on a different part of the spectrum of French cuisine to the gourmet dinner at the Chèvre d'Or last night or, indeed, the still-warm-from-the-oven pain au chocolat this morning, but the rich French onion soup with its Gruyère-encrusted croutons, the light soufflé with blue cheese, figs and honey and the crème brûlée for dessert were perfect.

They looked through all the photos on Noah's camera and chose their favourites for the brochure. There were probably too many but each one of them was enough to catch the eye and spark a dream of being here that could make someone consider buying a little stone cottage in the South of France.

There was one of the lavender field this morning, with the ruined dwelling and the blurred outline of the distant mountains. One of the red bicycle propped against the wall of La Maisonette, between the shutters of a window and the rose-covered archway of the front door. One of the little red car parked on the road, and one that Laura especially loved of the flowers Ellie had painted all around the walls of the child's bedroom.

She had to swallow the lump in her throat.

'This photo means so much,' she told Noah. 'The person Ellie was when she came here to France could never have done this. It shows just how far she's come in healing and… I think I understand why, now.'

'Why?' Noah was watching her intently as he listened.

Laura bit her lip, a little shy to share her thoughts. 'You probably don't notice because you've always lived here, but there's something about this part of the world that makes you feel different. I don't know what it is, exactly – maybe it's got something to do with the pretty villages, or the sunshine, or the people and the way of life here. *I* feel like a different person and I've only been here for a couple of days.'

Noah's smile made her think of a fond parent responding to something a child had said. It should have been embarrassing. It could have been belittling. But it was neither of those things. Because of the warmth in his eyes that almost made it look as if he was proud of her.

'You're not different, Laura,' he said softly. 'You've just found the person you've always been. Maybe because you've let yourself relax enough to forget who you've always thought you *should* be. Or because you feel safe here.'

He was right, Laura thought. She *did* feel safe. And she had discovered things about herself that could only have happened because she was inside a fantasy, but it wasn't just because of where she was. It was because of who she was with. She wouldn't tell Noah that, of course. She didn't say anything at all, in fact, because listening to that rich voice with its gorgeous accent was as musical and compelling as the waterfall beside them.

He was still watching her as he spoke again. 'The South of France is like a sigh, *n'est-ce pas*?' he asked. 'Like breathing out slowly because you've found what you've been looking for all along, even if you didn't know what it *was* that you were looking for.' The corners of his eyes crinkled. 'You have lived a little, *mon amour*. It feels good, yes?'

'*So* good,' Laura whispered. 'I will never forget any of it.'

Noah smiled again but glanced up to signal to the waiter that he was ready for the bill. 'I need to get you back,' he said. 'You and Ellie have things you need to do.'

Laura stood up at the same time Noah did and found herself so close to him that she caught her breath. And then he reached out and gently touched her with the tips of his fingers, just inside the open neck of her shirt. Over her heart.

'Look after her,' he said very quietly. 'The *real* Laura. The one that's been hiding in here.' He leaned even closer, brushing her lips with his before they moved to her ear. 'She knows what she wants. What she needs.' His breath was tickling her ear. 'Listen to her...'

10

Au revoir.

Goodbye.

The finality of the last words Noah had said to her was hovering on Laura's emotional horizon like a storm cloud.

He could have said *à la prochaine fois* if he'd imagined there could be a next time one day.

Or *à bientôt* if the idea of seeing her soon was appealing even if it wasn't likely.

But no... He'd said goodbye when he'd taken her back to La Maisonette after the most magical day – and night – of her life and ridden off into the distance on that big, black motorbike.

Okay... he'd added that gorgeous endearment of *mon coeur* to his farewell and the look in his eyes had made her feel that she had, indeed, won a permanent place in his heart, but... it wasn't enough to stop that cloud blocking too much of the light in Laura's life when she was back in Scotland.

She hadn't expected it to be this hard to step back into her real life and put that fantasy where it belonged – in a locked space that could only be accessed when, or *if*, she chose to.

Was that part of the problem? Wondering if this was actually her *real* life?

Of course it was. She would never have done the things she had done if she hadn't been stealing a scrap of time from reality to pretend to be someone completely different. Someone who had no need to stay trapped within the perimeters of the life she had constructed so carefully to give her the security she needed.

But what if there was even a bit of truth in what Noah had told her at the end of that amazing lunch almost under a waterfall? Was who she'd been pretending to be in France actually the *real* Laura? Had she been buried forever beneath layers of responsibility and fear and putting her own desires aside in favour of the people she loved?

The echo of other things Noah had said that day were also threatening to haunt her.

'She knows what she wants...'

'She knows what she needs...'

'Listen to her...'

But Laura wasn't listening. She couldn't afford to, when the messages might undermine everything she'd been striving for in her life until now.

She had to stick with the plan of 'what happened in France, stays in France'.

It was back to 6 a.m. visits to the gym and long hours at work, in the office and traipsing all over a significant part of Argyll to provide estimates on properties, secure listings, help the owners get their houses ready for viewing and then take clients through for inspections. She dealt with endless hours of paperwork and admin and design work for estate publications, newspaper advertisements and flyers, made hundreds of phone calls and attended too many meetings.

It should have helped that the market seemed to be taking off and Laura was riding the wave. She'd even sold a gorgeous but isolated six-bedroomed property on the Isle of Mull that had been on her books for over a year.

She should be happy.

She *would* be happy, she told herself. Very soon.

She was just... a wee bit out of kilter, that was all.

And maybe the fact that she'd started taking an oral contraceptive pill a couple of weeks before that memorable weekend had a lot to do with her low mood, thanks to messing with her hormones. She was getting various degrees of the other side effects she'd been warned about, like faint nausea and breast tenderness and annoying spotting that never quite turned into a proper period but wasn't going away either. She could make another appointment with her GP, or she could just stop taking it and see if that made a difference.

It wasn't as if she needed any protection now that she was back home. Who would she be having sex with? Colin Armstrong?

Oh, dear Lord... Laura had been in a meeting with the agency's CEO within days of returning and she'd found herself wondering how she could have had even a fleeting thought of hooking up with the local silver fox. Noah Dufour had raised the bar to such an extent that Laura had the horrible feeling that she was never going to find any other man remotely desirable. The thought of having such a passionate encounter with Colin that neither participant noticed the loss of a condom made her feel more than faintly nauseated.

Maybe that was why she was still taking the pill. Because she'd felt so relieved that she had taken that precaution in the first place. She'd not only seen the flash of fear in Noah's eyes when they realised what had happened, she'd felt it herself.

The reassurance she'd been able to provide for both of them had been priceless.

And... okay... maybe there was a wee spark of hope she couldn't quite douse: that it might happen again. What if there was some aspect of the sales process for La Maisonette that meant another flying visit was required? Paperwork that only she could sign because she had legal permission to represent all three of the beneficiaries of their uncle's will.

What if Noah was thinking about her as much as she was thinking about *him*?

The messaging between them, as they finalised their shared project, had changed. It felt as though they were both being careful not to overstep agreed boundaries but couldn't entirely dodge the new depth of connection between them.

Being unable to easily separate the lines between fantasy and reality did not sit well with Laura. Neither did the uncertainty that plagued her when she was writing those emails or text messages. She found herself adding an *x* or two after the *L* she signed off with and then deleting them.

She imagined messages she wanted to write but never would. She woke up in a cold sweat one night having had a nightmare about finding she'd written one and sent it by mistake, the way she had with that photograph of herself in the black dress.

I miss you...

I need you...

I think I might be in love with you...

* * *

It felt like loss.

Even though he'd been as careful as he always was not to

let someone become close enough to miss them when they were gone.

There had been something about Laura Gilchrist, however, that had crept into a place in his heart that it should never have been able to reach.

He made another visit to La Maisonette to take a few more interior shots for the advertising. Ellie opened the door to him with a smile that made him wonder if she suspected something *trop peu professionnel* had happened between himself and Laura during her visit. Or did she know exactly how unprofessional some aspects of their time together had been?

Sisters talked about such things, didn't they?

He'd love to know what Laura had said. What she might be thinking now.

Was she missing *him*?

Casually, as he noticed Ellie watching him as he started by taking photographs of the kitchen, he engaged her in conversation.

'I hear that you're thinking of driving all the way back to Scotland.'

'How did you know that? Oh...' Ellie shook her head. 'Laura. Of course.'

'I think she's worried about you driving such a long way by yourself.'

'I know. She told me I was completely bonkers. But I won't be by myself. Pascal's coming with me.' Ellie looked down and smiled at the little white dog positioned beside her feet. 'Laura might be my oldest sister,' she added, 'but the days are long gone when she gets a say in what I should or shouldn't be doing.'

Noah shifted to get a shot that used the kitchen as the foreground but included a view out of the French doors to the terrace.

'Was she very bossy?'

'Still is.' But the grin on Ellie's face faded. 'But... she was also *so* protective as well. She was like another mother for me and Fi.'

'She certainly loves you very much,' Noah said. He hesitated for a moment. 'She... told me about your son,' he added quietly. 'I was so very sorry to hear that you lost him.'

Ellie simply nodded. 'I don't think I would have got through any of it without Laura,' she told him. 'My partner walked out on me the day I told him I was pregnant, and she was there to pick up the pieces. She was with me the day I gave birth to my baby and—' Her breath caught. '—she was there the day I buried him.' It looked as though she was blinking back tears and Noah wished he hadn't said anything, but then Ellie smiled. 'Laura's the best sister in the world,' she said. 'She would do anything and everything for the people she loves.'

It was Noah's turn to nod as he agreed with her. 'She's very special.' He reminded himself that anything he said – or how he said it – might get back to Laura. He didn't want her to think he might have upset Ellie, so he tried to lighten the atmosphere. 'And yes, she is still bossy. She's not happy unless she's in charge.'

The affection in his smile was genuine. He'd seen through the impression that Laura had wanted to make all the rules, hadn't he? He'd had the pleasure of discovering that what she'd really wanted was to get swept off her feet and made to feel... special.

Adored, even if it was just for such a short time.

Even if it was only a game. Because she would never truly relinquish control of her own life. He respected that.

He knew exactly how important it was to be in control.

Ellie caught Noah's gaze and held it as if she wanted him to listen carefully.

'She's only bossy because she cares so much and she wants to try and make the world a better place. It's hard for her to trust other people. Or relationships. It wasn't just picking up the broken pieces for me after my partner walked out, she was trying to do that for our mother when she was only a child herself. Even before our father walked out on us.' Ellie grimaced. 'He was an alcoholic and he could get… abusive. I don't remember much of it – I was too young.' She paused. 'Sorry… Too much information. You don't want to know about our family history. I'm getting in your way.'

'Not at all,' Noah assured her.

But Ellie and Pascal went out into the garden and Noah finished taking his photos alone.

Except he didn't feel alone because he was thinking about Laura. It made him feel sick to his stomach to think that she might have been the victim of some level of abuse from her own father, but it made him understand on a much deeper level why she needed as much control of her own life as he did of his. And why the 'real' Laura had become so good at hiding. He could only hope that she wouldn't be allowed to disappear again. Not entirely, anyway.

When he left La Maisonette a short time later, he drove a little way towards Grasse to stop and take a photograph of Tourrettes-sur-Loup from a distance that could take in the whole walled medieval village on the hilltop, with the dramatic hump of a *baous* above Vence in the background. On his way back to his office, he stopped at a shop where he made a small purchase. To outward appearances, it was something any visitor to the South of France might enjoy as a souvenir.

But he knew that this would have far more significance for a particular visitor. Someone for whom this gift might bring back memories of far more than the scenery.

He asked for it to be well wrapped.

He didn't want it to break before it got to its destination.

* * *

A florist's van was pulling away from the Oban office of The Property Centre as Laura arrived back from an afternoon of viewings.

'Laura… these are for *you*.' The receptionist, Maureen, was admiring a large bouquet of sunflowers in a rustic hessian wrapping. 'Have you made someone very happy by selling their house for way more than they expected?' She didn't give Laura time to respond. 'There's a little parcel tucked in here as well. And a card.'

Laura's heart had skipped a beat. Now it was speeding up rather alarmingly. Surely there was only one person in the world who would think to send her sunflowers?

She tried to intercept before the card could be read but she was too late.

'Are you listening?'

'Erm… yes?' Laura waited to hear the message but Maureen shook her head.

'That's what it says on the card.' Maureen's eyes were wide. 'I know… *weird*, right?'

There was definitely only one person in the world who would send her that message.

Telling her to look after the person she really was. The version of herself that had been hiding for so long.

It took an enormous effort not to show any sign of the

squeeze on her heart that took her breath away. She even managed an almost dismissive shrug.

'Private joke. You had to be there.'

Laura's entire being was wishing *she* was there. With Noah. Right now...

'Who's it from?'

'An estate agent I was helping with a marketing project. We've just finished it.' It was getting too hard to keep pretending this was no big deal and her tone became clipped – a warning that this conversation had gone on long enough. 'He's just saying thank you, that's all.'

She took the bouquet in one hand, went into her office and shut the door behind her, leaning against it as she closed her eyes and held the bouquet tightly against her chest for a long moment. She finally moved, put the flowers down on her desk and took the parcel out to unwrap it.

It contained a tiny spray bottle of lavender oil. It was automatic to push the button on the top of the bottle to release a burst of the fine spray.

The scent of it threatened to utterly undo her.

She was back there. In France. With Noah. In the middle of the field of lavender in that space of time they'd been lucky enough to have to themselves.

Laura sank down on her chair. How on earth was she going to respond to this?

In the end, she only sent two words back to Noah, along with a photograph of the flowers.

I'm listening xx

* * *

The flowers had been unexpected.

The phone call from Noah only days later was even more of a surprise.

'We have an offer, Laura. The sign has only just been put in place. I haven't even put an advertisement in the window yet but I've just had a buyer's solicitor in my office to make an offer on their behalf – for the *full* asking price. You have the authority to accept it on behalf of yourself and your sisters, *n'est ce pas*?'

'I do… but I thought this was going to be complicated and take ages.'

'It can. But this is good news, *oui*?'

'It is.' Laura forced a smile so that she could sound sincere. 'Tell me what happens next.'

'I will send the initial paperwork to you for a digital signature and then I can draw up the *Compromis de Vente* and start the legal process. After that…'

Laura made some notes as Noah was talking. She really shouldn't feel this disappointed, she reminded herself as she ended the call. This *was* good news.

She made a call herself, much later that day. To Ellie.

With an effort, Laura managed to sound almost as pleased as Noah had been about the unexpected ease of the sale. This was exactly what they'd wanted, after all. It was just happening a lot faster than she'd anticipated.

'It's done, Ellie,' she told her sister. 'It's over…'

The problem of dealing with the unwanted inheritance of the little house in the South of France did seem to have been resolved.

But it wasn't the only thing that was over, was it?

Any connection Laura had to France – and, by default, to Noah Dufour – was also about to end.

* * *

Except, it wasn't.

Several things happened during the whirlwind of the next few weeks as the sale of La Maisonette was finalised, paperwork was completed and the cooling-off period came and went.

Ellie astonished them all by announcing that she was utterly in love with Julien, the man next door, and she was going to spend the rest of her life with him – and his young son, Theo – in France.

They learned that it had been Julien, in fact, who'd purchased La Maisonette.

Fiona came, for the first time in nearly a year, to have dinner with her mother and sister and the evening became a joyful, family celebration for Ellie and the new life she was about to begin.

And Laura discovered she was pregnant.

11

Laura wasn't *just* pregnant.

She was *well* pregnant.

Having finally given up taking the oral contraceptive pill when the annoyance of symptoms like the mild nausea and sore breasts didn't completely disappear, she had been prepared for it to take weeks for her normal cycle to resume.

She had not been remotely prepared for *this*.

Still stunned by the results of the test she'd done in the privacy of her own apartment, her fingers were shaking as she tried to count up the weeks. Seven? *Eight*? And didn't you have to add on a couple to get back to the first day of your last period, which meant...

Oh, *God*... was she approaching the end of her first trimester already?

Almost at the point of no return?

Was it, in fact, inescapable that she was going to have a baby?

Laura had never wanted to have a baby. She'd had enough

of a taste of parenthood by taking so much responsibility for her younger sisters.

She'd certainly never dreamed of becoming a single mother. Good grief, she'd seen more than enough of how hard it had been for her own mother, not only financially and emotionally but practically – every single day – as she juggled the demands of raising three daughters and providing for them.

It hadn't been easy for Ellie, either, despite having only one child and plenty of family support.

She *couldn't* have a baby.

Her life – the life that she'd worked so hard for, for so long – would be over.

The solution was obvious, but...

...but maybe it would have been a whole lot easier to consider that if she'd been facing it a hell of a lot sooner.

Or if she wasn't facing it entirely alone.

But who could she tell?

Laura had colleagues. She didn't have the kind of close friends you could trust to keep a potentially career-damaging secret.

She desperately wanted to tell her mother. She could imagine Jeannie opening the door and taking one look at her oldest daughter's face and asking what was wrong, and she could burst into tears and find herself in her mother's arms and... and somehow, magically, she'd know that everything was going to be all right.

But how unfair would it be to give her mother something new to worry about?

Jeannie Gilchrist was happier than she'd been for so long; Laura couldn't actually remember the last time she'd seen such joy in her face. The day Jack had been born, perhaps? If she was disconcerted by Ellie having no intention of coming back to live in Scotland, she was hiding it convincingly. Maybe the potential difficulties of coping with that distance had been tempered by Fi taking a step closer. The welcome back into the family home had been genuine but gentle. No awkward questions had been asked that might make Fi regret her visit.

The focus of the conversation over dinner that night had, of course, been on Ellie, and it was Laura who'd been able to fill in some of the gaps.

'No, I didn't meet him but I did think there might be some shenanigans going on.'

'Why didn't you say something?'

'It was Ellie's business. If she'd wanted me to know, she would have told me.' Her response had also been a promise to Fi that Laura wasn't about to start prying into her personal life.

'She sounds so happy.'

'Aye... she's happy. Did I show you the photos of the painting she did in the second bedroom of the wee house?'

'Have you got any photos of the donkeys? I said I might go over and make sure their feet are okay but... things have been kind of busy.'

'I have so many photos – of everything... Let me get my phone. I have to show you the lavender fields, too. Oh, my goodness... you can't imagine how beautiful they were.'

Laura had shared lots of other photographs over the next week or two, on the new group chat they had created that evening for the family.

Her phone was lying beside the basin, where she'd put it down after turning off the timer for the test. As she picked it up to open a calendar that would be more accurate than trying to do the maths on her fingers, there was a ping to announce a new post in that group chat.

From Ellie.

A photograph of her hand. Her left hand, with a beautiful diamond ring on her finger.

I said yes!!!

The text was surrounded by so many heart emojis that Laura was transported back to the night of the pinnacle of her career so far – the night of the awards dinner. When she'd received that shower of hearts from Noah.

Oh...

Noah...

Laura had been leaning against the wall of her bathroom as she'd stared at the test result. Now she found herself sliding down to end up in a crumpled heap on the floor, her head, as well as her phone, in her hands.

She heard another ping and she could see the messages coming up briefly on her screen as notifications. She knew they wouldn't be marked as read unless she clicked on them.

Fi sent the first one, with several open-mouthed emojis.

Wow!!! Congrats. So happy for you.

The next was from Jeannie.

Oh, oh, oh. I'm happy crying.

Laura was crying, too, but they weren't happy tears. Any thought of sharing her own news with her mother had just gone right out the window. She couldn't spoil this moment. And she couldn't tell anyone else, could she?

Certainly not Ellie.

Not after Jack...

Fi still felt too distant. She might not even be interested.

And Noah?

Oh, dear Lord, *no*. She'd promised they were safe. She could still see that fear in his eyes. It would be just as bad as telling Ellie.

Worse...?

Her phone was still pinging.

FI

Have you set a date?

ELLIE

No, but it will be soon. We don't want to wait. Will you come?

FI

Of course.

ELLIE

Where's Laura?

FI

Probably still at work. Or in the gym.

A strangled sound, far too close to a sob, escaped Laura. Imagine if she messaged to say she was sitting on her bathroom floor amongst the shards of her life, having just blown that up?

Call me?

A plea from Jeannie interrupted the rapid-fire exchange between Ellie and Fi.

I can't type fast enough and I have too many questions!!

It was a reprieve. Nobody would notice if Laura didn't respond for an hour or two. She could let herself shrink back from the maelstrom of her thoughts in the hope that they might stop spinning quite so fast.

Because it felt as if she had no chance to catch them. And if she couldn't even catch them, how on earth would she be able to control them?

And fix this?

* * *

After a sleepless night, the hardest thing Laura had ever done was to turn up for her customary 6 a.m. session at the gym.

But that was exactly what she did. Because this was the first step in taking back control. Surprisingly, once she was there and had settled into her warm-up on the treadmill, it became easier.

Maybe this was the answer. To carry on as if nothing life-changing had happened. She knew perfectly well that she couldn't ignore the problem for long, but even a few days might give her the time to process things enough to take the next step.

Nobody present at the staff meeting later that morning had any reason to suspect that Laura Gilchrist – The Property Centre's regional estate agent of the year – might be struggling to stay at the top of her game.

And the clients she met later that day, to take through a property listing she had in central Oban, had no idea of just how much they were messing with her head from the moment they arrived. Laura had known they were a young couple who were desperate to find their first home.

'It's Jamie, isn't it? Jamie McAlpine?'

'Aye...' He was opening the car door for his wife, Catriona, as Laura hurried to meet them at the gate of the property. She came to a very abrupt halt as she saw how difficult it was for the woman to get out of the low-slung sportscar.

'Oh, my goodness...'

'I know.' Catriona was laughing as she hung onto her husband's hands to get to her feet. 'We need a new car as well as a house. We're working on it.'

'Ah... how long have you got?'

'About eight weeks.' The young mother-to-be grinned at Laura as she rubbed the enormous bump of her belly. 'I know... it's twins.'

Laura had to resist the urge to rest her hand on her own belly. As if she thought she might be able to feel the tiny limbs of her own baby already? Her voice sounded slightly strangled. 'Congratulations.'

'Thank you.' Jamie's face shone with pride. 'If you can find us the house we need and we can move in before our entire universe turns to chaos, we might name one of them after you – even though they're both boys.'

The laughter broke the tension.

'Come on in,' Laura invited. It was a relief to turn away and walk in front of the McAlpines to where the front door of the house was already open. 'I think you'll find that this is a perfect family home.'

The three-bedroomed, end-of-terrace house was modest and needed a lot of redecoration, but they loved it.

'It's close to my new job,' Jamie said. 'I've been commuting for well over an hour in Glasgow and I'm over it.'

'Three bedrooms.' Catriona shared a look with him. 'I thought the third would only be a box room but... it's big enough to be a real bedroom.'

'And the other ones are more than big enough for two cots.'

Laura had a flashback to the child's bedroom that Ellie had redecorated in La Maisonette, with the tiny daisies painted on the curved top of the cot and the soft yellow blanket that covered the mattress. But the time travel didn't stop there. It went further back. Way back, to when she was only six years old and she was staring, in complete wonder, through the bars of a different cot, at the miracle her mother had just brought back from the hospital that day.

Her baby sister, Eleanor. She could even remember the feeling of falling in love with her – so hard it had been overwhelming, making her cry.

She could hear her mother's voice.

'What's the matter, hinny? Do ye no' like her?'

'I love her, Mammy... I love her so much...'

'Come and sit down, then, and you can have a wee hold of her.'

'It's got a garden on three sides.' Catriona looked close to tears. 'If we fix up the fence at the back, it'll be perfect for the kids to play in. I'd be able to see them from the kitchen window.'

Laura smiled, as though she could see the happy family picture herself, but all she was really aware of was the memory of baby Ellie being placed in her arms. The weight of her.

The soft, snuffly sounds she was making, like a wee piglet.

And, *oh*... the *smell* of her...

She'd been far too young to understand that she'd just fallen head over heels in love, of course. She did realise that her world had just shifted on its axis but she couldn't have articulated the knowledge that another human being had just become the centre of her universe. That her own happiness was going to be forever linked, inextricably, to the happiness of this person.

Laura had to push the disturbingly vivid memories of how it had felt to hold that tiny baby back to where they belonged, in the distant past, and slam the door on them. That was a completely different life.

She had been a completely different person.

'*Listen to her...*' Noah's voice came from nowhere. '*She knows what she needs...*'

That did it. Laura snapped back into the present.

'You've got a nursery and primary school only about a five-minute walk away,' she informed her clients. 'And I believe there's a medical centre in the local shopping precinct. I can check on that and any other questions you might have and get back to you later this afternoon?'

'I'm not sure we want to wait that long,' Jamie said. 'What do you think, Cat? Shall we put in an offer?'

* * *

Ellie and Julien hadn't wanted to wait too long, either.

The wedding date was set for the middle of December.

'Almost a Christmas wedding.' Ellie looked radiant when she video called Laura. 'How romantic will that be?'

'And you're going to do it in France?'

'It's my home now,' Ellie said simply. 'And... to be honest, there's this gorgeous church in Tourrettes-sur-Loup and the first time I went inside it I had a bit of a fantasy about getting married there. You could almost hear the echoes of wedding vows from hundreds of years ago. When I told Julien about it and that I'd been dreaming about marrying *him*, he said that makes it the perfect place for us to get married. We have to do the civil ceremony at the town hall first, but... oh... wait until you see this church. You will come, won't you?'

'I wouldn't miss it.'

'They don't have bridesmaids at French weddings. Or groomsmen. But we can choose up to two witnesses who will stand beside us and then sign the register afterwards. Will you be a witness for me? *Please*?'

'Of course.' It was more than two months away. The mind-numbing inability to make the decisions she needed to make would be a thing of the past by then. Life would be back to normal.

'I'm going to ask Fi to be a witness, too.'

'You're not going to ask us to wear pink, frilly dresses, are you?'

Ellie laughed. 'You'll be guests, not bridesmaids, so you can wear whatever you like. I just want you to be a part of the best day of my life.'

'It will be an honour.'

'I really hope Fi will feel the same way.' Ellie's smile faded. 'Do you think she's okay? Mam sounded a bit worried about her.'

'She came to a family dinner,' Laura said quietly. 'That's more than she's wanted to do for a very long time.'

'So you think she'll want to come to the wedding?'

'She said she would.'

'She said she'd come and see the donkeys but she didn't.'

'That means she's got two reasons to come to France now. Let's tell her how much we want her to come but not push too much. The last thing we want is for her to disappear again.'

'I'll try calling her.' Ellie sighed. 'I wish I could have had dinner with you all. I miss Mam's cooking.'

'We got the whole Sunday special that night. Roast beef and Yorkshire pudding, cauliflower cheese and those really crispy garlic potatoes she makes. Oh, and the gravy... How does she always make it taste *so* good? It's just as well she doesn't do it too often – I'd end up being the size of a bus.'

Laura was prattling. About *food*, of all things.

It was no surprise that Ellie was blinking in astonishment.

'Anyway... I'd better go,' Laura added. 'We'll talk soon. I want to hear all about what you're planning for your wedding dress. Will you have a veil? What sort of flowers will you have in your bouquet? And will Julien's little boy be involved? Do they have page boys or flower girls if they don't have bridesmaids?'

Diverting attention from saying something so out of character seemed to be working. Ellie was laughing.

'I'll get back to you. Looks like I have a whole questionnaire to fill in first.'

* * *

Why on earth had she gone on and on about Mam's dinner? Or made that stupid reference to gaining weight. No wonder Ellie had been gobsmacked. Her sisters were perfectly well aware of how disciplined Laura had always been when it came to her diet.

Had she been paving the way to excuse a change in her own body shape when she turned up to the wedding?

In case she was still pregnant then?

As if...!

She'd be... what, about five months gone?

If she wasn't going to spoil the run-up to Ellie's wedding by revealing that she was pregnant, would it even be possible to hide her secret well enough to make sure she didn't drop that bombshell during the actual event?

Good grief... where had *that* thought come from?

She wasn't still going to be pregnant in December. It was the last thing she wanted.

This was just one of those annoying voices in the back of her head that meant she couldn't seem to make the appointments she needed to make.

Okay... it was only one voice.

And Laura knew it was very likely to be the voice that Noah had told her to listen to, but she was fighting back. Arguing with her real self. Clinging on for dear life, in fact.

I don't want to be a single mother. The argument always started the same way. Look at how hard it was for Mam.

She managed. She adores all of us. Having us was what saved her after Dad walked out.

I didn't choose this. I don't want it.

But it's happened. And, hey... lots of women choose to be single parents these days – it's a perfectly legitimate life choice.

Not for me.

But what's the real reason for you not wanting to be a mother? It's hardly the challenge of doing it by yourself, is it? It's always been the fear that you might end up in a relationship that was as bad as your mother's. Or Ellie's. This way you still get total control over your life and how you bring up your child. You would be choosing this because you want it. So what if it's not easy? When have you ever backed away from a challenge?

I don't want this challenge. I love my life just the way it is.

Do you? Really? And will you still feel like that in ten years' time? You might regret this decision. What if it's the only chance you'll ever get of being a mother?

I couldn't do that to Noah. I'd have to tell him. It would be the worst thing anyone could possibly do to him.

Ah... Noah... The man who showed you how good life can be if you take the time to notice? How good sex can be. What it's like to fall in love...

Oh... Laura could feel it now. That unique sensation, some kind of internal fireworks, as if every cell in her body was contracting with a flash of joy unlike anything else life could provide.

Life's never going to be the same, is it? Kind of like knowing how it feels to be pregnant, isn't it? It doesn't matter how hard you try – there's no going back...

Laura had no answer to that but it didn't shut the voice up fast enough.

You miss him so much, don't you?

She did...

Long after that call from Ellie had ended, Laura still hadn't moved. She was sitting in the dark but she didn't get up to turn on any lights.

She felt almost paralysed by how alone she was. How lonely...

The ticking of the clock that had only come into existence the moment she'd discovered she was pregnant still wasn't loud enough to drown out something else she could hear, even though it was no more than a whisper now. That voice. The voice of who she really was.

This is what you want. More than you've ever wanted anything. Ever.

12

The pretty embossed white card was lying on Noah Dufour's desk.

He blew out a long cloud of smoke and reached for his glass of red wine.

Donc... he'd known that Ellie Gilchrist had become engaged to Julien Rousseau, but now the wedding date had been formally announced and it was a lot sooner than Noah had expected.

He was delighted to be invited both to the religious part of the ceremony in the church and also to the *repas de noce* – the wedding meal, which was only for the close friends and families of the couple. The time he'd spent with both Ellie and Julien over the course of finalising the sale of La Maisonette had resulted in an easy friendship between the men after they'd bonded over a shared interest in the old Citroën 2CV. Julien had learned to drive in one, his first car, when he was only fifteen years old. He'd taught Ellie to drive what she called the 'tin snail'. They planned to keep this little car forever, and Noah suspected that was because it was a symbol of the obvious and deep love they had for each other.

It would be a pleasure to watch them make their promises for a lifetime of happiness together but...

...but this meant that Laura would be coming back to France for another visit.

And Noah wasn't sure that he was quite as delighted about that.

Oh, he *wanted* to see her. He had no doubt about that. He wanted it so much there were loud alarm bells ringing. Which was why he'd waited until he was alone in his office to think about this properly. To decide whether it was wise to RSVP in the affirmative.

He was still missing her.

He had expected to feel her absence after such an intense time together on her last visit. He had expected to end up with some fond memories that he could look back on – as he had with many past liaisons. What he had not expected was to still feel a pull that was not showing any signs of a normal fading process.

He'd barely texted in the weeks since the final business matters to do with the sale of the property had been concluded. He'd sent a photo he'd taken of Ellie and Julien, looking as besotted with each other as any new lovers should, the day he'd learned of their engagement and turned up with a bottle of champagne to celebrate the news. He'd received a single heart emoji by way of acknowledgement but, since then, there had been a noticeable silence that he had chosen not to break.

Because it was time to move on.

Past time, in fact.

Why was he finding it so difficult? Why did he feel a connection to Laura that he'd never experienced before?

He knew the answers to those questions. He knew them off by heart because he'd thought of them so often. Not on purpose, of course. They were just there. All the time. Waiting to ambush him when he was least expecting it.

He could still feel the shock of seeing her eyes fill with tears as she stood in front of that painting of a mother and baby, and how he'd realised he could see through barriers he was only too familiar with to a woman who'd forgotten – or maybe she'd never truly met – the person she really was.

His dreams still reminded him of every touch of making love to Laura and the extraordinary pleasure he'd got from sharing what he was quite sure had been her first time to experience *l'émerveillement* of ultimate sexual satisfaction.

He could still see the delight of a dream coming true when she was standing in that field of lavender but, most of all, he could still feel the glow of those small candles in that chapel on the cliff towering over Moustiers. A glow that had somehow seeped right inside his body – inside his *soul* – as he felt her empathy. She knew his story and understood exactly why he could never allow someone to get past the barriers he'd built to keep his heart safe for the rest of his life.

They'd had so little time together and yet she knew him better than anyone else on earth.

Did she miss him anything like as much as he was missing her?

If she didn't, maybe seeing her again would be all that he needed to consign these disturbingly compelling memories to a mental vault that would no longer be a problem.

If she did, maybe another *brève rencontre* would be all that he needed to break the spell.

Especially at a wedding.

It might be the best wake-up call Noah could have devised. A complete cure.

He reached for his pen and the small card he needed to post back to respond to the invitation. He filled in his name and then ticked the first answer to the question of whether he would be able to attend.

OUI. Avec plaisir.

PART III

13

Laura had never been this nervous.

Ever.

The nerves had been there all along, to some degree, ever since Laura had come to the life-changing realisation that she couldn't bring herself to end her pregnancy. The weeks seemed to pass more and more quickly and the closer it got to this date, the more important it was that nobody guessed the truth. The best gift Laura could give her family was to not let her situation detract in any way from the best thing that had happened to the Gilchrist family in... well, it felt like almost forever.

Ellie's wedding.

Keeping her secret had been – at least physically – easy so far. Even now, at around twenty weeks, her bump was modest enough to be hidden with relative ease. It probably helped that all those hours in the gym had given her exceptionally strong abdominal muscles. It definitely helped that it was winter. The trendy, oversized jumper that Laura was travelling back to France in was perfect, teamed with knee-high boots and her first purchase of maternity clothing – a pair of skinny jeans that incorporated a stretchy panel that was invisible beneath the jumper. By the time she got through meeting up with Jeannie at Heathrow airport and they had boarded their flight to Nice, Laura was feeling perfectly confident that she had everything under control and that the dress she had chosen for the wedding would be equally successful.

She had tried on so many but finally settled on a style with draped cape sleeves, a gathered crossover bodice that knotted in the front under the bustline and scarf-like ribbons that blended with the ripples of the calf-length skirt. She'd found a dark green velvet jacket to wear outside on the off-chance that a breeze could reveal the change in her body shape, and the matching green fabric of the dress, with the addition of a hint of shimmer, was the final touch in distraction, It also fitted the brief that Laura had discovered online for suitable attire to wear to a French wedding. She'd passed that wisdom on to her mother and sister.

'*Think Sunday best*,' she'd instructed. '*But not a day at Ascot or a night out clubbing.*'

Had the idea of finding a wedding outfit that flattered her own curves been enough to have tipped the balance for Fi? It had been shortly after that advice that she'd broken the news that she wouldn't be able to make it to the wedding, after all. She was very sorry, she said. She'd tried to ask for time off work but it simply wasn't possible and she couldn't afford to lose her job.

At least Laura could be by her youngest sister's side on the most important day of her life. She knew Ellie would be very happy that their mother had chosen to be here as well given that she probably had reasons not to come that were just as compelling as Fi's. Jeannie was currently staring intently out of the plane's window as they made the final approach to Nice airport – over the sea, parallel to the shore, as dusk was falling.

'Look at that!' she exclaimed.

'What is it?'

'A star. A really huge star. It looks like it's just hanging in the sky, but it can't be.'

* * *

It was Ellie who explained the mystery to Jeannie as she met them outside the terminal with the rental car that Laura had organised online. 'It's the Christmas star. It's attached to one of the mountains right behind Vence. They light it up every year at the start of December. Isn't it gorgeous? You should be able to see it from your hotel windows.'

That was what did it. What threatened to shatter Laura's confidence that she could get through the next couple of days without being derailed by difficult, emotional drama.

'The *baous*...'

Laura's soft words were drowned by the rattle of suitcase wheels on the ground. Nobody noticed that she was quieter than usual on the trip towards that shining star thanks to the excited chatter between Mam and Ellie about all the final plans for the wedding.

It was completely dark outside now and Laura was focussed on following the satnav and staying on the right side of the road, but that didn't stop her remembering exactly what that mountain they were heading towards looked like. She had a mental image of it in the daylight from when she'd been standing at the lookout near the ancient ash tree. It was just as well she couldn't close her eyes for even a moment, because she knew she would still be able to feel Noah standing behind her, close enough for her to imagine she could feel the heat of his body. She couldn't stop herself hearing his voice as he explained the old Provençal word. As he told her about the Christmas star that would hang on the Baou des Blancs.

The fear that control was being lost hit her like a physical blow. This was it. Laura had almost run out of time. Somehow, after the wedding and before she went home, she had to find a way to tell Noah that he was going to become a father.

She still wasn't quite sure how she would do that, despite trying to imagine it a thousand times. She had wondered if it would be more manageable if she kept it businesslike and made an appointment to see him at his office, but that seemed too cold. Brutal, even, when he had no idea of the bombshell she was about to drop. Maybe they could meet for a meal. A coffee might be safer, though. What if he walked out on her as soon as he heard the last thing he wanted to hear?

'Laura? Are you listening?'

'Sorry… I was away with the fairies. It must be all the lights.'

There were fairy lights everywhere as they arrived in Vence, edging shop windows and looped against ancient stone walls. The cobbled streets of Vence had Christmas decorations strung across them and shop windows were sparkling with tinsel and silver stars. Lamp posts and fountains were wrapped in greenery and baubles. The bare upright branches of the plane trees around the central square had lights that made them look like giant crystal vases. And Ellie had been right – as they carried their bags up the steps into the hotel, they had a clear view of the massive star, hanging above them on the tip of the *baou*.

'It feels like we're in Bethlehem,' Jeannie said. 'I love it.'

'Isn't it pretty?' Ellie's smile was as bright as any festive lights. 'It almost feels like the whole world is celebrating with me and Julien. Oh... I can't wait for you all to meet him at dinner soon. And his family tomorrow – although, I have to confess his grandmother is a bit scary. Did I tell you, Laura, that Julien has become good friends with Noah?'

'Erm... no...' Laura actually froze, as if the wheels on her suitcase had jammed. Her heart was sinking like a stone. Being weighed down with dread. Surely not...?

'Yes. He and Julien's friend, Christophe the vet, have kind of made their own wine club.' She laughed. 'I call them the Three Musketeers, although Noah very cleverly suggested that maybe it should be the Three Muscadet-eers. You know, like the wine?'

Laura didn't respond.

'Anyway, they get together every week or two and have a tasting session. They're such good friends that, because Christophe is away for a family emergency, with his grandmother in hospital, Noah's stepping in to be Julien's witness for the wedding.'

Laura could actually feel the blood draining from her face. 'Noah's coming to the wedding?'

Amazingly, Ellie didn't seem to notice anything odd in her tone. 'Not to the civil ceremony, just at the church. Because I've got you to be my witness, Julien wanted one as well.'

Laura was finding it impossible to move again. It was hard enough to take a new breath.

Ellie still didn't seem to notice. She raised her eyebrows as if imparting something that she found intriguing. 'Julien said that Noah's really looking forward to seeing you again.'

Oh, *no*... this was just getting worse.

This was a real curveball. The memories invoked by the Christmas star had caught her off guard, but this was something else entirely. A scenario that Laura had not even considered mentally rehearsing. Breathing the same air as Noah Dufour was supposed to happen *after* the wedding. Preferably after Ellie and Julien had left for their honeymoon. Confessing her impending motherhood to her family was going to happen at an undetermined date in the near future – when she was back in Scotland and it was well past a time when the news could rain on any part of Ellie's parade.

Jeannie was shaking her head. 'French weddings are so different. Two ceremonies? And no bridesmaids? Is Noah that estate agent? The one who arranged the sale of the wee house? I seem to remember the name.'

'He is,' Ellie confirmed. 'But did you know that he took Laura all the way to see the lavender fields when she came over in the summer? On the back of his motorbike?'

'You never told me that!' Jeannie sounded shocked. 'I would never have imagined you'd do something as wild as that.'

'To be fair, neither did I.' Laura managed to find a smile. 'But I guess it doesn't matter *how* well you know someone. They can still surprise you.'

It was a gentle warning. She knew they had no idea of its significance.

* * *

The day of Ellie's wedding dawned with a clear sky.

Jeannie and Laura arrived to help her get ready and then get changed themselves. A hairdresser was coming and a car had been booked for the short drive to the village centre. Laura braced herself for the memories she knew would be waiting to ambush her as they arrived at La Maisonette.

A sleepless night had given her the time and strength to muster her courage to get through the day. Or perhaps it was simply the knowledge that she'd come this far so she had no choice but to see it through. It helped that she was seeing this through the eyes of Jeannie, who'd only seen photographs of the little stone cottage and its interior. It also helped that she knew her mother would be finding this difficult. Her memories might be so much older than Laura's but they had to be far more painful. This house had belonged to her husband's brother. The husband who'd walked out on her and their three daughters more than twenty years ago. The man who'd made life miserable for them all for too long before he'd had the decency to leave.

Jeannie did simply stop and stare moments after she walked through the front door.

'What is it, Mam?' Laura could feel the hairs on the back of her neck lift a fraction. 'What's wrong?'

'That painting...' Jeannie's gaze was fixed on the stone wall above the fireplace. Her tone was hollow.

Laura hadn't seen the large canvas before. It was pure Provence, with misty mountains and a stone building that was smudged but gave the impression it could be on the point of crumbling into a ruin. It sat in grass speckled with daisies and poppies. It had been done with thick, almost three-dimensional strokes of paint so that the image was lightly blurred – as if it was part of a remembered dream.

'Where did you get that?' she asked. 'It's... beautiful.'

Ellie looked as misty as the mountains in the painting. 'It's special, isn't it? I fell in love with it when I saw it at one of the summer markets, the first night I went out with Julien. And then he managed to buy it for me secretly and hang it up as a surprise on the night that he told me he loved me.'

But Laura wasn't really listening. She was watching her mother. Were those *tears* in her eyes?

'I've seen it before,' Jeannie whispered. Then she shook her head, quite sharply. 'But I can't have, can I?'

'You might have,' Ellie said. She, too, was looking at the painting, so she hadn't noticed the emotional reaction from their mother. 'I've often been wandering around when we've done video calls. Maybe you just saw it in the background but I never showed it to you properly.' She sighed happily. 'We're going to hang it in our house as soon as we come home after the honeymoon – somewhere we can see it every day. Oh...' she grabbed Laura's hand. 'Come and see my dress. It's hanging in the bedroom...'

The dress was stunning enough on its hanger. When Ellie wore it, framed by a gossamer-thin veil on a headband of tiny daisies pinned to an updo that left long coils of her hair to hang loose, it was even more breathtaking.

The underdress was a simple ivory silk sheath that fell softly in the front but fanned out into a small train at the back. Over the top was another layer with long sleeves and a high scooped neckline – white lace that was exquisitely embroidered with flowers in the same shade of ivory as the underdress.

'I've never seen you looking *so* beautiful,' Laura said softly to her sister. 'I'm in danger of ruining my mascara by crying as much as Mam today. I keep thinking of when she brought you home from the hospital and I got to hold you and it was like I'd been given the best present ever. I love you so much. You know that, don't you?'

'I love you, too,' Ellie whispered back. 'And I love your dress. And that jacket. You *always* look amazing but there's a kind of glow about you today. *Oh...*' She ignored the knock on the door – it had to be the driver of the car waiting to take them to the town hall – so that she could hug Laura. And then her mother, who was looking like the perfect mother of the bride in a lavender dress with a matching chiffon coat.

'We *all* look amazing,' Ellie declared as they headed for the door. 'I'm sad that Fi couldn't make it but I'm *so* happy you're both here with me.'

The civil ceremony, conducted by the mayor of Tourrettes-sur-Loup, took less than half an hour and was attended only by close family. It was a complete blur to Laura because every minute that ticked past was closing the gap while, ironically, tearing her apart.

She wanted to see Noah again. So much so, it felt like desperation.

But she didn't want to see him again. Because she was terrified of what she had to do.

Not today, though, she reminded herself. Or tomorrow.

Would it be any easier if she could pretend that she'd stepped out of her real life once more? Like she had on her last visit to France, when she'd given herself permission to be someone else. To do things she would have never ever allowed herself to do?

When she could be someone who was able to relinquish control enough to fall in love...

Could she, this time, *retain* control enough to keep her secret hidden?

For Ellie's sake.

For her whole family's sake on this, the happiest day of her youngest sister's life. A family occasion being made even more joyous by the fact that it was happening not only in such a magical part of the world, but at such a special time of year – a time to celebrate families and then ring in the new year and new beginnings.

Yes... she could do this.

She had to.

* * *

They walked the short distance from the *mairie* to the beautiful church near the main road, much to the delight of tourists, who took photographs of the wedding party as they walked the cobbled streets between tall stone buildings and through romantic archways. A crowd had gathered outside the doors to the ancient church, and Julien's small son, Theo, looking adorable in a suit and tie, was waiting at the door with his grandmother. His father crouched down to speak to him and Laura guessed that he was making sure he was still feeling brave enough to be the *garçon d'honneur*, tasked with walking alone in front of the bride as she entered.

Laura had been instructed to go inside with Julien to wait for the grand entrance of the bride, who would enter on the arm of her mother in the absence of a father to escort her. Julien would stand on the right, beside his witness. Laura would stand on the left, leaving room for Ellie between herself and Julien. There would be only two people between herself and Noah. Was it possible that she might have the whole of this ceremony to get used to being that close to him again and to prepare herself for making eye contact with him?

She saw him the moment she walked into the astonishingly pretty church with its internal archways and vaulted ceiling, gilded statues and enormous medieval flagstones on the floor and... white flowers everywhere. Bunches of gypsophila were tied with silk ribbons onto the dark wooden chairs at the aisle end of the rows and there were huge bouquets of lilies framing the front of the church where the other witness to the wedding was standing.

Noah looked as if he was wearing the same tuxedo he'd worn the night he took her to dinner at the Château de la Chèvre d'Or. It was possibly the same dress shirt, but it was buttoned up today. He was wearing a tie. Not an ordinary tie. Or even a bow tie. This one was a thin ribbon – the kind she could imagine a cowboy wearing.

A maverick.

Exactly the man she knew Noah Dufour to be.

She had no more than the time it took to take a breath to get used to seeing him again in real life, because he was looking straight at her. It almost felt as if he'd been waiting for this moment, and she could feel the intensity of that eye contact instantly and so definitively it could have been a physical touch. The sensation of something melting deep within her belly was so familiar. Even if she'd refused to acknowledge it, she'd felt it the first time they'd ever met, in his office when he'd looked at her as if she was perfect.

That delicious melting sensation had been amplified when he was waiting for her at the airport that day and they'd both known they were unleashing an attraction that would lead inexorably to an intimate encounter. It had reached a whole new level when he'd kissed her that first time and sent a thrill that even now could reach every cell in her body with the speed of light, and it had disappeared totally off any chart she could have imagined when he'd made love to her that night. It had still been there when he'd been getting ready to say goodbye to her.

When he'd told her to listen to the real Laura because she knew what she wanted.

Oh my...

As she followed Julien down the aisle of this amazing church, she could imagine *she* was walking towards the man she loved enough to marry.

She'd realised that she was in love with Noah but, somehow, those feelings had been put aside – buried, even – during the emotional journey of dealing with the fact that she was pregnant. They were coming back in full force right now but, even so, she would never want to *marry* Noah. The dark flip side of that coin – when it went terribly wrong – was far too well engrained for Laura to want to go there even if it seemed that Ellie had, miraculously, managed to get past her own relationship disaster. She'd found the holy grail of being able to not only love someone enough to marry them, but also to have the level of trust it took to give them so much power over how happy you could be.

But Ellie's happiness was, as always, contagious and Laura's heart so was full of it she was feeling misty as she kept walking towards Noah. She could almost believe it was possible to feel it was worth taking that kind of risk. That you could love someone with all your heart and soul and it could feel like it would last forever. That the fairy tale could be real.

And Noah Dufour was the only man that was part of any fairy tale for Laura.

What was Noah thinking as she walked towards him? He looked almost sombre but there was a warmth in his eyes that looked like the glow of every memory they had made together.

If she let herself, she could believe that it looked like love.

The kind of love she could see in Ellie's face as she walked slowly down the aisle. The kind she could hear in Julien's voice as he made his vows to his bride. It was easy to understand the

French that followed the traditional rhythm of lifelong commitment to have and to hold, for richer or poorer...

'...dans la maladie et dans la santé, pour aimer et chérir, jusqu'à la mort nous sépare...'

The tears gathering in Laura's eyes weren't simply due to the emotion of her baby sister pledging her undying love to the man she had chosen to share her life with.

There was an embryonic grief there as well. Because Laura knew that Noah was going to feel completely betrayed if she told him she was going to have his baby. Any hint of love in the way he looked at her would be replaced by shock and then... oh, God... would it flip into hatred?

If she told him? Where had that slip come from? It was a matter of *when*. There was no *if* about it.

There was no escape. She couldn't keep it hidden much longer. She didn't want to, because it was getting harder to deny herself the support she knew her family would provide. She didn't have to tell them who the father was, but Ellie would join the dots as soon as she did the maths. She already suspected that something had gone on between her and Noah. Julien was friends with Noah, so he would find out and he would feel even more betrayed if that information came from someone other than herself. She would lose even the faintest possibility that he might, one day, forgive her.

The guests, including Laura, left the church first to gather around the door ready to throw rice and flower petals over the happy couple as they emerged through the doors to the joyous sound of the bells ringing. They would be driven to the champagne reception next, and the Gilchrist family had been warned that there would be a lot of honking of car horns as they travelled. It was the same restaurant where the more intimate dinner – the *repas de noce* – would happen later. Where there would, no doubt, be speeches and dancing and everything that came with the celebration of a marriage.

Not that Laura would be dancing. She never danced, but just imagining having Noah as her partner and his hand brushing her belly was enough to send a chill down her spine. No amount of fabric could hide the truth then.

How ironic was it, that the reception was going to be at the Colombe d'Or? The restaurant that Laura had expected to be taken to when Noah had, instead, taken her to the Chèvre d'Or.

The night that the baby girl hidden beneath the soft folds of her shimmery green dress had been conceived.

As if she knew she was being thought about, the baby moved. This ripple of sensation was still new and amazing but the soft kick of miniature feet felt more like a protest this time.

Tell him... I'm his child, too. You have to tell him tonight...

14

This wasn't Laura.

Not the *real* Laura. This was the Laura that Noah had almost forgotten – the buttoned-up, in-control estate agent who'd made no effort to conceal her disapproval of his self-indulgent lifestyle.

It was surprisingly disappointing. A little heartbreaking, even.

Especially given that it hadn't felt like that in the church, when he'd seen her enter behind Julien and his mother. When her gaze had found him in no more than a blink of time, as if she was responding to the irresistible magnetic pull he was aware of himself.

The feeling of that pull was gone by the time she took her position as one of the witnesses. And that was a good thing, he had reminded himself more than once during the ceremony. That was why he'd wanted to be a part of this wedding. That *was* the cure. He knew that both versions of Laura felt the same way about marriage as he did. If she'd been hanging on to any desire to revisit that *affaire* they'd both enjoyed so much, she would be finding this ritual of commitment just as much of a wake-up call as he'd intended it to be for himself.

No wonder she was tapping into the image she had honed over so much of her life. It was a signal that he would not be welcome to get close again even if he gave in to the pull of temptation. Noah was absolutely on board with her stance, because it made the intensity of his desire to have this woman in his bed again irrelevant and therefore so much easier to dismiss. It wasn't going to happen.

He did have to steel himself when they arrived at the reception venue, however. This was a restaurant he'd told Laura about. One of the lures he'd shamelessly played with to get her to come back to France, to give him the opportunity to discover whether she was as perfect as he'd thought from that first moment she'd stood in front of him.

There was nothing to do other than mingle with the guests and drink champagne until Julien and Ellie returned from the first round of wedding photography: shots of the happy couple in and around the medieval walled village. Group photos would be taken here, on the terrace. The ancient grapevines that provided welcome shade during the summer were bare of leaves but the generous strands of tiny lights woven between the thick stems were a seamless part of the silver and white wedding décor.

He had to steel himself again when he saw Laura standing alone on one side of the terrace. Taking a deep breath, he collected two flutes of champagne from a silver salver held aloft by a passing waiter and went towards her without a beat of hesitation.

'Bonjour, Laura. It's good to see you again.' He smiled as he offered her the glass. '*Une coupe de champagne pour toi, peut-être?*'

Using that particular phrase had been deliberate but perhaps unwise. Because he saw that Laura remembered the first time he'd used it, when he'd sent that photograph of the romantic table at La Farigoule, the day she'd returned to Scotland after they'd first met. The photograph that, quite possibly, had been the catalyst for the entire flirtation that had followed, as well as its memorable finale.

For a heartbeat, he saw the *real* Laura again.

More than that, he felt the brush of her skin against his own as he reached to offer her the glass. When she took it, he would be able to kiss each of her cheeks because it was only polite to *faire la bise* on greeting someone he knew so well.

And, *oh, mon Dieu...*

This was worse than he could have imagined.

That fleeting touch might have only lasted a nanosecond but it was enough to bring every one of his senses to an almost painful level of awareness. Flashes of memory that were crowding his head but being felt throughout his entire body. The sounds and scents of making love. The taste and touch. Even the visual memories were somehow blurred into something more like emotion than mere images.

He didn't want to be here, trapped in this crowd of people. He wanted to be alone. With Laura. Somewhere no one could find them, for a very long time.

But...

But Laura was pulling her hand back. Sharply – as if she'd been burned.

'No, thank you,' she said. 'I don't want any champagne.'

It felt like she would reject anything he offered. How had his touch become so distasteful to her?

Noah didn't understand and the rejection was hurtful. He hadn't promised her anything that he hadn't delivered, had he?

Were her memories of their, albeit brief, time together completely different to his own?

He stood there, holding two untouched glasses of champagne in his hands, feeling foolish, but rescue came from an unexpected source as Laura's mother walked towards them.

'*Bonjour*, Madame Gilchrist.'

'*Bonjour*, Monsieur Dufour.'

'Please, call me Noah. This is such a happy occasion for your family,' he said. 'I'm also delighted to be here. And look... I happen to have two glasses of champagne. One for each of us.'

Jeannie was happy to accept the drink and Noah couldn't help a flick of a glance towards Laura as he remembered the way she had flinched at the offer. She averted her gaze swiftly, but not fast enough to hide a flash of... what was it?

Fear?

Noah could feel himself frowning. Was Laura afraid of her mother – and perhaps, Ellie – finding out how well she knew him? Would they be shocked? Any hint of the real Laura that he had discovered was certainly not visible. Had she always been hiding from her family? Had she ignored his advice to take more notice of what *she* wanted than what those around her expected?

How sad was that?

But wasn't this what he had been seeking all along?

The cure?

He didn't want to be endlessly thinking about Laura Gilchrist in the future, especially if he was worried that she wasn't happy. Her demons were not his problem. He didn't want to care *this* much. He had no idea how she'd slipped through his defences to this degree, but he had to repair the damage before it got any worse.

It would only take a few hours and then he could slip away from this gathering, having done everything he had been asked to do. In the meantime, it wouldn't be difficult for him to play the part of nothing more than a friend of the bride and groom. His ability to be charming and polite but not actually engage with people on more than a superficial level had been polished over years of working in the real estate industry.

He could make it easy for Laura to keep hiding.

Because he would be hiding himself.

* * *

She couldn't go home.

They were all supposed to go home the day after the wedding, following a lunch at a small restaurant in Tourrettes-sur-Loup that was between the *mairie* and the church. This was just a casual family meal and Laura was wearing her oversized jumper, skinny jeans and boots again. Her small suitcase was with her mother's, tucked into a corner. Julien's mother and grandmother would be leaving afterwards, taking Theo and the little dog, Pascal, and driving back to their home in the mountain village of Roquebillière while Julien and Ellie would fly to Paris for a very brief *lune de miel*. Laura had a ticket to accompany Jeannie back to Scotland but she knew she wouldn't be able to forgive herself if she boarded that plane.

She couldn't go home yet because she still hadn't told Noah and it was completely unacceptable to convey what she had to tell him by a written message or a long-distance call.

She had hoped there would be a chance to have a private word last night, even if was only to arrange to meet this morning but, despite how charming he was being to everyone and especially her mother and sister, it felt as though the only opportunity Noah had wanted to offer had come with a glass of champagne and a private reminder of how their affair had started.

And she'd refused to accept the offer.

She couldn't blame him for being offended.

It had been a relief that they weren't seated too close to each other at the tables for a meal that went on for course after course of amazing food that Laura could barely taste. She'd listened to speeches and watched a montage of images of Ellie's childhood that she'd helped to gather in recent weeks.

The final course of the dinner had been the wedding cake, a stunning croquembouche – a tower of small profiteroles filled with crème pâtissière and thinly coated with crispy caramel – decorated with spun sugar tendrils and silver glitter, which had arrived encircled by fizzing sparkler firework sticks. Laura had been as enchanted as everyone else, but when she'd looked away from its grand entrance, Noah had gone. He'd slipped out without saying goodbye and simply vanished into thin air.

After a largely sleepless night, she had taken her phone out this morning to text him, with the intention of making an arrangement to meet, but her mother had knocked on her door while she was trying, and failing, to find a way to even begin the message.

'Did you get the link from Ellie?' she asked. 'With the first wedding photographs? Oh, my goodness. I can't believe how beautiful they are.'

It had been all too easy to gift herself just a few minutes of procrastination, but those minutes led to more and now they were all looking at the photographs again during lunch, hours later with Jeannie one side of her and Ellie on the other, trying to pick their favourites to forward to Fi.

'This one,' Jeannie said. She turned her phone around so they could all see the image – a view of Julien and Ellie walking away from the photographer, hand in hand through a narrow, cobbled alleyway in St Paul de Vence.

Ellie's choice was one where she was leaning back against a stone wall with a trail of clinging ivy, beside a giant, terracotta plant pot on one of the steps of the steep street, beneath a quirky sign advertising an antique shop. Julien had one hand on the wall, his other cupping Ellie's chin as he kissed her.

The palpable tenderness of the moment captured forever was enough to bring tears to Laura's eyes.

Oh, *help*... She blinked them back.

'Laura?' Her mother's voice held a note that suggested her uncharacteristic level of emotion hadn't gone unnoticed. 'What's your favourite, hen?'

'Ah...' Laura was grateful for an excuse to spend a few seconds scrolling through images on her phone. Gathering her composure. 'This one's lovely.'

The happy couple were standing beside a tiny chapel just down the road from the Dufour Immobilier offices. 'I remember standing right there with Ellie myself on our first visit. It's such a lovely view of St Paul de Vence in the background.'

Ellie's choice was definitely one of her own favourites. Or maybe it was one of the less formal pictures that had been taken on the outdoor terrace of the Colombe d'Or, the lack of greenery in the roof of twisted old grapevines more than made up for by thousands of tiny lights. Or the indoor shots of the beautifully set tables in the private area of the restaurant, with the background of beautiful artworks on walls of pale plaster mottled with the patina of time and smoke. There was a picture of Noah, with his guitar, playing and singing what had to be the most romantic song she had ever heard, even if she couldn't understand the words well enough.

He had taken off his jacket by then and rolled up the sleeves of his white shirt. The string tie had been loosened, and his hair...

Ohh... it looked as if someone had run their fingers through it to make it so tousled, and Laura's heart had been breaking with the longing that she could have been the one to have done that.

She had wanted desperately to let every one of her senses soak this in but she hadn't dared let her gaze rest on him as he sat on a wooden bench beneath windows that looked out onto the terrace, wall sconces with flickering candles on either side. If he'd looked up and made eye contact, he would have been able to see into her soul, and Laura knew the rejection that would come as he recognised how she felt about him might very well feel like the end of the world. So she'd kept her head down and allowed only the sound to fold itself around her bones.

But... she could secretly print this photograph and keep it somewhere very private. She could show it to her daughter when she was old enough to understand.

That's your papa...

Ellie reached across the table to touch her hand. 'Are you okay?' she asked.

Laura found a smile. 'Just tired,' she said. 'It was an amazing party but I'm not used to such late nights. And... I haven't been sleeping that well lately, anyway. Work's been a bit... stressful, I guess.'

'You need a break,' Jeannie said firmly. 'You work far too hard, Laura. You've been looking a lot more stressed than usual lately.'

'It's nearly Christmas. I'll get a couple of weeks off soon.'

'Why don't you stay here for a couple more days?' Ellie suggested. 'You wouldn't have to pay for the hotel. You can have La Maisonette all to yourself. It's got everything you could need. You could keep the rental car and go anywhere you want, but I can guarantee a peace and quiet in La Maisonette that you could never find anywhere else. There's something else there, too... Something special about that wee house. Something magical.'

Laura opened her mouth to say that she couldn't possibly not return to work as planned but then pressed her lips together. That wasn't true. She had nothing scheduled that couldn't be postponed. And this was it. Another chance. If she didn't take it she might end up getting on that plane later this afternoon and then she'd have to live with the lifelong guilt of not having done what she knew was the right thing to do.

'You know what?' Somehow, Laura managed to keep her voice neutral, even though her heart rate had picked up and nerves were making her stomach clench. 'I just might do that.'

* * *

The text message was unexpected.

Noah had assumed that all the Gilchrist women were out of town, either in Paris or Scotland. He believed that the awkward, overly formal, interactions with Laura at the wedding were the last he would ever have with her, face to face.

But maybe not?

For some inexplicable reason, Laura had decided to stay. Not only that but she was asking to see him.

I need to talk to you, Noah. But not on the phone, please. I'm staying at La Maisonette.

Noah took his time, finishing his cigarette and glass of wine. Absorbing the shock – or was it possibly delight – of this message.

Judging by his disturbed sleep last night, being present at a wedding ceremony hadn't quite provided the cure he needed to be free of this... obsession with Laura Gilchrist.

Maybe he *was* the only person that Laura felt she could be entirely herself with. She might want to apologise for that hurtful coolness towards him because of the presence of her entire family.

Talking to her might help.

But could he be that close to her and not want more?

Of course not. But whether something more happened was entirely up to Laura.

Could *that* turn out to be the cure?

Did he just need to be with her once more because it couldn't possibly be as good as he remembered the first time being? He'd made it into some kind of fantasy that was endangering the potential enjoyment of any future liaisons, and that really needed to be sorted so that he could move on. Properly. All it might need was a dose of reality. It would be good – he hadn't the faintest shadow of doubt about that – but it wouldn't be *that* good. Nothing ever was.

He stubbed out his cigarette. There was a wine shop just over the road and he knew they would have an excellent, and well chilled, bottle of champagne available.

He finally answered the text.

À très bientôt

* * *

The path to the front door of La Maisonette looked so different to the last time he'd been here with Laura. There were no lavender flowers on either side of the pathway or pretty roses smothering the stone archway of the entrance. There was none of that heady anticipation, either. That deliciously playful dance of words and looks and gentle touches as they stretched out a time that could exist only once – before they made love for the very first time. Knowing that it would also be the last time had made everything so sharply focussed.

So... intense.

So utterly unforgettable.

Noah could hear the echoes of Laura's laughter and see her smile and feel her pleasure in what she was doing, like taking photographs of this door knocker, a hand holding an apple.

He could feel the coldness of the brass as he lifted the hand to announce his arrival. He only tapped softly but the door swung open seconds later, as if Laura had been waiting beside it. She stepped back as he entered but she was still holding the door and she was in the shadow so much that he couldn't interpret the look in her eyes.

He paused, leaning forward to brush her cheek with his lips, one side and then the other.

'*Bonsoir*, Laura,' he murmured.

'*Bonsoir*, Noah. Thank you for coming.' She shut the heavy wooden door behind her but didn't move towards the couch that was within a welcoming circle of warmth from the fire flickering in the grate.

He held up the bottle of vintage Dom Pérignon. If she accepted the offer this time, he would know how this meeting would end. Noah didn't realise he was holding his breath until he saw the shake of Laura's head.

A tiny shake but it was enough to make the smooth fall of her hair swing, the light catching its red-gold threads and making them glimmer.

'You don't want the champagne?' His voice was as heavy as his heart.

'I can't,' Laura said quietly. 'I'm pregnant.'

Putain!

He hadn't seen this coming and he had no idea how to respond. To try and gain a few seconds he walked further into the room. Far enough to put the unwanted bottle of champagne onto the table and then turn to face Laura, who still hadn't moved.

He tried, and failed, to find a smile.

So Laura had another man in her life. She was going to have his baby. To *marry* him, *peut-être*? Because a child was something that could change even a well-founded stance on whether or not they wanted to make a lifelong commitment.

'Ah...' Noah cleared his throat. 'I must offer my *félicitations*. This is more happy news for your family. Especially your mama.'

'She doesn't know yet. Nobody knows. I couldn't tell them when they were so happy about the wedding.' Laura was finally moving, walking towards the couch, but she didn't sit down. She stood at one end of it. Noah was standing on the other end. The distance between them felt very much greater than the length of this piece of furniture, however.

'I understand,' Noah said, nodding. 'And it's early days, *n'est pas*? Many couples prefer to keep the news private for a while anyway.'

Why was she telling *him*?

There seemed to be a soft, almost imperceptible buzzing sound in the room. A kind of hum, like you might associate with the electricity of an approaching storm.

'It's not early,' Laura said quietly. 'I'm five months pregnant.'

The humming was louder now. It was interfering with his brain's ability to make sense of the information. Five *months*?

Had Laura already been pregnant when she came back to France?

He could actually see the movement of her throat, as if it was very difficult for her to swallow.

'It's *your* baby, Noah.'

'*Pfft...*' The sound was as dismissive as the gesture Noah made with his hand.

'Not possible,' he added, but then felt a chill trickle down his spine. 'Unless you were lying to me? About being protected?'

She shook her head harder this time but Noah didn't notice any glimmer of her hair catching the firelight.

'I wasn't lying,' she said. 'But... sometimes. Rarely... it happens. The pill can fail to give protection.'

She was telling the truth. He might not want to believe it but he knew she wasn't lying the moment he met her gaze and held it hard enough to make her flinch.

'And you chose not to tell me when you found out?'

He'd never seen anyone look this guilty. Or distressed.

'I didn't want you to know.' Laura's voice cracked. 'Not then. I didn't want anyone to know because I was just going to make the problem go away, but...'

'*But*?' The word was savage. Bitten out, coated in ice.

'But I needed to make my own choice.' Laura raised her chin and held his gaze. 'I needed to listen to the words I could hear coming from here.' She laid her hand over her heart. The way Noah had when he'd told her to listen to the *real* Laura. The one that was hiding. The one who knew what she wanted and what she needed.

'I want this baby,' she whispered. 'I don't expect anything from you, Noah, but you have the right to know that you are going to be a father.'

Non... non, non, non...

Not that the words were allowed to emerge. The buzzing sound had become a roar. Noah didn't dare open his mouth to say anything because he had no idea what might come out after that impassioned denial.

He had no control over what was happening here, even though it was happening to *him*. And that was... terrifying.

He hadn't felt this afraid since...

...since he was no more than a child. When his beloved sister was having a seizure right in front of him. Dying... and there was nothing at all he could do to stop it.

But he wasn't a child now. And Noah Dufour had been in complete control of his life until this moment. He wasn't going to sink into that fear. He *could* take control again.

He did.

He turned and walked towards the door. He opened it and then shut it behind him in a quiet, controlled manner.

And kept walking.

15

'Laura? Where are you?'

'Ellie... You're back!' Laura hurried down the narrow cottage stairs as she heard her sister calling through the French doors that led to the terrace. With an effort, she dragged herself out of the misery she'd been fighting not to drown in for the last couple of days and deliberately brightened her face with a smile as she hugged her. 'How was Paris?'

'Perfect...' Ellie's smile was dreamy. 'It's like walking into postcards that have come to life. The Eiffel Tower, Montmartre, the Louvre. The street food... oh my God... we ate raclette, with ham, in fresh baguettes, sitting on a stone wall watching the boats go past on the Seine.' She paused to catch her breath. 'But you know exactly what it's like – you spent your gap year there.'

'That's ancient history now. And I wasn't there on honeymoon with my brand-new husband. I want to hear all about it. But where's Julien?'

'He's gone to collect Theo and Pascal. I wanted to warm the house up and cook dinner. That's what I've come over for – to invite you to come and have dinner with us. But how are *you*? Have you been okay here by yourself? Do you feel better?'

She looked so hopeful. She clearly wanted to hear that Laura loved this little house as much as she did. That she'd soaked in peace and quiet and it had melted away whatever stress had been affecting her. She wanted her sister to be as happy as she was. But that was... never, ever going to happen, was it?

The dismay on Ellie's face as Laura burst into tears felt like a physical punishment that was entirely deserved. This was her fault. She was ruining the newly wedded bliss that Ellie had been still basking in when she'd arrived.

'What's happened?' Ellie sounded frightened, as well she might. She'd never seen her cry, had she? Certainly not like this, anyway. 'It's not Mam, is it? Or Fi?'

Laura shook her head. She gulped in air and tried to control her tears. 'I'm so sorry, Ellie.'

'What *for*?'

'I'm... I'm pregnant.'

It was Ellie's turn to shake her head. 'Why are you sorry? Oh...' The sound was redolent with comprehension. 'Were you afraid to tell me? Because of Jack?'

Laura nodded. 'And you were getting married and Mam was so happy for you. *You* were so happy. I couldn't do something that would make it less perfect.'

Ellie reached for Laura's hand and pulled her towards the couch in the living area. 'Sit,' she commanded. 'Can I get you anything? A cup of tea? Where are the tissues?'

Ellie ducked into the kitchen, came back with a handful of paper towels and then sat beside Laura, close enough to put her arm around her shoulders, and that touch, along with the relief of finally giving up her secret, started a fresh wave of tears. Ellie let her cry, rubbing her back until the sobs began to subside, which was when Laura could hear her speaking softly.

'It's okay... it's going to be okay...'

Laura blew her nose into the scratchy paper.

'I'm sorry,' she said again.

'Och, stop saying you're sorry. How far along are you?'

'Five months.'

Ellie gasped. 'And you haven't told *anybody*?'

'I have now.'

'And nobody's noticed? Oh, wait... this was why you were all weird when I called you that time, isn't it? Going on about Mam's roast dinners and you putting on weight.'

Laura nodded miserably, opened her mouth to apologise again but managed to stop the words emerging. Ellie was staring at the oversized jumper she'd been wearing for days now.

'I should have guessed,' she said. 'You never wear clothes like this. Show me?'

Laura lifted the jumper. Her belly was softly rounded, showcased by the different fabric of the stretchy insert in her jeans. Ellie pressed the fingers of one hand to her mouth and, with a glance at Laura to ask permission, she laid her other hand on the modest bump. The only other people who'd touched Laura's body in the last few months had been the medical professionals she'd seen. This touch was very different. It was questioning. Almost reverent.

So full of love that maybe the baby felt it too. Laura could feel the ripple of movement beneath her skin and the contact of Ellie's hand above it. Her gaze met her sister's and, for a long moment, they sat very still, in complete silence. It was the closest Laura had ever felt to Ellie – as overwhelming as the very first time she'd held her baby sister in her arms. Like then, it was enough to start tears flowing again, but there was something different about the tears this time.

They almost felt like happy tears.

And Ellie was crying too. 'I remember this,' she said. 'It's the best feeling ever, isn't it?' She swiped at the tears on her own face as she sat back and Laura pulled the comfort of the woolly jumper back over herself like a thick blanket.

'I'm not really sad,' Ellie added. 'Well, I am but not because I can't bear remembering Jack. I *want* to remember him forever, even if it hurts sometimes. I'm sad right now because you've been doing this by yourself. When *you* were always there to support *me* when I was single and pregnant. Were you scared? When you found out?'

'I was... so shocked. Flabbergasted. I was on the pill so I ignored all the early symptoms because I thought they were side effects. I thought I was completely safe.' Laura's voice was trailing away. 'I'd never intended to have a baby. I never thought I'd want one...'

'It changes everything, doesn't it?' Ellie asked softly. 'When you find out.'

Laura's response was a nod. And a smile.

'Are you ready to tell Mam? And Fi? Do you want me to be with you when you do? Like a family video call?'

'Maybe...' But Laura was screwing her eyes shut to try and stave off yet more tears. Were they ever going to stop?

'It didn't go so well when I told the father,' she said.

She could feel Ellie watching her. She could actually feel the moment when the penny dropped.

'It's Noah, isn't it?'

Laura simply nodded again.

'I *knew* there was something going on, but I couldn't say

anything. Not when I was keeping what was happening between me and Julien a secret. It was your business. If you wanted to have a naughty weekend with a gorgeous Frenchman, I wasn't about to talk you out of it.' Ellie leaned her head back on the couch and let her breath out in a sigh. 'He is gorgeous, isn't he? When he was singing at the wedding, I think every woman there fell in love with him. Did you know he could sing like that? And play the guitar?'

Laura nodded. 'He sent me a recording once. A voice note. It was late and I was in bed and...'

Ellie's inward breath was audible. 'You're in love with him, aren't you?'

Laura said nothing. She didn't want to say the words aloud. It would make them more real, somehow. And make it impossible to take them back or pretend they had never been true.

'When did you tell him about the baby?'

'The first night I was here.' Laura opened her eyes to catch Ellie's shocked expression. 'I know... I should have told him as soon as I knew myself but... I knew what he would say.'

'Which was?'

'That he'd made it very clear he never wanted to become a father. That I would have to end the pregnancy. That was a decision I needed to make for myself.'

'Of course it was. It's your body. It's your baby.' But Ellie sounded cautious. 'What did you say when you told him?'

'That it was his baby. That he had the right to know but that I wasn't expecting anything from him.'

'What did he say?'

'Nothing,' Laura whispered. 'Not a single word. He just walked out and I haven't heard from him since.'

'Oh, Laura... that's awful... I'm so sorry...'

Squeezing her eyes shut wasn't going to stop the tears that only flowed faster when Ellie wrapped her arms around her.

'He needs time,' she said. 'It's a huge shock.'

'It's more than that.'

Haltingly, Laura told Ellie about the tragedy of Noah's sister and that it had affected him enough to make him build impenetrable barriers to loving anybody that much again. How she felt that she'd betrayed him. That she was responsible for him being slammed against those walls around his heart hard enough to hurt very, very badly.

Ellie listened, and when she spoke again it was with wisdom way beyond her years. She said something Laura hadn't even considered.

'He might think that this baby is the last thing he wants, but it could be that it's exactly what he needs,' she said quietly. 'He doesn't know that, and he wouldn't have chosen it because sometimes what you really need comes with a pain that nobody would ever choose. He's dealing with the worst of that pain right now. He needs time. And he needs to know that you're still here.'

'*What*? No... I'm going home. To tell Mam. To start getting my life sorted. Everything's been on hold while it's been a secret, and the clock's ticking. I have to sell my apartment, which is totally unsuitable for a baby, and that could take ages.'

Ellie shook her head. 'Stay,' she said. 'There's no point even thinking about putting your apartment on the market when everything's going to shut down until well into January. You've got your own holidays due to start, haven't you? You *could* stay.'

'But I haven't got any clothes other than the ones I'm wearing. And my wedding outfit.'

'I had less than that when *I* decided to stay here,' Ellie

reminded her. 'I'll take you shopping tomorrow.' She caught her lip between her teeth. 'You're going to need a lot more in the way of maternity clothes very soon.'

'I can't crash your first family Christmas.'

'*You're* part of our family, Laura. A very important part. And... it feels like it would be a mistake for you to leave right now.'

'Why?'

'You'd be running away – just like Noah did. When he's ready, Noah will need to talk to you again, and if you're in another country that will probably only be a phone call and it would be too easy to hang up if it got difficult. Or to be less than honest. It's a lot harder to hide how you really feel when you're actually with someone.'

Laura knew that was true. Telling Noah she was pregnant face to face had been the hardest thing she'd ever done but, even now, she knew it had been the right thing to do.

She knew that Noah Dufour was an honourable man and, deep down, she knew she could trust him to do the right thing as well. Not in the outdated sense of offering marriage, but she could imagine that he might decide to formally acknowledge his child. To allow his name to be on the birth certificate and, potentially, to accept a share of parental responsibilities. That would also involve accepting the link that he was always going to have to his child's mother.

And aye... she wanted to be able to see his body language when he told her what part he might – or might not – be prepared to play in the life of his child and, by default, *her* life. She'd know, then, whether there was any chance he might forgive her one day.

Laura pulled in a long breath. 'Let me try and fix my face,' she said. 'And then let's call Mam and Fi.'

16

That the heart of Christmas was all about family took on a whole new level of significance for Laura this year.

She was wrapped in the comfort of the love of her own family, despite being scattered between two different countries, when the shock of her confession had morphed into unconditional support. There was a thread of compassion for Ellie woven into every exchange that felt like it was bringing the Gilchrist women closer together than they'd been since the sisters had reached adulthood and gone their separate ways. Even Fi seemed to want to be included, maybe because she was at a distance and in total control of how much contact she had with her mother and sisters.

Ironically, given that her waistline was clearly expanding, Laura felt lighter, as if the secret she'd been carrying had been much heavier than she'd realised. It helped that the initial, unbearable heartache created by Noah's reaction to the news was dissipating slowly as the days went past. Laura had the reassurance of her family's love. She could finally allow herself to embrace the astonishing prospect of impending motherhood and, increasingly, she could do so with the confidence that she was more than capable of doing it as a single parent.

She could believe that it would be enough.

That *she* would be enough.

That she would be able to create a life that would be more than simply enough. It might not be a fairy tale, but it would be satisfying. Fulfilling. *Happy*...

It did feel a bit like a fairy tale, however, being here in a medieval village in the South of France – at Christmas time, with grey weather that made the decorative lights sparkle so brightly, a small boy next door whose face was shining with the excitement of it all and... oh, my goodness... a huge star on the top of a mountain and two donkeys in the olive grove that made it feel like she was taking part in a real-life nativity scene.

Ellie took her shopping for clothes in Nice and then they met up with Julien and Theo as daylight was fading to go to the central park that hosted the biggest Christmas market in the South of France, and Laura was almost as overwhelmed as three-year-old Theo as he was carried on his father's shoulders, his mouth open at the wonder of it all.

An enormous Ferris wheel dominated the space, with every capsule framed by lights. There was an ice-skating rink, a forest of pine trees and an entire village of Alpine chalets with decorations on their roofs, like snowmen or Christmas trees or Santa in his sleigh being pulled by a reindeer. The music of a carousel competed with seasonal songs from elsewhere, and there was something different to smell or taste every few steps, like mulled wine and hot chocolate, ice cream and crêpes, candy floss and gingerbread.

'Oh, look...' Ellie tugged on Laura's arm. 'How cute are these?'

'What are they?' Laura asked.

The counter of the chalet was crowded with thousands of tiny figurines – people and animals of every description, as though the population of an entire nation of dolls' houses and toy farms had gathered.

'They're called *santons*,' Julien told them. 'Little saints. They are a Provençal tradition. We use them to build nativity scenes. You can have Mary and Joseph and baby Jesus and the donkeys, but it's not just the wise men that come to see them. It's everybody from the South of France. Every farmer and baker and the village women and children and dogs—'

'Oh... there's a *doctor*.' Ellie picked up the figurine wearing a white coat and a stethoscope around his neck. 'We have to have this for our nativity.'

'Let me buy it for you,' Laura said. 'For a Christmas gift. I'll see if I can find something for you, too, El. In fact, why don't you guys go and do something fun for Theo and I'll do the rest of my Christmas shopping while I'm here.'

'We did promise him a ride on the Ferris wheel,' Julien said.

'Let's meet back here in an hour,' Ellie suggested. 'It'll be time to take Theo home by then, I think.'

Laura bought a selection of *santons*, including a little white dog that could be Pascal. She found some handcrafted finger puppets for Theo and some lavender oil to take home for her mother. And then she stood in front of another chalet and simply stared. It was another offering of children's toys and games, like the one where she'd purchased the little knitted puppets, but this one had an array of soft toy animals and it was a section that was clearly intended for babies that had caught Laura's eye.

In particular, it was the sweetest teddy bear she'd ever seen.

The seller noticed what she was looking at.

'*C'est trop mignon, oui?* Very cute?'

'*Très mignon*,' Laura agreed.

The woman picked it up and shook it. The toy was soft and fluffy but it was also a rattle.

'*Parfait pour un bébé*,' she said.

Unconsciously, Laura's hand shifted to touch her belly as she nodded. It was, indeed, perfect for a baby.

Her baby. She purchased the little brown bear and tucked it at the bottom of her carrier bag.

Because this was private. It was a Christmas gift she'd chosen for her unborn daughter. A breath of hope for their future.

* * *

Theo fell sound asleep on the drive home.

'Did he love the Ferris wheel?'

'He loved everything,' Julien said. 'This is the first Christmas that he's really aware of it all. It makes it special for all of us.'

'Which reminds me,' Ellie said. 'We're going to go up to Roquebillière on Christmas Eve. That's the night for the big family Christmas dinner in France. We'll stay the night there as well and do the presents for Theo in the morning. Will you come with us?'

'Oh...' Laura bit her lip. 'That's so kind of you... but... you wouldn't be offended if I stay at La Maisonette, would you?'

'Won't you be lonely?'

'No... I can call Mam. And Fi. I can go out and talk to the donkeys. It'll make me feel like Mary.'

Ellie laughed. 'I'm glad you're not quite that pregnant. What is your due date?'

'May Day.'

'As in "help, everything's turning to custard"?'

'As in the first of May. Labour Day.' Laura was laughing now. 'How appropriate is that?'

'We celebrate *la Fête du Travail* in France as well,' Julien said. 'But it's also *la Fête du Muguet*. I don't know what those flowers are in English, but we give them to the people we love and they are a symbol for good luck and happiness for the year ahead. They are small and white, like tiny bells, and they smell beautiful.'

Ellie was scrolling on her phone. 'They're lilies of the valley,' she said. 'Oh…' She turned to Laura. 'They're Mam's favourite, aren't they?'

'I believe they are.'

'I hope that does turn out to be the baby's birthday. And wouldn't Lily be a lovely name for a girl?'

'Or Lilou,' Julien suggested. 'That means the lily flower in French.'

The silence that fell in the car then started to feel a little awkward. Were they all thinking about the baby's father?

It was Laura who broke the silence. 'Have you seen Noah, Julien?' she asked, quietly. 'He might need a friend at the moment.'

Julien shook his head. 'I'm not sure he's around. He told me once that he doesn't like Christmas and he prefers to go away. Somewhere it's warm enough to go to the beach.'

The silence fell again, but this time nobody broke it.

* * *

He shouldn't be here.

Noah made a point of being somewhere very different for the days before and after Christmas. Somewhere hot so it didn't even feel like winter. A Fijian island was always very pleasant. The Maldives was a favourite, but he had planned a first visit to one of the French overseas territories this time and he'd been looking forward to setting foot on the fabulous Champagne Beach on the island of Espiritu Santo in Vanuatu.

But here he was.

In the South of France. At the end of a chilly, wet day far too close to Christmas. Walking through the rain-slicked stone streets, under archways with loops of fairy lights, past store fronts stuffed with seasonal treats and gaudy decorations. Past gatherings of friends and families in the bars and restaurants or ice skating on the tiny, artificial rink.

Past the vintage carousel with its painted ponies that looked as if they were leaping over raging streams, with their legs curled up and their manes and tails flowing. Red-cheeked children in woolly hats and mittens were laughing with delight, hanging on to the gilded poles as the ponies moved up and down and around, prancing to the tinkling, tinny music.

He'd been dragged into the past far too much over the last few days, and right up until this morning he'd been counting the minutes until he could board the plane and escape. He'd had his bag packed and a taxi booked but, in the end, he couldn't do it.

There was no escape.

There would be no reprieve from crunching through what felt like the shards of his life to be found in lying on the white sand of a tropical beach or diving into the turquoise-blue seawater. He would be running away. That was something only a coward would do and Noah Dufour had never been a coward.

The shock of Laura's revelation had given way to an anger that had been burning so brightly it seemed to be reaching a point where the fuel was exhausted.

Noah was certainly exhausted. Physically, from lack of sleep, and emotionally, from a trial run of every stage of grief.

Denial had seen him scouring the internet looking for evidence that he couldn't possibly be the father of Laura's baby, but even if she'd followed every rule for taking oral conception, it was only 99 per cent effective. In reality, with the mistakes that could be made, it was more like 93 per cent.

The anger wasn't simply due to the feeling of being utterly betrayed. He was angry with himself as well. He hadn't been careful enough. He'd trusted someone else with what was, arguably, the one thing that could turn his entire world upside down. Someone he'd believed understood exactly how important it was to him. Had he only imagined the connection he'd felt when they'd been lighting those candles in the church in Moustiers to remember the terrible loss of children in their lives?

Tonight, it was pure sadness, as he watched the children on the carousel and fell into the past again. It was quite likely that it was one of these very ponies that Elise had ridden, in those happy days before she'd become so sick. He could hear an echo of her laughter and see the look that was on every child's face when they had no reason not to believe in the magic of Christmas.

There was something else in the emotional mix, however. Something new. The beginning of acceptance, perhaps?

This couldn't be changed.

But it could still be controlled.

Noah had questions, though. And there was only one person who could answer them.

* * *

It was so quiet that Laura could hear the sound of a motorbike that was probably miles away.

She stared into the glowing embers of the fire but didn't get up to add a new piece of wood. She had closed her eyes, in fact, because the sound of a powerful bike was always going to make her think of Noah. She hugged herself, curled up on the big old sofa, as if it could bring to life the memory of having her arms around Noah.

Her heart tripped as she heard the roar of the bike coming to a halt, and it was racing by the time she heard the sharp tap of her brass door knocker.

For a long, long moment, Laura couldn't move after she'd opened the door. She searched Noah's face, not daring to look for any signs of forgiveness but... unable to see the sharp edges of hatred. She hadn't realised she'd been holding her breath until she stepped back and felt new air rushing into her lungs.

It was only then that she remembered that she hadn't bothered with any make-up today and her hair hadn't seen a straightener for days. She was still wearing the oversized jumper that had become an adult version of a child's comforter, but the jeans had been swapped for some new leggings and her smart boots had been replaced by sloppy socks with suede soles.

'Sorry... Please, come in...' She pushed tangles of hair away from her face. 'I'm a mess. I... wasn't expecting any visitors.'

'You look beautiful, Laura.' Noah walked past her and she closed the door. 'You always do.'

The tone suggested a statement of fact rather than a compliment. He went to stand in front of the fire.

'Can I get you something to drink? Some tea... or wine?'

'*Non. Merci.* I won't stay long. I needed to ask you something.'

'Okay...' Laura sank onto one end of the couch.

Noah cleared his throat. He took a deep breath. And then he said only a single word.

'*Why*?'

Laura didn't know what to say. Was he asking her why she hadn't told him earlier, or why she was telling him at all?

Noah filled the silence. 'You knew,' he said slowly, 'you knew that it would be the worst thing that could happen for me.'

There was a note of puzzlement in his tone. It wasn't simply that he was angry that he hadn't been informed or given any chance to contribute to choices being made. He was hurt, Laura realised, and that made her feel really bad.

A flash of a forgotten memory. Ellie, as a baby, reaching up for the pretty lolly that Laura was unwrapping to eat, her little face lit up with the desire to taste what her big sister was about to put into her mouth.

'I'm sorry, hinny,' she'd told her. *'But you can't have one. It's too dangerous. You might choke...'*

Ellie's face had crumpled in disappointment and Laura hadn't even wanted that lolly any longer.

Did she love Noah as much as she'd always loved her baby sister? A love that meant that their happiness, along with any other emotion, would always be linked at some cellular level? Knowing that she'd hurt Noah was hurting *her*. She could actually feel the physical pain of it.

'I'm sorry,' she said softly.

'So... *why*? I thought we were the same. That we both had our own reasons not to want a child. Or to be married.'

'I thought so too,' Laura said. 'And I did believe we were safe. My doctor told me that you have immediate protection if you take it during the first five days of a period and... it was more than five days before I came to France.'

Oh, help... Laura could feel her cheeks going red. She was, effectively, telling him that she only started taking the pill because she knew she was hoping to have sex with him. She rushed on before he had time to comment.

'I didn't tell you when I found out because I didn't think I would need to. It was the last thing I expected to happen. The last thing I *wanted* to happen.'

She stopped and swallowed hard.

'But then you changed your mind.'

Laura could feel the intensity of Noah's gaze on her but she couldn't look up at him. 'It was because I knew it might be the only chance I ever got to be a mother,' she said quietly. 'And... because of Ellie. I could remember what it was like to hold her when she was a baby. That love that was so huge it felt like... like the only thing in the world that mattered.'

She risked a glance and saw that Noah had closed his eyes. When he spoke, there was a raw edge to his words.

'I was remembering *my* sister this evening. And yes... I know that kind of love.' He opened his eyes and cleared the roughness from his voice. 'I will accept this child, Laura. I will help in whatever way I can – we will discuss arrangements before you go home – but... I cannot give it the love a father should be able to give his child.' He let his breath out in a sigh. 'I buried my heart with Elise,' he said, so quietly she could barely hear his words. 'I am not capable of feeling that kind of love again.'

Laura didn't try and stop the tears from escaping and rolling down the side of her nose as she followed him to the door. He could easily let himself out of the cottage – he'd done it the last time he'd been here, after all. Maybe it was an instinctive need to offer comfort that had pushed her to her feet. Or maybe it was simply love. Her heart was breaking for him and she had to be closer, even if she couldn't touch him.

It was Noah who turned in the open door and the look in his eyes broke another piece of her heart.

'*Bon nuit*, Laura,' he said. '*Et joyeux Noël. À bientôt.*'

She watched him walk to the gate but she could hear Ellie's words rather than any echo of his farewell.

'He might think that this baby is the last thing he wants but it could be that it's exactly what he needs...'

17

There was something about donkeys.

Something peaceful.

Something magical, even? Like Ellie had promised La Maisonette could deliver?

This was the strangest Christmas Day Laura had ever experienced but, even more strangely, it didn't feel sad. Or lonely.

She fed the last of the supply of carrots she had to Marguerite and Coquelicot. She rubbed the soft tufty hair on the front where those extraordinarily log ears were attached to their heads because Ellie had showed her that this was their very favourite way to be petted. Sure enough, they stretched their necks out and closed their eyes and gave every indication of being blissed out.

It was a brainwave to take a selfie with the donkeys and send it to Fi with a Happy Christmas message. Laura told her that the donkeys approved of her channelling Mary. She told her about the huge star on the mountain, too, and ended up by telling her middle sister that she missed her. That she wished Fi was here.

The swiftness of the reply was unexpected.

Merry Christmas. LOL – I think I want a donkey!

There was a Christmas tree emoji at the end of the message and a gift with a ribbon and one that looked more like a horse than a donkey.

Best of all, there was a second text.

Miss you too.

And this time the emoji was a heart.

Her mother kept up contact all day via text messages and a video call.

'Next year,' Jeannie said, firmly, 'we'll all be together. The *whole* family – with your wee bairn with us, too.' Her sigh was wistful. 'How wonderful would it be if Ellie was on the way to being a mammy again by then?'

It was the call from Ellie that finally brought tears to Laura's eyes.

The happiness in Ellie's voice and the chorus of *Joyeux Noël* from all the members of her newly extended family was so genuine. As was the concern for whether Laura was having a good day.

She was, Laura assured her, but Ellie was distracted by the call of Theo's small voice.

'*Tatie Laura,– Regarde...*'

The phone screen shifted and Laura could see small fingers, most of which had little knitted puppets on them.

'Brilliant gift,' Ellie said.

'*Dis merci à Tante Laura.*' Was that Theo's grandmother's voice in the background?

'*Merci...*' Laura could see Theo's face now. Lit up with the joy of the day. '*Merci pour mon cadeau, Tatie Laura.*'

Laura felt one of those tears escape as she ended that call. It trickled down the side of her nose as she laid both her hands gently on her bump.

'I have a present for you, too, little one,' she whispered. She went to find the soft little brown bear. Her baby might not be able to see it but she knew that the sound of the rattle could be heard.

And the sound of a mother's voice telling them how much she was already loved.

* * *

The roads were quiet on Christmas Day.

The sky was clear but the wind chill factor was enough to be uncomfortable despite the merino balaclava beneath his helmet, the under-glove liners and winter-weight socks.

Not that Noah was complaining. The discomfort, along with edge of danger at the speed he was travelling, was exactly what he needed to not only distract himself but to try and clear his head. He knew he was breaking the speed limit at times but that felt inevitable. This journey was, after all, being fuelled by more than what was in the bike's tank. He could feel the weight of anger pushing him onwards. Into the wind that was so cold it felt as if it was burning his face with the same kind of heat as that anger.

Betrayal. That's what it felt like.

He'd been so clear about how he felt about relationships. He'd told Laura that he never wanted marriage. Or a child. *Especially* a child. He'd believed she understood – like no one else could have understood – and yet she'd pushed him into this space. He was going to be a father and there was no escape.

Perhaps this impulsive decision to hit the road had been a bid for escape from his worst nightmare.

If it was, it was clearly futile. Fate seemed to be laughing at him because it wasn't just anger he could feel behind him. He could feel what it had been like to have Laura Gilchrist on the back of this beloved motorbike, her arms tightly around his waist. Her body pressed against his.

Was that the reason he was, without thinking, following the same route he had that day?

Not that it would have mattered what direction he'd gone in. It was this speed he needed. This freedom. Feeling like part of this machine as he leaned into the curves. Feeling a part of nature as the wind unendingly swallowed him.

It wasn't as if there were any purple clouds of lavender blooms to catch his eye as he headed into the landscape of Haute-Provence, taunting him with images of Laura standing in the middle of one, her arms out to embrace the dream that had come true that day. The neat rows of the bushes were still there, of course, but they had been pruned hard enough to look dead. Dark and gloomy.

Like the way Noah was feeling.

He wasn't intending to stop in Moustiers-Sainte-Marie, but he was losing the feeling in his fingers and toes and he was in need of some strong, hot coffee and the lift that he could rely on nicotine to provide.

He certainly didn't intend to climb the steps to the chapel again, either, but he needed something more than speed on the road could give him, and pushing himself to the physical limit of climbing hundreds of steps as fast as possible was suddenly a challenge he couldn't resist.

There was no need to go inside even though he knew the chapel would be open on Christmas Day.

There was a need to catch his breath, however, when he reached the last of the steps. Two hundred and sixty-two of them. He'd counted every one of them as he'd forced his body through the threshold of burning physical pain that too little oxygen and too much lactic acid had created.

The wind was colder up here. A different kind of cold that threatened to reach his bones. An icy cold that felt as if it was trying to cool his anger, but what would be left if the anger vanished?

Something worse… like fear?

Maybe he needed to escape the cold now, to try and keep the anger alive because being angry was more acceptable than being afraid.

Or was it because of what day it was that he suddenly turned and entered the chapel?

This was a day for family.

For children.

He couldn't be here and not light a candle for Elise.

Noah's hand was shaking a little as he lit the candle. And then he stood and watched it flicker. There were other candles alight but, in this moment, he was alone in this sacred space. But he didn't feel alone.

In the same way he'd been able to feel Laura's arms around him on the bike, he could feel the memory of her standing beside him in front of these candles. Holding his hand. He hadn't imagined that connection. It had been real.

As real as the other memories that were flooding into his head. And his heart.

Happy memories, like the day Elise was brought home from the hospital and he was allowed to sit in a chair and hold her in his arms. The way he could make her smile simply by being there, right from when she was only a few weeks old. Later, he could make her giggle and it had been the best sound in the world. And, when she was old enough, it was his hand that Elise would insist on holding, and he could still feel the absolute trust of that small hand clinging to his – the pure, totally unconditional love that it could both gift and create.

It was impossible to prevent other memories stored in the same place from emerging. The ones that came as part of the terrible diagnosis that Elise had received when she was only five years old. He couldn't blame his parents for being so focussed on their precious daughter, of course, but it shrouded the less than happy memories with impenetrable shadows.

Having Elise taken away, again and again, for surgeries. Months of chemotherapy that made her so sick and radiotherapy that blistered her skin. Watching, without understanding, as she slowly stopped eating and then talking, moving and then, finally, breathing...

Without realising that he'd been moving, Noah found himself outside again.

It was the icy wind that was making his eyes water. Noah Dufour didn't cry. He hadn't cried even when Elise was taken away for the very last time. He'd bottled up tears along with the memories and retreated into the shadowland of a child that wasn't important enough, watching his parents pull on suffocating cloaks of grief to face the world for the rest of their lives.

Walking down the side of the mountain was so much easier but, strangely, it made Noah feel more tired. He reached his bike and piled on all the protective gear he needed for the ride home and then revved the engine and took off without a backward glance. He was going to leave all those memories here. They were still too painful.

How much worse would it be if he had a living child in his life again? Not simply a sibling but a child of his own that he had to take responsibility for. To try and protect even though he knew, better than anyone, that you can't always protect the people you love.

The fear was real.

Too close.

But then he could hear a whisper of Laura's voice right inside his helmet.

'I don't expect anything from you, Nouh...'

That rang true.

He'd known exactly how competent and in control Laura was from the first moment he'd seen her. It might have been the image she was living rather than the *real* Laura, but she was disciplined enough to create whatever image she deemed necessary for a successful life and not break it. She would be the perfect single mother, taking sleepless nights and the worry of an unwell child in her stride even if she was still working fulltime. Their child would have the best of every thing and a life full of encouragement and fun, and educational activities like swimming and music and dance.

He – or she – would be clever and confident and adorable.

And they would be loved.

With a deep, unwaveringly unconditional love.

'...love that was so huge it felt like... the only thing in the world that mattered...'

The way he'd loved his baby sister. The way Laura still loved hers.

The kind of love he'd lost when Elise was gone. The kind he would never have again because he would never let it seep through the protective walls he had built around himself. Fathering a child was the last thing he'd intended to do but he had no choice other than to cope and do what was the morally right thing.

He wouldn't need to feel guilty that he was not a part of that child's life on a deeply meaningful level, however, because Laura was more than able to fill any gap that his absence would create.

She would probably go back to Scotland very soon so that she could get her new life as a mother-to-be arranged with admirable precision, and he would be more than happy to provide whatever financial resources it would take to make it as perfect as possible.

He would play his own part to perfection as well.

From a safe distance.

Noah could actually feel the anger finally beginning to shed tiny fragments that were sent spinning into his wake as he put his head down and headed for home.

* * *

Laura clicked on her choice of seat for the plane ride back to Glasgow. She'd chosen the second day of January, which would give her several days to get settled back home and organised before the Oban office of The Property Centre opened for the start of business in the new year.

With the 'New Year, New Me' philosophy popping up on social media, she'd planned to return before the last day of the current year and get a head start on the extensive list of changes she needed to make in her life, like finding a child-friendly house near an acceptably good school, but something stopped her rushing back.

Tickets were more expensive and getting snapped up fast with people trying to get to friends and family to celebrate New Year's Eve, but that wasn't the only reason Laura wanted to stay just a little longer. Neither was it because of the joy to be found in sending photos home that captured how happy Ellie was in her new life – there was something far more selfish in postponing her departure for a few more days.

Maybe she needed to catch a little more of the magic to be found within the stone walls of this little French cottage. To breathe in some of the peacefulness that seemed embedded in those ancient stones. It was time during which she could sleep in the gorgeous old brass bed with its soft pillows and crisp cotton sheets, the bliss of knowing no alarm was going sound to announce that it was time to get to the gym and push herself through a punishing fitness regime. She could sit in front of a crackling fire and soak in the comfort of its warmth and know that she could do whatever she felt like doing the next day. There were no back-to-back appointments crowding her diary. Nobody was expecting anything of her.

This was like stolen time. Away from everything that made up her normal life. Away from being the person she had to be in that life. This was a chance to take a deep breath and prepare herself for the huge corner in life that she was about to turn. A chance to tuck away a taste of the magic for when it might be exactly what she needed to get through a tough challenge. She could add it to the glow she would always have from that brief blink in her life when she'd stepped away from reality to come to France and... let herself live a little.

Oh, help... she was always going to hear Noah's voice in that phrase, wasn't she?

Would it always create that sensation that travelled like a jolt of electricity through her whole body?

Perhaps. But its effect would fade when she was far enough away from him.

There was no reason she couldn't work right up until the last week or so of her pregnancy and, with everything else she needed to do to get all her ducks in a row, there wouldn't be much time to even be thinking about Noah Dufour. And, after the baby was born, there would be whole new focus in her life.

A whole new love.

Brand new. Pure. Perfect...

* * *

'It's *le réveillon du Nouvel An*,' Ellie told Laura. 'It's as big as Christmas and just as important to spend it with family and friends. We have to go back to Roquebillière because Julien's grandmother doesn't want to come to us. She says it hurts her hip to spend that much time in the car. Please come with us this time?'

'I'm happy here,' Laura said. 'It's really kind of you but you told me how small their house is. Julien's mother was sleeping on the couch so you two and Theo could share *her* bed, wasn't she?'

'We can find a hotel.'

'There's no need. I want to stay here. I'm might go into Vence or St Paul de Vence and find a place to watch the fireworks.'

'But there's a feast. We decorate the table and eat traditional things like oysters and foie gras and caviar. Julien's got a special champagne out of the cellar for midnight. Oh...' Ellie's expression was rueful. 'Shellfish and pâté and champagne are all right up there on the forbidden foods list, aren't they?'

Laura wrapped her sister in a hug. The reminder of her own pregnancy would never lose its poignancy.

'At least I wasn't in France.' Ellie found a smile as she let go of Laura. 'The home of the world's most delicious soft cheese.'

'Honestly, I'll be fine. I'm making the most of my last few days here to get my head together. Time on my own is a gift right now.'

18

Le réveillon.

Noah had been invited to half a dozen New Year's Eve parties but, instead, had come to his favourite café just outside the fortress walls of St Paul de Vence, where he could have a drink and a cigarette and watch people gathering in the square to dance to live music from a band. He'd stay for the fireworks at midnight and then walk home.

Both Christmas Eve and New Year's Eve could be called *le réveillon* but, while Noah avoided everything to do with Christmas, starting a new year was entirely different. This was a time to make new resolutions and strengthen old ones and he was ready to embrace a new start.

Ready to talk to Laura and make plans. She may have already left to go back to Scotland but that wasn't a problem. It might even be preferable, given their experience in communicating via technology. Okay... it would definitely be preferable. Being close to Laura in person created all sorts of distractions that would not be helpful when practical things such as finances and legal matters needed to be discussed.

'*Merci bien.*' He nodded at the waiter who delivered the *coupe de champagne* he'd ordered. Because it was nearly midnight and you had to have a glass of champagne in your hand when the bells rang to welcome in the new year. *C'était une règle, n'est-ce pas*?

'*Bonne année, Monsieur.*' The waiter took the notes offered but Noah shook his head as he opened the pocket on his belt to find the change.

'*Gardez la monnaie,*' Noah said. '*Et bonne année à vous.*'

Noah took a long swallow of a very good champagne, lit a cigarette and narrowed his eyes to peer through the plume of smoke he exhaled to take in a noisy crowd of expats – or tourists, perhaps – in fancy dress who were either leaving or heading towards a party that was clearly intended to be patriotic. Wearing navy-blue and white striped Breton tee shirts, red berets, and sunglasses, even the women had curly black moustaches and goatee beards painted on their faces. They were attracting a lot of attention and phones were being raised to take photographs or videos. Some people were shaking their heads at the spectacle, or possibly at the flimsy attire in temperatures that were low enough to have most people wearing layers of warm clothing, with coats and woollen hats and gloves. Like that woman with an anorak over a warm-looking jumper, a dark green scarf and a matching knitted hat with a furry bobble on the top. A woman who looked remarkably similar to Laura.

Noah put down his glass and leaned forward, the ash on his cigarette dropping, unnoticed, onto the table moments later.

It *was* Laura.

Walking in his direction. He was right on the edge of the café's terrace, so it was impossible to hide. Noah didn't want to hide, anyway. He wanted Laura to notice him. He wanted...

Oh, mon Dieu... he just wanted... *her*.

So much that it hurt.

* * *

She liked that he was stubbing out that disgusting cigarette as soon as he saw her approaching him.

Laura could never have lived with his kind of lifestyle habits, so it might turn out to be a blessing in disguise that he wasn't interested in long-term relationships.

But... *ohh*... the way he was looking at her. That look that could make her feel as if she was naked, which should have been an unattractively freezing proposition on a winter's night but was, in fact, making her feel far, far too *hot* for comfort.

Surely this attraction would have to fade at some point? With this level of heat it felt like it should burn itself out in no time at all and, when that happened, it would be so much easier to co-parent their child. To share photographs and videos and, on occasion, to cross the conveniently protective moat of the English Channel and have brief, well-controlled visits.

Laura was lucky, really. There was never going to be any ugly custody battles over this child. Her father didn't want to be a parent and she wasn't aware of any grandparents who might demand access. If she and Noah could establish a civilised relationship – some kind of friendship, even – she could see a glimpse of a future that was... well... possibly as close to perfect as she could hope for.

So Laura offered Noah a smile.

'*Bonne année*,' she greeted him.

'*Bonne année*, Laura.' Noah stood up, stretching his hand towards the empty chair at his small table. 'Please, sit down.' He had to raise his voice over the increasingly noisy crowd of people in the square. 'Can I get you something to drink? A coffee? A taste of champagne?'

'No, thank you.' Laura glanced over her shoulder. People were blowing on whistles that had streamers attached to them and the noise was getting too much for her. She'd never liked being in crowds. Even on a happy occasion such as this, there was a feral element to a large group of people. It could tip into chaos in a heartbeat and it wasn't just herself that Laura needed to protect now.

'I came to see the fireworks,' she told Noah. 'But I think I'm ready to go home.'

Noah was frowning as he, too, stared at the crowd. A shout had gone up and there was the sound of glass breaking. 'Where is your car?' he asked.

'Not far from your office,' she said. 'I remembered that was a good place to park to come here.'

'I will come with you.'

It was a statement, not an offer. He was going to make sure Laura got safely to her destination. He was going to walk beside her.

To protect her and, by default, to protect their child.

And Laura felt a wash of gratitude that was strong enough for her to accept his offer of an arm to hold as they made their way past the edges of the dancing, singing crowd.

It was strong enough to feel like more than gratitude. This felt like love. Longing. And a sadness that was poignant enough to bring the prickle of tears too close to Laura's eyes. She let go of Noah's arm once they were across the road and walking up the slope of the cobbled street.

It was nearly midnight and they could hear the increasing excitement of the revellers below them. The road felt steeper than Laura had remembered it being and she was too out of breath to hold a conversation with Noah, but the silence they walked in didn't feel awkward. It felt like the worst was behind them now. The bomb had been detonated and the embers of destruction were cool enough to walk on. They could start picking their way through this new landscape and find some solid ground to start building whatever their shared future might be.

As they came to the tiny chapel where one of her favourite photographs of Ellie and Julien's wedding day had been taken, Laura had to stop to catch her breath. It was worth stopping for the view of St Paul de Vence, especially now, lit up in sparkling party lights with the sound of the music and a happy crowd drifting up to where she and Noah were standing, side by side. Close enough to touch, but the gap between them felt like a ravine to Laura.

A new sound floated up from the old city. People were counting. Shouting numbers over the cacophony of whistles and cheers.

Dix... neuf... huit...

The countdown to the new year had begun. It didn't matter what language the numbers were in, they were simply bursts of sound.

Three... two... *one*...

A single shell shot into the black night sky and then exploded with a boom that Laura could feel right through her body. Trails of sparks erupted from the centre of the star towards them and she instinctively ducked. She felt Noah's arm wrap around her shoulders.

He didn't need to say anything.

He was keeping her safe.

She wouldn't have heard him say anything over the sound of more and more shells exploding. From this vantage point they could see the midnight pyrotechnics as far away as Nice or Cannes lighting up the sky, the faint pops in the distance filling any gaps in the show right in front of them. Massive stars of all sizes and colours were filling the sky along with swirling patterns, as if a school of tiny fish had been shaken loose, and flickering lights that spread sideways and hung there like a gathering of giant fireflies.

Laura looked up to see if Noah was as captivated by the fireworks as she was, only to find him looking down at her. He put his lips so close to her ear she could feel his breath on her cheek.

'*Bonne année*, Laura.'

'Bonne année, Noah.'

It seemed that neither of them hesitated for even a heartbeat to follow the tradition of the midnight kiss. Noah held her face between his hands, his fingers weaving themselves into her hair beneath her hat as his lips touched and then settled on hers.

And then that kiss exploded just as effectively as any one of those huge, manmade stars they had just been watching. Laura could feel the trails of sparks burning tracks over and through every inch of her skin, heading for her bones, leaving pools of fire deep in her belly.

She knew she should pull away but she couldn't. Maybe Noah felt the same way because she could feel the growl of a groan rather than hear it before the touch of his tongue soothed it into oblivion.

It was a kiss like no other.

A kiss that Laura would never forget.

One that left her completely stunned.

They both were. When they finally broke apart, they stood there, staring at each other as the fireworks finally ended. And then Laura gave her head a tiny shake, unable to find any words, and gestured towards her car. Noah gave a single nod. She was safe. It was time for her to go home.

She could hear the crowd in the square singing as she unlocked the car. The words were muffled but the tune and rhythm were as familiar as every other New Year tradition.

'Ce n'est qu'un au revoir...'

The French version of Auld Lang Syne. Laura could remember translating it in a long-ago school lesson.

It's only a goodbye.

She could remember another line, too.

Faut-il nous quitter sans espoir? Do we have to leave without hope?

She slid into the driver's seat of her car and she could feel the shock of that kiss wearing off.

It was only then that Laura could feel something it had left behind. She knew it wasn't real, but she also knew it would be impossible to ignore what was right there in front of her.

Hope, that's what it was.

And how could anyone resist taking that with them?

19

Where *was* it?

Laura's open suitcase was on the floor of the spare bedroom in La Maisonette. The child's bedroom that Ellie had decorated so beautifully with the frieze of flowers on the walls and the freshly painted cot that Laura had come in to gaze at, more than once, during her stay here – her eyes misty, her hand on her belly – dreams of the future drifting past like cotton wool clouds in a summer sky.

It was the first day of the new year and, as corny as it had always sounded, it was also the first day of the rest of Laura's life and she was packing to go home and get on with it.

But she couldn't find her woolly hat. The dark green one with the faux fur pompom that matched her scarf and gloves. Laura bent down to shift the jacket of her wedding outfit, which could be disguising the hat by being the same colour. Losing things was careless and carelessness was unacceptable – because that was tempting fate to take control completely out of your own hands – so Laura was determined to find the hat, but it didn't appear to be in the suitcase.

She'd been wearing it last night, hadn't she? Yes... If she closed her eyes, she could feel the way Noah's fingers had slid beneath the hat to bury themselves in her hair while he kissed her completely senseless.

It must be in the rental car, she decided, straightening up to go downstairs. A wave of dizziness made her catch the door frame and, while it subsided swiftly, it left a throbbing sensation in her head. She took great care going down that narrow staircase in the cottage and made a mental note that she wanted the new house she was about to start looking for to be single level. You wouldn't want to fall with a baby in your arms any more than when you were pregnant.

The hat wasn't anywhere to be found in the car.

Had she dropped it? Was it on the road near the chapel?

It wouldn't take long to take that small diversion on the way to the airport tomorrow, but it would be a good idea to make a note of that intention. Laura looked around the living area of the cottage. She always carried a notebook and pen in her shoulder bag, but where was it?

Another wave of dizziness hit her and, this time, Laura could feel the prickle of perspiration on her skin. It was too warm in this wee house. Which was odd, because she'd only lit the fire a little while ago as daylight began fading and she needed a cheering light as much as the warmth. Her head was definitely aching now, so Laura abandoned the hunt for either her hat or her bag. She needed to go upstairs and find her toilet bag because she knew it contained a blister pack of paracetamol.

Oh, wait... was it safe to take paracetamol when you were pregnant? Where was her phone, so she could do an internet search?

And who was knocking on the door? Ellie?

Laura tried to take a deep breath to slow down thoughts that were oddly fuzzy around the edges but it wasn't working. Even the air felt too hot and it was hurting her chest.

* * *

Noah stood under the bare branches of the rose-covered archway outside La Maisonette's front door, a dark green hat clutched in his hand.

He'd picked it up last night as the taillights of Laura's rental car vanished around the corner. He'd forgotten all about it today – the first day of this new year. No, that was not true. Ignoring the hat had been deliberate. If he'd picked it up, he wouldn't have been able to resist scrunching it in his hands and holding it to his face to smell the scent of Laura's hair that he knew would be clinging to the soft wool.

He would remember, too clearly, sliding his fingers under the hat to cradle Laura's face while he kissed her, and he didn't want to think about that kiss.

About how *empty* he'd felt when he saw the lights of her car blink into darkness.

But it had been his fault that Laura had lost her hat. He must have pushed it off her head without realising it, and returning it was the right thing to do.

So here he was, but it didn't seem as if Laura was home. He reached to rap the brass hand of the door knocker against its apple a little harder but, as he did so, the door opened. Laura was standing there and she looked...

...like a ghost. So pale he could see tiny freckles on her nose and cheeks that he'd never noticed before.

'*Laura...*' Noah's heart clenched as hard as his hand was holding that hat. 'What's wrong?'

'I... I don't know...' Her voice sounded as pale as her skin. 'I'm not... feeling very well.'

Any plan to simply hand back the hat and assure Laura that he would be in touch very soon to discuss the arrangements that needed to be made regarding their future had already evaporated. The hat fell to the ground a second time as Noah caught Laura before she fell and picked her up in his arms to carry her to the couch. He put a cushion under her head and a rug across her body and then pulled out his phone.

'Julien? *Tu es à la maison mon ami? Nous avons besoin de toi. Laura est malade...*'

His friend arrived within a couple of minutes, a doctor's bag in his hand.

'Laura?' He crouched beside the sofa and put the fingers of one hand on her wrist and then on her forehead. 'You have a fever,' he told her. 'How long have you been feeling sick?'

'It came on r-really s-suddenly.' Despite the fire and the blanket, Laura was starting to shiver violently. 'I f-felt dizzy...'

'Do you have a headache?'

She nodded.

'Aches and pains?'

Laura nodded again. She looked so miserable that Noah wanted to get closer. To hold her hand and tell her that everything was going to be okay. He couldn't interfere with what Julien was doing, however, as his friend took small packets from his bag.

'Tip your head back,' he instructed Laura. 'I'm going to put a swab into your nose. I'm sorry, it won't be comfortable.'

'You think I have Covid?' Laura tilted her head and screwed her eyes shut.

'This test is for Covid, influenza A and B and RSV. I think

it's likely you have one of those viruses. Luckily we can do it all with one swab.'

It didn't take long to get the result.

'Influenza A,' Julien pronounced. 'I'm not surprised. There's a lot of it around at the moment. I'm sorry, Laura, you won't be flying home tomorrow.'

'But...'

'You can't spread the infection,' Julien said sternly. 'Influenza can be a serious illness. You don't have any medical conditions I should know about, do you? Like asthma or diabetes?'

'No... I'm just... pregnant.'

'And that also means that you have to take extra care.'

It didn't seem possible but Noah could swear Laura had just become even paler. 'It's dangerous?' she whispered. 'For the baby?'

He could hear the fear in her voice.

He could feel how much she cared about this baby.

How much she wanted it.

Noah would never have chosen to have this baby in his life but he didn't want anything bad to happen to it, either. Because that would hurt Laura and he cared about her.

Too much...

'There is a higher risk of complications,' Julien admitted gently. 'It's a very good thing you are well past your first trimester, and it's very unlikely to be harmful to the *bébé* but, to be safe, you need to go to bed and rest. I'm going to go to the *pharmacie* and get you a course of antiviral tablets and some *anti-inflammatoires*.' He lifted his hand as Laura opened her mouth to protest. 'They're perfectly safe to take when you're pregnant and they will make the illness less severe. I will send

Ellie over to take care of you. She's with Theo and Pascal and she will be worried.'

'No...' Laura was shaking her head. 'She can't come. I don't want her to get sick as well.'

'I'll stay.' The words came out of Noah's mouth before he'd realised he was even thinking of it, and they came out with enough emphasis to be a little embarrassing. He shrugged it off. 'I'm already here.'

Not that he was going to tell Julien, but if he was going to catch the illness, it would have already happened during that kiss last night. There was no way he could walk away from Laura in any case. Not when she needed help.

When she needed *him*...

'*D'accord*...' Julien snapped the catches shut on his bag. 'I will be back soon.' He smiled at Laura. 'Ellie can go to the *supermarché* first thing tomorrow and bring everything you might need for the next few days and we can help with changing your tickets. Try not to worry. You will feel better soon, I promise.'

Noah followed Julien to the door where he could ask his own questions without Laura hearing the answers. Not that she would have followed the rapid French, but she might have picked up on his concern about possible complications. It was apparently a good thing she was this far along in the pregnancy because it could have caused major issues earlier. There was still a risk of miscarriage, however. And pneumonia. He had a list of symptoms to watch out for, like a really high fever. Confusion. Difficulty breathing. Signs that Laura was sick enough to need to go to hospital. Signs that her baby might be in danger.

Non... There was no way Noah was going anywhere.

* * *

The warmth and softness around her was as comforting as a mother's embrace but it wasn't enough to stop the pain, as deep and sharp as a toothache, that had spread throughout Laura's whole body. It wasn't enough to stop the shivering, either, but how could she be so cold and feel like she was melting in overwhelming heat at the same time?

There was something worse than confusion to be felt, however. There was fear. Fear that control had been ripped out of her hands.

Fear that she was in the middle of losing something very, very important.

She had to fight to open her eyes. And then she had to ride another wave of pain at the impact of light that felt far too bright. She screwed her eyes almost closed again but she could still see the iron bars right in front of her face.

Like the bars of a jail. The idea of being locked away added another note to that fear but Laura knew where she was. She was in the antique iron and brass bed in the upstairs bedroom of La Maisonette. It was daylight but the last thing Laura could remember clearly was getting the fire started downstairs because daylight was starting to fade and it was getting so cold. And... and she'd lost something. Or had that been a dream? Noah had been there. And Julien and Ellie, who had looked as scared as Laura was feeling now.

A sound that was intended to be a groan escaped her throat. Or tried to. Her throat hurt and her mouth was too dry to make it anything more than a croaky breath, but there was an instant response.

'Laura? *Es-tu réveillée, chérie*? Are you awake?'

With another effort, Laura turned her head. What on earth

was Noah doing in her bedroom? He had a glass of water in his hand and she suddenly realised how thirsty she was. Her hand was shaky as she reached for the glass. She needed help to take a sip. And then another.

'It's time for your pills,' Noah said. 'Let me help you sit up.'

He put more pillows behind her and a small blanket around her shoulders. A soft, yellow blanket that Laura had seen somewhere before...

In the other bedroom. Tucked over the mattress in the baby's cot.

She gasped, sharply enough to create a stab of pain on top of the steady throbbing in her head.

'What is it?' The concern in Noah's voice was just as sharp.

'The baby...'

'The baby's fine. Julien has checked the heartbeat. When you are better, he is going to take you to his hospital for a... I don't know what it is in English – *un examen échographique*.'

Laura's hand had gone to her belly and she was aware of two things within seconds. The first was that the baby seemed aware of the pressure of her hand because it moved beneath it. Just a tiny ripple but it was so reassuring. The second was that she was wearing her soft organic bamboo pyjamas and she had no memory of putting them on. Or of taking off her clothes.

The light hurt all over again as her eyes widened. 'How did I get into bed? Did you—?'

'*Non, non*... Ellie helped you get into bed. And she brought everything. Drinks and soup and a... *bouillotte*.'

'I don't know what that is.' Ellie took one of the pills from the palm of Noah's hand. She didn't know what these pills were either, but she had an absolute trust that Noah wouldn't be giving her anything that could cause harm. He looked... tired, she thought. Had he been sitting beside her bed all night? But he was smiling. As if he was happy to be here.

Caring for her...?

'A *bouillotte* has hot water in it,' he said, as she took a second tablet. 'It helps when muscles are painful. These pills will help also. For *la grippe*. The influenza.'

The hot water bottle was there beside her in the bed. Noah took it after she'd taken the last pill.

'I will make it hot again. Do you think you could drink a little soup if I bring some?'

'I think I just want to go to sleep...' She couldn't stop her eyes drifting shut as her words faded. She felt the duvet being pulled up around her shoulders as she wrapped both her arms around herself. Around her bump. She thought she felt the brush of a kiss on her hair but maybe she was dreaming again already.

* * *

It was dark when she woke the next time. The lamp on the bedside table was on but the light was gentle enough not to hurt her eyes. Or maybe she was feeling better? There was a chair in the room that hadn't been there before. No... it was a beanbag, Laura decided. And Noah was sitting in it. Asleep.

She'd never seen him asleep before, she realised. His face was softened and that wicked glint in his eyes shuttered. He was...

...absolutely the most gorgeous man she'd ever seen. Even now, with a dark shadow of stubble on his jaw and his tousled hair looking like it hadn't seen a comb for days. She was probably looking just as bad herself. Laura put a hand to her own hair and felt her fingers tangle in the knotted waves.

'*Ouch*...'

Noah's eyes opened instantly. '*Ça va*? Are you okay?'

'My hair is a rat's nest.'

She could see Noah smiling. 'I didn't know you had curls in your hair like Ellie does. Not until I saw you at Christmas time.'

'That's because I've always straightened it.' Laura put her hand over her eyes. 'I hate anybody seeing me like this.'

'Why?' Noah sounded genuinely puzzled. 'Your hair is even more beautiful like this. *Les cheveux bouclés te vont vraiment bien*.' He gave that very French kind of shrug that said he was right but that others were free to disagree. 'More importantly, are you feeling better?'

'I think so. My body doesn't hurt so much at the moment.'

'I will make you some tea. And get you some more pills.'

When Noah returned, Laura was trying, unsuccessfully, to comb her hair with her fingers. Noah put a mug down on the table and some pills beside it. He lifted an eyebrow as he saw what she was doing.

'You really want to make it straight again, don't you?'

Laura nodded. Her smile felt creaky. 'I do love my straighteners,' she confessed. She picked up the mug and took a sip of the warm, sweet tea. Then she took the pills as Noah settled back on the beanbag. 'Sometimes,' she said, 'I wish I had some really, really big straighteners so that I could use them to make the knots in life go away. Annoying things like unpleasant people or a house so full of rubbish you can't possibly show a client through.'

Noah's breath was a huff of soft laughter. 'If only the knots in life could be straightened so easily.'

'Most knots can be. You just need to do it a little bit at a time.'

There was a moment's silence as Laura took another sip of the tea. She didn't normally have sugar in any drink, but this tasted so wonderful it was a shame when the mug was empty.

'Would you like some more?'

'Later...' Laura snuggled back under the duvet. 'Don't go...'

She could feel her eyes drifting shut again when the silence was broken by Noah. He was speaking so softly it almost sounded as if he was thinking out loud.

'Why is it that you need to control your curls, *mon coeur*? What are you afraid is going to happen if you don't keep such a tight hold on it?'

Laura didn't open her eyes. She didn't speak for a long moment, either, but there were words that wanted to come out in this quiet, semi-dark space. With this man whom she trusted so completely.

'It's not so much the bad things that happen,' she said slowly. 'Even if they hurt.' She let her breath out in a sigh. 'It's because it's your fault. Because you didn't do something you were supposed to do.'

'Like what?'

'Like putting the toys away so that Dada falls over when he comes home from work... or the pub... and he's hurt his head and he's angry. So angry...' Her breath hitched. 'He pushes me over when I try and pick up the toys and I'm crying and he hits Mam when she tries to get to me and her mouth is bleeding and she's scared and... she tells me to look after Fi and Ellie. To hide until it's over...'

Laura could feel the tears on her cheeks. Oh, help... she'd never said anything like this. To anyone. Ever...

She was too weak thanks to this horrible virus, that's what it was. She had lost control. And now that she'd started, she couldn't stop.

'...until *real* Dada comes back,' she added.

'Who's "real Dada"?' There was a catch in Noah's voice that was an echo of what Laura could feel in her heart.

That broken bit...

'The one who smiles and swings you up in his arms to kiss hullo.' Laura's voice was only a whisper. 'The one who tells you that you're the best and the most beautiful girl in the whole, wide world.' She could feel her words slowing down as sleep reached out to claim her again. 'The one who says, "I love you so much, Lulu"...'

* * *

It was like a rollercoaster, this illness. Laura seemed to be getting better but then her temperature would spike and she would be shivering and miserable again. She slept a great deal and was so weak and wobbly she needed help to get to the bathroom and then back to bed again. Noah had been on high alert for the symptoms he'd been warned to watch out for, but the medications seemed to be doing their job and her fever never got too high, her breathing was good and she wasn't at all confused, although he suspected she would never normally have talked about things that were so private.

Like her father.

Noah's heart was still aching for the child that Laura had been. He had wanted to reach back into the past and comfort her. To tell her that none of it was her fault. He wanted to tell her that she didn't need to spend the rest of her life trying to control and *straighten* everything in the world to keep the people she loved safe.

But he'd also wanted to tell her that she had the biggest heart of anyone he'd ever met and he wouldn't want to change anything about her. That it felt like a privilege that he had been able to meet the real Laura, who was so well hidden from everyone else.

He hadn't said anything, of course. That would be overstepping boundaries and that couldn't be allowed to happen just because he was tired and he'd spent too much time, too close to Laura. Noah hadn't been home for two days and he was about to start the vigil of the third – hopefully the last – night before the corner was turned and recovery could be trusted.

He needed to go home but he was caught in a web he couldn't break. He'd stayed because he couldn't *not* stay when Laura needed him, and now he couldn't leave because...

...because it was when he'd left Elise lying in *her* sick bed that she'd died. When she was having that seizure and he knew she might be dying but his mother said it was no place for a child and had sent him away. It had taken too many years to get rid of the irrational thought that, if he'd stayed, he could have kept her safe and he wouldn't have lost the person he loved the most.

Laura wasn't going to die. Julien had assured him that she was over the worst of this virus. She might even be well enough soon to go and have the check he wanted her to have for the baby. But, for some reason, deep down, being here felt like a long overdue apology to his sister. He was making up for not being there when he should have been. For *her*.

Maybe it was because of what Laura had said only a short time ago, after Ellie had been here to help her have a bath and brush her hair and she was back in bed and ready to sleep.

'She's the best sister anyone could ever have,' Laura had said. 'I love both my sisters, of course, but they're so different. Fi was always worried about everything but Ellie was the happy one. She was always smiling. And dancing. And her laughter was like music.' On the verge of sleep, there was a smile curving her lips. 'I *never* dance.' Her words were soft, as if she was sharing a shameful secret. 'But when I hear Ellie laugh? I'm always dancing – on the inside.'

Her words had been echoing in his head ever since.

It had been exactly like that with Elise but he'd never been able to articulate it. The way the warmth of her smile could light up a room had been a joy, but her laughter *had* been like the purest kind of music and it had made his soul dance and he knew that was what it felt like to love someone that much.

And why he could never feel it again.

He knew that the flip side of being able to dance inside like that was a hole that was so deep and dark and painful that the prospect of falling into it again was terrifying. If you let yourself love someone, you would have to take that risk, and Noah had decided, as that forgotten teenager, that he was unlikely to survive a second fall like that.

He still got a glimpse of what it was like, though. He just hadn't realised why it was that music was so important in his life. When he played his guitar and got lost in his music, was it because he could hear a note of Elise's laughter?

Was it making *him* dance inside?

20

Hospitals could be daunting establishments at any time. A world of its own with a sense of urgency lurking behind closed doors or amongst the flow of people wearing scrubs, with stethoscopes looped around their necks, some of them with disposable booties over their shoes and hats covering their hair as if they'd just popped out of an operating theatre for a short time. There was a strong smell of disinfectant and the sounds of pagers beeping or trolley wheels rattling.

When all the signs were in a different language, everyone was speaking too fast to follow and there was a possibility that you were going to be given bad news, the environment could easily become overwhelming. Especially when you were still feeling wobbly after a nasty, but mercifully brief, illness.

But Laura was not alone.

Julien had arranged this appointment in the *gynécologie et obstétrique* department at his hospital.

'They've got the most amazing technology,' Ellie had told her. '4D high-definition ultrasound. They can even take videos of the baby moving.'

'Come with me. Please?'

'You can only have two people in the room with you. Julien is going to be with you to translate what the technician and doctors say.'

'So you can be the other person.'

'Don't you think that should be your baby's father?'

Laura hadn't expected Noah to want to attend the appointment even though she knew he had insisted on paying the fees associated with it. But she hadn't expected him to watch over her like a guardian angel during those first days of being sick, either. It was a side of Noah that had been enough of a surprise to make her wonder if basing her judgement of his potential as a father on his lifestyle had been far too harsh. Maybe Ellie had said something to Julien, because he seemed to take it for granted that Noah would be coming with them.

And here he was. In this dim room where the main source of light was coming from the two screens attached to the ultrasound machine, one that the technician was sitting in front of and a larger one that was turned so that Laura could see it from where she was lying on the bed. Noah was standing on the other side, close to the head of the bed, facing the larger screen. Julien was standing behind the technician.

'Ooh!' The squirt of gel on her abdomen startled Laura.

'*Désolée.*' The technician smiled at her. '*Il fait un peu froid, n'est-ce pas? D'accord...*' She rubbed the transducer in the gel and then pressed it more firmly against the skin. '*C'est parti...*'

The scan was astonishing from the first moment. It was in colour and it was as real as if the skin on Laura's abdomen had been peeled back to reveal what was safely tucked away in her womb.

The technician would freeze an image on the screen and use cursors to mark points and measure parameters. She would change the angle and position of the transducer to find exactly what she was looking for. Julien's quiet voice relayed to Laura everything the technician was seeing and doing.

'That's the heart. You can see the four chambers and that the ventricular function is completely normal. So is the heart rhythm and the rate.'

There were two kidneys that were also normal, and no evidence of any defects in the spine or brain or any other anatomical structure. It was all totally reassuring. The only time Laura felt a moment of fear was when the gender of the baby was confirmed. She already knew it was a girl from her first scan but, when she saw him freeze for a moment, she knew she'd been right to think that sharing that information with Noah would only remind him instantly of the sister he'd lost.

The one he had buried his heart with.

But then the astonishing clarity of this technology showed tiny fingers and toes that were captivating enough to be a distraction from any pull into the past from learning the baby was a girl. There was the cutest button of a nose as well, but the most amazing thing was the movement – not only as evidence of life but that there was personality to be seen in it as well.

This baby girl was tilting her head and yawning. Her hands went over her ears as if the world was too noisy. She put her fingers in her mouth and... she *smiled*...

Laura's inward breath was a gasp.

Julien was saying something about it being caught on video but Laura wasn't listening. She'd even taken her eyes off the screen because she wanted to see if Noah was feeling what was bringing tears to her eyes.

This tiny human – currently the size of a carrot and only

weighing about a pound – was a real *person*, and the love that Laura could feel for this baby was filling her heart so hard it felt like it could burst.

Not just for the baby, either. Somehow, there was room for the enormous love she felt for Noah in there as well. He seemed so mesmerised by the screen that he wasn't aware of her gaze on his face and... were those tears she could see in his eyes?

Maybe the power of what Laura was feeling was enough to break the focus Noah had on the screen. Or maybe he was already dragging himself away, because his gaze shifted to catch Laura's and, just for a heartbeat, the shutters were open. She could see, so clearly, the love that this man was capable of, if he could only let himself embrace it.

And, *ohh*... there it was again...

That frisson she had felt in the wake of that amazing kiss they'd shared to welcome in the new year.

That... *hope*...

* * *

The scan was over. They had pictures. A USB stick with a video. A detailed report would follow.

Laura wiped the gel off her skin and climbed down from the bed. She still felt dazed as she followed Julien and Noah back to where the car was parked, and she was quite sure that Noah was equally affected by the experience they'd both had but he was hiding it well. They would go back to La Maisonette now. Noah would go home and Laura was planning to go online to rebook her tickets back to Scotland. Ellie was going to help her tidy up the cottage and get packed.

But something was becoming clearer to her with every step

she was taking. Whether or not he wanted to acknowledge it, Noah had felt an emotional connection with his baby and it had weakened the barriers he had around his heart, but if she took herself – and the baby she was carrying – far enough away, it would make it too easy for him to shore up that protection again and hide himself away in the space where he felt safe.

The same tiny voice that was whispering words of hope in her head, or possibly her heart, was also telling her that she shouldn't go home to Scotland. Not yet. That, if she did, that hope would be destroyed. Noah would never recognise, let alone trust, the love that was being offered to him. Or the love that he might even find himself able to return, at least to their baby. Perhaps even to her?

* * *

'You don't have to go home yet.' Ellie looked delighted at Laura's confession that she would prefer to stay longer. 'You're welcome to stay here for as long as you wish. I'd *love* you to stay. You could have your baby here – it's more than half French already, and I've heard that if they're born here, they automatically receive French nationality as well as keeping UK citizenship. Otherwise, I think you have to apply for it later.'

'But that's months away.' Laura felt a beat of panic. She hadn't given much thought yet to the actual birth of her baby.

'Not that many months. They'll go faster than you can imagine.'

'I have to get back to work.'

'You've been sick. I'm sure Julien could give you a doctor's note and you could ask for more leave. And shouldn't you tell your boss that you're pregnant? You'll need to arrange maternity leave and they'll have to organise other agents to take over your listings.'

'I need to sell my apartment.'

'Not right now. Isn't January the worst time to put a property on the market, with awful weather and people worried about how much they just spent on Christmas?'

'It can certainly be more challenging.'

'And you could take leave without pay if it came to that. You've got your share of the money from selling La Maisonette.' Ellie's expression softened. 'And Julien told me that Noah looked really emotional when he saw the baby.' She looked as if she was blinking back tears herself. 'It makes it so real, doesn't it? Like your heart just cracks open and gets filled with the most amazing love you can ever feel.'

They were both crying as they hugged, so tightly that they both had to let go in order to take a breath.

'Ring your boss,' Ellie ordered as she wiped tears away. 'Right now, before you talk yourself out of it.'

* * *

The last thing Laura expected was that Colin Armstrong would be delighted to hear that she wanted to stay in France longer.

'Couldn't be better timing,' he said. 'I never did get that chance to talk to you about the real estate market in the South of France. I've recently bought a property in Nice. A block of flats that I'm planning to renovate and sell separately down the track, but I'm not sure the agency I've purchased it through is the one I want to work with. I've been wondering how to find the right people on the ground to get the project up and running and... there *you* are. Our salesperson of the year! Perfect.'

'I might not be here long enough to do something that big.' Laura was still trying to find the right moment to tell Colin that she was pregnant. 'Passing on my current listings to other agents is only intended to be temporary.'

'You can get the ball rolling. A single step will start any journey, you know – but choosing the right route? That's what makes the real difference. It'll be some time before I can take possession, but I can arrange for you to get access and I'll come over when you find an agency in the area that you think might be suitable. What about the agent who sold the house you inherited? Didn't I hear that got snapped up in the blink of an eye? And that you had a big part in the marketing copy? I want the same dream team in charge of marketing this project.'

The reasons for the success of La Maisonette's sale had more to do with the passionate love affair happening between Ellie and Julien than any real-estate-marketing prowess on either side of the English Channel, but there was no need to explain that to Colin, was there?

Laura caught her breath. This wasn't fate giving her just a nudge in the direction she thought she wanted to go, was it? It felt more like a definitive shove.

'Aye,' she said. 'I think he might be just the right person.'

* * *

'*Ouah...*'

Noah was standing in the foyer of a small apartment block in one of the more prestigious areas of Nice, within easy walking distance of the Promenade des Anglaise and the beaches.

Laura was looking at the intricate pattern that edged the tiled floor between the front door and a lovely old wooden staircase. 'I love these mosaic tiles.'

'This place must have cost a fortune. And your boss has purchased the *whole* building? It must have about eight apartments.'

'I knew he was wealthy,' Laura said. 'But I don't think he's gone into this alone. He does want to keep one of the top floor apartments for himself, as a holiday home.' She was sorting through the bunch of keys she was holding. 'Apparently they all need "refreshment" and Colin wants me to find the local people he needs to talk to when he comes to meet you. He also wants me to stay long enough to see the project get off the ground. Shall we have a look?'

Noah followed Laura into one of the apartments. Mid-nineteenth century, it had the high ceilings, tall windows and parquet floors he had anticipated in the spacious rooms. The chandeliers and wrought-iron balconies were a nice touch but the kitchens and bathrooms needed updating.

The opportunity for Dufour Immobilier to be part of the refreshment and sale of apartments that would be highly sought after was a no-brainer, but Noah wasn't sure how he felt about Laura staying on in France long enough to be part of the process of setting up the partnership and the employment of contractors.

He still hadn't quite got his head around the changes in their relationship over the last week or so. The intimacy of being with her, night and day, while she was ill had inevitably brought them closer. The glimpse into the life of a child who was frightened of the one person she should have been able to trust to protect her had made those bonds feel unbreakable. But seeing the baby on that extraordinarily detailed scanning machine had been so overwhelming he was only just beginning to find he could think about it without a level of emotional reaction that was physically painful.

Whether or not he wanted it, this was really happening and it was a connection he would have with Laura for the rest of his life. This friendship – if it could fit into such a mundane-sounding category – was a relationship with another person unlike any Noah had ever experienced and he had no idea what he was, or was not, supposed to do. Maybe he still needed time to recover from the shock of seeing his child.

His *daughter...*

Ouais... Finding out that the baby was a girl had left raw patches on his heart, but experience had taught him that you could recover from almost anything, given some time and the necessary care. And the ability to parcel up any disruptive emotions that an illness or injury might have let loose and securely lock them away.

Recovery could mean that you were stronger than ever. Laura was almost completely healed from her recent physical illness and she definitely looked better than ever. Noah wondered if it was partly because she had stopped straightening her hair. It may well have had nothing to do with him telling her how much it suited her to have curly hair, but he hadn't been wrong. He was fascinated by the way the sunshine was catching those soft, red-gold curls that tumbled to her shoulders as she swung towards him from where she was standing by the tall windows.

'Isn't this amazing? It's going to be perfect.'

Her smile was just as bright as the glints of light in her hair and... was there something different about the curve of her lips as well? Was her physical appearance a reflection of changes on a deeper level? She seemed softer. Less determined, perhaps, to straighten out her whole life as well as her hair?

She certainly seemed happier, and that was exactly what he'd wished for her when he'd persuaded her to come back to France and live a little.

'*Parfait*,' he agreed, returning her smile. But he wasn't referring to this piece of real estate, however impressive it was.

Maybe this could be the perfect way to move forward with his own life. A combination of both a professional and personal relationship with the mother of his child. One project like this could easily lead to another, and working together would ensure regular contact and give him a way of being part of his daughter's life without the expectation of visits being for purely personal reasons, which could lead to disappointment for everybody involved.

Laura knew him now, perhaps better than anyone ever had. She'd been shocked by his approach to life but she knew exactly what to expect – and not expect – from him and she clearly accepted him for who he was. She had also accepted that gift he had given of teaching her the pleasure that can come from living in the moment. He'd had no idea of how that blink of time back in August had been going to change both their lives, but it was still a philosophy that he had no intention of abandoning.

He didn't need to let the weight of future responsibility crush the pleasure in this moment, of seeing the fragments of sunshine caught in Laura's curls or the unfiltered joy that was in her smile. He could simply enjoy the company of this extraordinarily beautiful woman. To savour the happiness, however fleeting it might be.

There was plenty to be happy about, after all. The potential of this new business arrangement was exciting. Laura was well again and nothing bad had happened to the baby. Noah could also be happy that he hadn't caught the virus himself, which was surprising, considering the kiss they had shared on *le réveillon*.

Ohh... that *kiss*.

Was it weird, when it should have been such a no-go area, to still feel so attracted to Laura now that she was pregnant?

More attracted, even, with the new depth their friendship had developed?

It wasn't so much that he was dreaming about taking her to his bed again.

It was just that he couldn't, for the life of him, stop thinking about that kiss.

21

It was almost worth getting really sick once in a while, Laura decided, because of how good it felt to recover.

She could feel a new energy humming in her veins. Things tasted better and smelled amazing. Colours seemed brighter and sounds clearer. The whole world seemed like a shinier place, and it felt so good to be alive it could give you a new perspective on life.

Quite possibly, where she was right now was enhancing the notion of there being a bright side to having been so ill. Apart from the hospital appointment, her first outing of the new year was to come and view Colin's real estate purchase in Nice and it was more than the beautiful location and architecture that was exciting Laura as they left the apartment block and walked past where she had parked her car to cross the Promenade des Anglaise and admire the closest beach to the property.

For a long moment they stood, side by side, breathing in the smell of salt in the air and taking in the glints of sunshine on seawater that was an amazing shade of turquoise until it turned into the whitest foam as the waves broke onto the pebbled beach.

Everything was so bright. So clear. Maybe that was why Laura suddenly had the feeling that her life was starting to finally fall into place after having been turned upside down and inside out by the discovery that she was pregnant.

She could almost see the process of how her brain was making sense of it all. It was like one of those Venn diagrams she'd learned about at school. Two circles. One of them enclosed her life in Scotland and it held her family and childhood. It was also full of rigid routines like getting up before dawn and going to the gym, the deadlines and pressure of her career in real estate. A strict, healthy diet and all the safe, boring men she had ever dated. Another circle had France as its outline and its interior couldn't be more different. It was full of impulsive things like riding on the back of a motorbike, the scent of lemons, and lavender fields. It was soft and sensual and... and Noah was there, along with the bittersweet bliss of falling in love.

But – and this was the epiphany – the circles of the Venn diagram overlapped each other and right now she was inside the intersection, with a mix of the familiar and new. She had family here in France, with Ellie and Julien and Theo, but she could now bring her career into the overlap, thanks to this potential joint project with Noah. And when her baby was born, that would become a whole new circle of her life and the single element in the more complicated intersection would be Noah. The father of her baby, a link to France for herself and to a circle still to come that represented the largely unexplored heritage she hadn't known she possessed.

She was liking this mathematical analogy. Life was all about adding new elements or circles. Maybe the key to happiness was to identify the most important links. The stars of the intersections.

Work.

Family.

The baby.

France.

Noah.

This mix of the different components of her life could be...

...*parfait*?

'Are you hungry?' Noah's voice broke into the buzz of finding the prospect of happiness within the overlap of her circles, one that she would still have access to after she went home.

'Starving,' she agreed. 'But I can wait. Could we walk for a while? This is the first time I've felt like I could do some exercise since I got sick.'

'Let's head for the old town,' Noah suggested. 'Walking is what the prom is all about, *n'est pas*?'

There were certainly many other people out walking, enjoying the sea air, with the sunshine and palm trees making it feel even less like the middle of winter. There were people walking their dogs and pushing prams or jogging. More than once, Noah cupped Laura's elbow to bring her closer to his side and protect her from others going much faster on scooters and bicycles and rollerblades.

They talked about renovation ideas for the apartments and the new marketing campaign that could take in a few of the many delights of the capital of the French Riviera, like the beautiful park of the Colline du Château and its views from the top of the hill, the historic Place Garibaldi and, perhaps, the pleasure of a food and wine tour of the old town, which was possibly why they ended up at the most famous market in Nice – the Cours Saleya.

In the heart of the old town, the colourful rows of striped awnings formed their own streets in this huge, paved area with tables beneath them offering a breathtaking array of fruit and vegetables and flowers. It was no wonder Laura's senses felt close to being overwhelmed with the movement and sound of crowds of people, both tourists and locals, doing their grocery shopping and the myriad scents and colours of so many different foods and flowers.

The rainbows of the flower stalls were so bright they made her blink, packed with flowers like ranunculus and dahlias and pots of polyanthus and pansies and...

'Daffodils,' Laura exclaimed. 'But it's the middle of winter. Aren't they gorgeous?'

Noah smiled and spoke to the woman at the stall. Moments later, he handed Laura a huge bunch of daffodils wrapped in hessian and tied with a rustic string bow. The flowers had cream petals and buttery yellow trumpets and the smell was glorious. She buried her nose amongst the blooms and inhaled more than the scent of spring. Noah had bought these flowers for her because he could see that she loved them. He had wanted to give her this small pleasure and...

...and it felt like when he'd been looking after her when she was sick.

As if he genuinely cared about her.

As if it wasn't impossible that he could, one day, fall in love with her?

Did that count as another heightened sense – this ability to feel the warmth of love as an actual physical sensation? The same kind of fizziness that came from the world being extra shiny?

Laura wanted to do something for Noah. But what...?

Another scent caught her nostrils and distracted her as someone walked past them, carrying something wrapped in a paper cone.

'What *is* that?' she asked. 'It smells delicious.'

'Socca,' Noah said. 'A local speciality. Like pissaladière and salade niçoise.'

'Oh... Ellie told me about socca. She adores it. I'd love to try some.'

They got the portions of smoky, salty chickpea pancakes wrapped in paper and tore pieces off to eat as they continued walking around the market, and Laura found the combination of heat and smoke, a crispy, salty exterior and the softness inside just as delightful as she'd been told it would be.

At the back of her mind she was still wondering what she could do for Noah. If nothing else, she really wanted to thank him for taking care of her. But they had finished their socca and were heading towards the outer edge of the market before inspiration finally struck.

'Let me cook for you,' she said aloud. 'I could make you dinner.'

'You can cook?' Noah lifted an eyebrow. 'How did I not know this?'

Laura could feel her lips twitch. To her surprise, she was coming to like being teased. It gave her a frisson of something... very pleasant. Because it reminded her of the first time? When they'd both know how much they wanted each other but Noah was pretending otherwise and letting it slowly simmer into something far more delicious.

Ooh… she could feel it now and it was even more powerful than it had been that first time. Tingles of sensation deep in her belly that were as sharp as lemon juice on the tip of your tongue and as decadent as the most wicked dessert. Laura had read about the increased libido that could happen for women in the second trimester of pregnancy but she hadn't believed it. Wasn't it a bit weird to want more sex when there was a small human that would actually be in the middle of it all?

It didn't feel weird right now.

Having sex with the other parent of that small human felt like the most natural thing in the world to do. Something else that she could be quite sure that every one of her senses would be only too happy to embrace in this astonishingly vibrant space of enjoying everything about life after feeling so unwell. The sight of that gorgeous body, completely naked, and the look that would be in his eyes – the one that told her how incredibly beautiful *she* was. The sound of him murmuring words in French, which was most definitely the language of love. The smell and taste of him. The *touch*…

Oh, *my*…

Laura made a huge effort to try and focus on cooking a dinner rather than the simmering sexual tension that was getting quite out of control.

They were passing another beautiful display of fresh produce where vegetables were arranged like a giant flower, with heads of green broccoli and leafy leeks like leaves and stalks around a centre of cauliflowers, with their snowy white florets looking like blossom.

Inspiration struck and provided a distraction from the simmering that was threatening to boil over at any moment.

'Do you like cauliflower cheese?' she asked.

'*C'est quoi?*'

'Cauliflower.' Laura pointed at the display. 'And cheese. Cooked.'

'Ah...' Noah nodded. '*Le chou-fleur au gratin. Oui. C'est bon.*'

'I can make it really well,' Laura told him.

'*Moi aussi,*' Noah said. '*C'est une de mes spécialités.*'

Was he teasing her again? Did he want a competition to see who could cook the best cauliflower cheese?

'With truffles,' Noah added. 'Black truffles. And it happens to be the season for those particular truffles right now. We can buy them here.'

Laura bit her lip. Maybe he wasn't teasing this time.

'Do you use Dijon mustard?'

'*Bien sûr*. And Emmental cheese. With some Parmesan on the top along with the freshly grated truffle. I also know where to buy cheese here. Shall we go shopping?'

Laura couldn't help it. She ran her tongue, slowly, over her bottom lip.

'That does sound... delicious.'

But Noah didn't seem to be listening. He was staring at her lips as if he could still see the trail of moisture her tongue had left behind, and Laura knew she'd lost the battle to prevent that uncontrolled heat from boiling over. Spears of sensation were escaping the confines of her belly and were reaching all the way to her fingertips and her toes with the speed of light. They were scrambling her brain.

And making her heart sing.

She was, in fact, dancing inside.

'*Ce soir,*' Noah murmured, his voice more than a little husky. 'We shall make this cauliflower cheese of yours this evening, but together. With my truffles. *D'accord*?'

Laura had to clear her own throat. She did her best to

sound nonchalant. *Française*. She even threw in a subtle, careless shrug and an almost imperceptible purse of her lips.

'D'accord...'

* * *

The scent of the daffodils that filled the white jug Laura had found in the crockery cupboard had drifted right through La Maisonette's kitchen and living area by the time Laura left to make her first visit to Noah's home in St Paul de Vence later that afternoon.

She wasn't feeling so nonchalant now. Something closer to the nervous point in a spectrum that ranged from dread to excitement was creating butterflies in her stomach and had, no doubt, been responsible for her taking the time to wash her hair, do her make-up and agonise over her limited choice of clothes before what felt like rather a significant rendezvous to cook a shared dinner. Should she go for her jeans and sloppy jumper and make this casual, or wear the dress she had chosen for Ellie's wedding? Would it be too obvious that she was thinking about the night Noah had taken her to the Chèvre d'Or and she'd worn that sexy black dress? Would he remember the sound of that zip being undone and the way that silky fabric had simply melted off her body? Had she imagined how mesmerised he'd been by watching her lick her lips at the market?

Was she about to find out?

Noah's home turned out to be part of an old mansion that had been beautifully converted into bespoke apartments. He met her at the front door of the huge house and Laura knew instantly that she'd made the right choice to go casual. Noah was also wearing jeans, with a black tee shirt, and the brief touch of eye contact made Laura wonder if he, too, was feeling a little nervous about the impulsive plan to make dinner together.

This wasn't about cauliflower cheese at all, was it?

His apartment turned out to be the whole top floor of the building and it was literally breathtaking for Laura as she walked into a living area that had a curved wall with floor to ceiling glass and a view that was a postcard image of St Paul de Vence. The tall ramparts of the medieval town rose from a green swathe of trees that covered the lower part of the hill-side, and the bell tower of the church stood out like a single fat candle offset on a birthday cake made up of a tumble of ancient stone houses in tawny, earthy shades of brown and gold and pale terracotta.

'Oh, my goodness... this is stunning...'

'Make yourself at home,' Noah invited. 'Please... sit down.'

There was a very comfortable-looking couch with a guitar propped against the end of it but Laura didn't want to sit down yet. She went to a telescope positioned on a tripod at the central point of the windows, and as soon as Noah showed her how to turn a wheel to adjust the focus, it felt as if Laura could reach out and touch those stone walls of the village – the way Ellie had traced the stone flowers in the cobbled streets when they'd walked in the medieval village for the first time.

'I can see the horse that's made completely out of horse-shoes,' she exclaimed. 'If it wasn't starting to get dark, I think I'd be able to see the bells in the tower as well.'

'But it's so pretty when it's getting dark, no?' Noah was still standing beside Laura. 'I can never decide what part of the day or season of the year is my favourite. There's always something different to see. I love that a village can have a... what is it – a *personnalité* – a character all of its own.'

They watched the rose-gold tinge of sunset begin to kiss the stone walls of the ramparts and houses. Lights were coming on in the streets and windows and the village took on the fairy-tale sparkle of night-time and made Laura think of being there as the old year gave way to a new beginning.

And that, inevitably, made her think of the kiss...

The way Noah cleared his throat made her wonder if he was trying to distract himself from the same thought.

'I have all our ingredients ready,' he said. 'Shall we start cooking?'

Laura had never imagined that the process of preparing food could be such an intimate experience. Right from the moment she washed her hands at the kitchen sink and Noah folded them into a soft, dry towel before putting his own hands under the running water. He didn't simply slice up the cauliflower into small pieces, he divided it carefully into perfect florets to drop into the pot of boiling salted water, and it was hard to focus on her own task of grating cheese when she wanted to keep watching the movement of his hands. The rather funky aroma of the black truffle as it was also grated to go into the butter of the béchamel sauce was new to Laura and she had to wonder how those sulphurous notes could improve the flavour, but Noah seemed to know what he was doing.

She leaned against the kitchen bench, watching him whisking flour into the truffle and butter, then slowly adding milk and cheese and mustard, stirring it constantly with a well-used-looking wooden spoon.

How had she never realised how incredibly sexy it was to watch a man cooking? To stand in his kitchen, knowing that they would be sharing this meal when it was finished?

It was like being cared for when she was sick.

Being nurtured.

It felt remarkably like being loved.

Noah finally lifted the wooden spoon he had been using to stir the sauce and swiped his finger across it. He touched his tongue to his finger, looking up with a thoughtful expression as he considered the taste to find Laura was staring at him. There was just a hint of a smile as he nodded in satisfaction and then he swiped the spoon again and reached towards Laura to offer her a taste and...

...she was completely undone. She parted her lips, closing them again around his finger as she touched it with her tongue, and she knew that this was another *tuerie*.

Something so good, it was to die for.

And, as amazingly delicious as this sauce was, that wasn't what she meant.

This time, it was Noah watching *her* and Laura couldn't have broken that gaze even if her life had depended on it.

It was Noah who broke it. In complete silence, he poured the cheese sauce over the blanched cauliflower florets that were in a cast-iron baking dish, sprinkled Parmesan, breadcrumbs and more truffle over the top, put the dish into the oven and set a timer.

And then, still without saying a word, he held out both his hands and Laura put hers into them. He drew her closer, so slowly it felt dreamlike. Nothing was being said aloud but everything was being said in that eye contact.

Would it be okay? Is it safe?

Yes... it's perfectly safe. And it would be more than okay.

Do you want this? As much as I do?

Yes... I think I want it even more...

It was the New Year's Eve kiss all over again.

Only, this time, when they finally broke apart, they knew it wasn't finished.

It was only just beginning.

* * *

Noah had not forgotten a single detail about Laura's body.

The taste of her mouth.

The delicacy of her collarbone, just under that perfect skin, that could lead his fingers and his lips to the hollow at the base of her neck and then down to the exquisite firmness of those perfect breasts.

But while this was astonishingly familiar, given that he'd only taken Laura to bed on that one occasion, it was also completely new.

Her breasts were so much softer and even more luscious.

And that belly...

Oh, mon Dieu...

The roundness of it was the sexiest thing his hands had ever traced. This was yet another version of Laura Gilchrist, and it was definitely the most beautiful so far. Making love to her demanded reverence. Time. A gentleness that spoke of a need to offer protection Noah had never experienced in his sex life. A gentleness he was determined not to break even as the tiny sounds Laura was making were pleading with him to take them both over the edge.

Despite the assurance that this was safe for the baby, Noah had no intention of putting any of his weight on Laura's belly but, in the end, it seemed an easy, mutual decision for her to turn, press her back against his body and lie in the circle of his arms, and... it was perfect. Not just for protection but to ensure he could take Laura to the release she desperately wanted before he allowed himself the pleasure of ultimate satisfaction.

He had no idea how long they lay like that, without

moving, waiting to catch their breath and for their hearts to slow down. He didn't want to move just yet. He wanted to feel Laura's skin against his own and her hands beneath his as they rested on that sexy roundness of her belly. It seemed that she felt the same way.

And then he felt it.

A ripple of movement beneath their hands. A soft knock.

'She's awake,' Laura whispered. 'Did you feel that?'

Noah could still feel it, a prickle of awareness that touched something else that was completely new for him. He had seen this baby on the screen of the scanning machine, but this was the first time he had ever *felt* an unborn baby.

His baby.

He moved his hand so that it was directly on Laura's skin, and when he felt another kick it was so much clearer. Because he'd seen that scan, he could visualise the tiny foot on the other side of that layer of skin and muscle. He could even imagine that this baby girl might be yawning at the same time. Or smiling?

He couldn't identify how it was making him feel, maybe because that was too new as well. But it wasn't a comfortable feeling and it was too close to being overwhelming.

Noah drew his hand away carefully. He pressed a kiss onto the back of Laura's shoulder.

'I can smell our dinner.'

'Mmm... so can I.'

'Are you hungry?'

'Mmm...'

Laura turned her head and the look in her eyes made Noah want to forget about dinner or even checking that the oven had turned itself off and wasn't going to ruin the food by burning it to a crisp.

The sheer force of the desire to stay here and make love to Laura all over again was almost irresistible. Until he remembered the sensation of feeling their baby move. Holding back what felt like a tsunami of emotion behind that memory was... kind of terrifying.

He rolled away and swung his legs over the side of the bed, reaching for his jeans that were puddled on the floor.

'Five minutes,' he said. 'You will love it, I promise...'

22

There was something different about Noah.

Or was it Laura who was different?

Whatever it was, it seemed to be creating a tension that Laura couldn't understand.

Some weird inverse correlation that meant the closer they got to each other, the further apart it felt.

The night of *le chou-fleur au gratin* – which had, indeed, been possibly the most delicious meal she had ever eaten – had been the latest peak of the emotional rollercoaster that represented her relationship with Noah Dufour. It had been building ever since that New Year's Eve kiss, as he cared for her while she was sick and when he came with her, as the father of her baby, to see the ultrasound scan. To make love to her – with such heartbreaking tenderness – when her body was so changed with her pregnancy and to feel his hands over hers as she felt the baby moving beneath them had taken her own emotional reaction to everything going on in her life to a whole new level.

A rather frightening level, because it was too high and that meant that a fall could be devastating. Laura was breaking one of her own steadfast rules here. She'd never let herself get this... *hopeful* before.

To make herself so incredibly vulnerable.

Perhaps it was because she could see, or sense, a future that was everything she could dream of. Every wish she'd had, for as long as she could remember, coming true. To have a family around her that she could trust was perfectly safe, people she could love with all her heart and soul – whom she knew, without a shadow of any doubt, loved her back just as much.

People that would never ever deliberately hurt her or simply walk away without so much as a word or a backward glance.

As the days clicked over from January into February and the better chance of her baby's survival, even if she arrived early, contributed its own boost to that rollercoaster, Laura knew she should be thinking about practical things.

Like going home. Selling her apartment. Buying baby clothes and nappies and accessories that were currently deemed indispensable, according to what Laura was finding online. Like wraps to keep your infant in contact with your body as much as possible and weirdly shaped sleep suits that swaddled them so they couldn't move their arms and bassinets that attached to your own bed so you could safely co-sleep.

There was something holding her back from diving into the deep end of that pool, however, and it was strong enough to make her resist even making a decision about when she would travel back to Scotland. It was so easy to find reasons why she couldn't go back just yet. There were appointments nearly every day with architects and builders, electricians, plumbers, tilers and interior designers as Laura made a shortlist and collated a portfolio in preparation for Colin Armstrong's visit planned for March. Noah went to every meeting with her both as a partner in the upcoming project and as translator, although her French was improving every day. There were shops to visit, as well, to look at soft furnishings and window treatments and kitchen designs, and there was always something that Noah wanted her to see in and around Nice that was special.

They hadn't made love again but Laura could still feel the vibration of physical attraction that was always there between them. She knew, instinctively, that if she pushed too hard, that hum could well be silenced completely, and that was the last thing she wanted to happen. This was a business relationship but it was also allowing their very personal bond to coalesce into something that was feeling more and more solid and potentially significant to both of them.

Time with Ellie was special, too. Laura could see just how happy her sister was in her new life. She could let go of the anxiety that had been in the background ever since her beloved baby sister had been born, had ramped up when Ellie had been pregnant and her partner had walked out on her and had become an unbearable crisis when her life had imploded with the loss of her precious baby. The poignancy of that shared tragedy would always be there but Ellie's genuine joy in Laura's pregnancy had made the bond between the sisters stronger than ever. It felt like a solid foundation stone of a perfect future family that Laura was unable to stop herself dreaming about.

One that included Noah as their daughter's father – and *her* partner. A family of her very own.

* * *

There was no hiding Laura's pregnancy by the time Colin flew in to formalise his partnership with Dufour Immobilier and his expression was dismayed as he turned towards Laura after greeting Noah.

'Oh my goodness... You look like you'll be on maternity leave any minute, Laura. And I thought the only thing I needed to worry about was keeping you as part of the team when you've clearly fallen in love with France.'

'Even single mothers are capable of working,' Laura said. 'I've still got plenty of time to get back and set everything up to run smoothly while I take *some* maternity leave.'

She threw just a passing glance at Noah, as if to reassure him that she wasn't about to reveal anything personal concerning their relationship or the paternity of this baby. His secrets were – and always would be – safe with her.

Then she smiled at Colin. 'At least you know, now. I'll be relying on you to give me first viewing on any properties that will be more suitable for me, because it's really not an option to be carting a pram up and down my stairs. I'll be with my mum for the first few weeks but I'd like to be moving into a place of my own by the end of May.'

She didn't look back at Noah as she was speaking but she could *feel* his reaction. She couldn't quite interpret it but, oddly, it felt not dissimilar to the dismay she'd just seen on Colin's face. Another quick glance made her dismiss that notion, however. If anything, he was looking perfectly happy with the idea that she would be leaving France soon to get her new life as a single mother set up.

Colin was also looking happier. 'So you'll be selling your apartment with that superb harbour view?'

'Yes. As soon as possible.'

'I can help with that too.' Colin gave her the ghost of a wink. 'We'll talk. Soon.'

Laura had expected to talk to Noah far sooner than Colin after they'd gone their separate ways following a long day of successful negotiations and introductions to potential contractors, but a day went past with no contact.

And then another.

There were any number of things Laura could have used as an excuse to message Noah. She could have asked him to remind her of the name of one of the interior design shops they had visited recently, or to send a business card for the architect who specialised in bathroom renovations but, for some reason, she held back. She wanted him to contact her.

Her heart actually skipped a beat when she finally saw his name on the screen of her phone.

Are you busy tomorrow? Could you meet me in Vence at 1500 hrs? I would appreciate your opinion on a property I'm about to list for sale.

Yes. Where?

Ave. Colonel Méyere. I will send a map reference.

The address wasn't hard to find.

And the house was beautiful. It had the traditional roofing of curved terracotta tiles and golden stone walls in a lovely garden setting.

'It looks like a bigger version of La Maisonette,' she said to Noah.

'*Exactement*.' He seemed pleased by the comparison. 'This

is a villa, not a cottage. It has four bedrooms and two bathrooms and it has had a complete renovation.'

Curious, Laura followed Noah into the house. Why did he want her opinion on a house that didn't need renovation or even staging to make it stand out in the market?

This was a stunning property. She walked through rooms that had stone floors or the rich patina of restored ancient wood complemented by simple limewashed walls. The spacious kitchen had marble benchtops and a butler's sink with brass fittings and the living room wall opened up to an enormous terrace that was shaded by a vine-covered pergola and had not only an outdoor dining table and chairs but cane couches and a built-in barbecue and pizza oven.

A stretch of beautifully manicured lawn featured huge olive trees enclosed by stone walls that would provide a shaded spot to sit and admire a wonderful view across the hills and forests all the way to the sea. One of the trees had a branch big enough to support a swing. Laura could almost hear the echo of a child's laughter and the bark of a dog from playtime in this garden. She actually looked over her shoulder at the swing behind them as if she might see it moving, as it would if someone had just jumped off.

'This is the perfect home for a family,' she said to Noah. 'It's absolutely gorgeous.'

His nod was thoughtful. 'It's the best area, too. There are two *écoles maternelles* – the first school for children in France – only a few minutes' walk away. There is the *médiathèque* and public swimming pool, and we're also so close to the Grand Jardin – the supermarkets, the doctors, the cinema.' He shrugged. 'Everything you could wish for, I think.'

Laura mirrored his nod. 'You won't have the slightest problem selling this. I'm not sure why you need my opinion?'

'I'm not selling it,' Noah said quietly. 'I'm thinking of *buying* it...'

Laura felt herself going still.

'...for you. And the child. *Our* child.'

Laura's mouth felt dry. Her question came out in a whisper. '*Why*...?'

He met her gaze. 'I want to take care of you,' he said simply. His gaze dropped to her belly. 'And the *bébé*.'

Laura caught the subtle movement of his fingers flexing gently as he spoke. Was he remembering how it felt when the baby had moved beneath his hands?

'I have been thinking about this,' he added. 'If you want, we could live here together. We could bring our child up together. In this house.'

His words flowed around Laura like a genre of music she couldn't name. Fairy words, offering her the magic of the future she had already allowed herself to dream about. Living with Noah and their daughter as a family. With her sister and a cousin for her child in the next village. In a country that was part of her own heritage and an even bigger part of her future.

Above all, it was offering her a future with the man she was so hopelessly in love with. Living close enough for it to be inevitable that he would learn to trust enough to let them both into his heart?

This felt – almost – like a proposal of marriage. Would Noah hold her in his arms and kiss her senseless if she said yes?

She wanted to say yes. It was right there, coming straight from her heart to reach the tip of her tongue.

Yes, yes... *yes*...

But the word wouldn't quite come out. Laura opened her mouth but then closed it again. She couldn't break the eye contact between them and, when she saw the way Noah's face softened, her heart melted completely.

If felt like he understood something she couldn't understand herself.

'It's big,' he said softly. 'You need time to think about it. You have things in your life that you need to take care of first, perhaps. Like selling your apartment?'

The first piece of a new jigsaw fell into place. This explained Noah's odd reaction when she'd been talking to Colin about being a single mother. In Scotland.

He didn't want her to be that far away, and that only increased that melty feeling in Laura's heart. She was on an even higher point of that rollercoaster right now. She could see into the future. The dream was close enough to reach out and touch.

'Thank you so much,' she said. 'I love this house, Noah. I love the idea of raising our child together but... you're right. It's a very big decision. And I do need to go home and get things sorted and... maybe the timing is perfect. Would a week or two be too long to wait? Are there other people who are looking to buy this house?'

'*Non*...' Noah smiled. 'It's not officially on the market yet. And...' He touched Laura's cheek with his finger. 'And some things are worth waiting for, *ma puce*. Come... let's walk a little. I can show you both the schools that are nearby.'

* * *

Just past one of the schools was a narrow lane that caught Laura's attention. 'What's down there?'

'That's the entrance to the *cimetière*,' Noah told her.

Laura's steps slowed. 'There was something you were going

to tell me about this cemetery. A long time ago, when I came to take the photos of La Maisonette.'

When they'd became lovers...

'Oh... I remember now.' Laura could feel a flush of pink in her cheeks at the reason her memory had been jogged. 'You said D. H. Lawrence was buried here.'

'Just for a while.' Noah's eyebrow quirked, as if he was also thinking about the most famous book banned for being too sexually explicit. 'Would you like to see where his grave was?'

'Yes, please.'

They walked into the tidiest cemetery Laura had ever seen. Gravelled pathways on several levels divided walls of raised graves and their monuments. Most had colourful arrays of artificial flowers, some had real plants, like neatly clipped rosemary bushes, and there were splashes of green from tall, conical cypress trees.

There was a simple plaque on a stone wall to commemorate where the author had been buried.

> Ici reposa David Herbert Lawrence de Mars 1930 à Mars 1935.

'Only five years?' Laura was intrigued.

'His wife, Frieda, moved back to New Mexico where they'd previously lived. She arranged to have him exhumed and cremated.'

Noah's expression told her there was more to the story.

'The story is that the captain of the ship was told he needed the same paperwork for an urn of ashes as for a body and he wasn't happy, so he threw the ashes into the sea. When he got to New York, he put some ashes into the urn from a fireplace so that it wasn't empty.'

'Is it a true story?'

'Who knows?' Noah shrugged. 'But it is a good story.'

It was, but Laura saw that Noah's smile faded quickly enough to be odd as they walked back towards the gates of the cemetery. His steps slowed as well, and when he stopped completely she glanced at the headstone and her heart fell like a stone.

This was the Dufour tomb.

Noah's parents were buried here.

And his beloved sister, Elise, who'd lived for only seven years.

It was one thing to have listened to Noah telling her about Elise and to feel heartbreak on his behalf. It had been another to stand beside him in the mountain chapel in Moustiers-Sainte-Marie, watching the flickering flames of their candles, but it was a very different feeling to be standing here, knowing that this was his little sister's final resting place.

The grave, with its weathered concrete walls and an ornate cross, looked as neat and cared for as those around it. There was a permanent flower arrangement of ceramic sunflowers and, beside it, something Laura hadn't seen on any of the dozens of graves she'd walked past already – a small, plain bowl that was filled with small differently coloured stones.

Heart-shaped stones.

Laura looked up to find Noah watching her.

'I put one in the bowl every year, on the anniversary of her death,' he said softly. 'There should be twenty-eight in there now because I don't think anyone has ever taken one away.'

Laura's heart broke all over again. For Elise. For Noah. And for herself?

She slipped her hand into his as they walked away from the grave and he didn't object to her touch but it didn't feel that

Laura was connected in any more than a physical way. It felt as if some of that hope she'd gathered around herself might not have been any more than wishful thinking.

She could hear Noah's voice as clearly as if he were saying the words aloud again.

'I buried my heart with Elise... I am not capable of feeling that kind of love again...'

23

'So... have you decided?'

'About what?' Laura looked up from an opened box on the kitchen table of her mother's cottage. 'You know I have a million things that I'm deciding about at the moment, Mam. Like' – she gestured at the pile of neatly folded small garments beside the box – 'does Ellie really want me to use all Jack's baby things that we stored in the attic?'

'Aye, I'm sure she does.' Jeannie stroked a small jumper she had knitted herself. 'It's like a gift from her baby to yours. Let's pack them away again for now, hen. It's time for dinner.'

Laura lifted the box only to find something beneath it. 'What's this?'

'Oh...' Jeannie had an odd expression on her face. 'I found it in the attic when I went up to get the baby clothes.'

'Is it one of Ellie's?' Laura picked up the sketch pad, which looked like the ones her sister had been using ever since she'd discovered her passion for art as a child.

'No...' Jeannie took the pad from Laura's hands and flipped

through the pages. 'It was something your father did as a hobby. I wanted to show you this.'

It was a pencil sketch of moor-covered hills.

'I remember him drawing,' Laura said quietly. 'That looks like the Campsie Fells.'

'But look…' Jeannie touched the heavy paper.

'It's a stone cottage. Or the ruins of one.'

'What does it remind you of?' Jeannie broke the silence before Laura could say anything. 'Do you remember the painting in the wee house in France?'

'Oh, Mam… it's just a stone building. They all look like that.'

Jeannie closed the pad and put it on top of the box. 'Aye… you're right. It's a coincidence, nothing more. And it's past time we should we eating our dinner.'

Laura picked up the box, put it on the floor in the corner of the room and then rubbed her lower back, which was aching more than usual. 'It smells delicious. What is it? Sausage stovies? Shepherd's pie?'

'Aye… Shepherd's pie. It was always your favourite, wasn't it? Are you hungry?'

'I'm always hungry these days. Could be because there's not so much room for food in there now. I have to carry snacks with me wherever I go.'

'It could be that you're doing too much.' Jeannie clicked her tongue as she opened the oven, took out a very-well-worn ceramic dish and put it onto a metal trivet in the centre of the kitchen table. The cheese on top of the mashed potato was crispy and brown. All around the edge, from beneath the potato, bubbles of the rich, tomatoey sauce that the meat and vegetables had cooked in were escaping. Jeannie poked a serving spoon through the crisp topping and fragrant steam billowed out.

'Sit yourself down while I get the plates,' she ordered. 'And you haven't answered my question yet – about whether you've made a decision.'

'Hmm...' Laura knew exactly what decision her mother was referring to, but it was becoming automatic to back away from trying to find an answer – for her mother *or* herself. 'I decided not to repaint the living room in my apartment,' she offered, hoping Jeannie would take the hint. 'It's fine the way it is and I want to get it on the market by next week. It's taken longer than I thought it would to declutter and give it a deep clean. There was way more to do in the office than I expected, too, to get ready to take maternity leave.'

'You should be on maternity leave already.' Jeannie spooned some of the shepherd's pie onto Laura's plate. 'You're running out of time if you do decide you want to live in that beautiful house. And have your baby born in France.'

'I've got a few weeks left.'

The look from Jeannie was enough of a reprimand to make her pause, her fork halfway to her mouth. Laura sighed.

'No, I haven't decided and I know I'm running out of time. I won't be able to fly soon. I really *want* to go and live in Vence. In that house... with Noah...' She put her fork back down on her plate. 'But maybe I want it too much to make a rational decision.'

'Because you're in love with Noah?'

'Aye...'

'And you don't think he feels the same way you do?'

'I know he doesn't. He can't. He won't let himself.'

Jeannie's expression was thoughtful as she ate a mouthful

of the pie. 'Maybe he won't be able to help himself when you're a part of his life. When his bairn is there as well.'

Which was exactly what Laura was dreaming might happen. She knew that Noah was capable of truly loving someone. Loving them deeply enough to keep him going back, year after year, even though they were gone, to put a small stone heart into a bowl. She ate in silence for a minute, barely tasting what *had* always been a favourite childhood meal, maybe precisely because of the memories it was invoking.

'But what if he doesn't?' she asked quietly.

That fear was what kept her pushing the decision to the back of her mind. She would never be able to stop loving Noah but how could she live with him, or even near him, if he was never able to love her back in the same way? How could she live like that? It would be a sentence of lifelong heartbreak that would destroy her in the end. Slowly, piece by piece, but very, very surely.

'What if things go wrong?' The words came out in a whisper. 'Like they did for Ellie with Liam?' She swallowed hard, her gaze shifting towards the box in the corner of the room with the sketch pad lying on top of it. 'Like they did for you with Dada...?'

It was Jeannie's turn to put down her fork. 'I never told you this, hinny, but I was pregnant with you when I married your dad. We barely knew each other but we were madly in love and... and mebbe Gordon was just doing the right thing at the time but he fell in love with you the moment you were born. He adored every one of his children. *And* me...'

Laura heard the faintest echo of a deep, male voice.

'I love you, Lulu...'

She swallowed hard. 'But that's what scares me. What if I

find out that Noah's not who he seems? That he might be a monster?'

'Your father was never a monster,' Jeannie said, a sharp note in her voice. Then it softened. 'He was a wonderful husband and father until...' She cleared her throat. '...whatever it was that went wrong. Gordon wasn't a violent person. For all those years he was a gentle giant of a man and I adored him. I wanted him to go to a doctor but he wouldn't. I thought something would happen and he'd end up in hospital or jail and then he'd have to get help but something *did* happen and... he was just gone...'

'Oh... *Mam*...' Awkwardly, Laura got off her chair and went to wrap her arms around her mother, who was wiping away tears. 'I'm so sorry...'

Jeannie sniffed and then fished in the pocket of her apron for a hanky. 'Don't be sorry,' she said. 'I have my three beautiful daughters and I'm about to be a granny again, thanks to you. And I'm so happy for Ellie. She'd been brave enough to try again and look at how happy she is.' She blew her nose and picked up her fork again, signalling that the upset was over and done with and Laura could stop hugging her now. 'If you go and live in Vence, you'll be close to her and I can come and stay in that lovely wee house and visit with you all. I believe that things will come right for Fiona one of these days, too, and that might even start when she comes to meet her new niece and...' She waited until Laura was sitting down again. 'I'm thinking that what we were talking about on Christmas Day really will happen. That we'll *all* be together next Christmas.'

Laura poked at her food, trying to find an appetite that seemed to have vanished. She remembered her mother's other hope – that Ellie might even be pregnant again by then.

'You're right about our Ellie,' she said. 'I think she might have been lucky enough to have found the secret to happiness.'

'It's no' really a secret,' Jeannie said, with a smile. 'There's certainly some luck involved but we all know what it is, deep down.'

'Do we?'

'Of course. It's love. Pure and simple. Now' – she pointed her fork at Laura's plate – 'eat up. And make your decision soon. You're keeping that man of yours waiting and that's not really fair, is it?'

* * *

'*Merci, mon ami. À bientôt.*'

Noah ended the call, dropped his phone onto his desk and opened the top drawer. A half-full pack of cigarettes had been in there for weeks now, ever since he'd decided to stop smoking – in case he was going to be living in the same house as a baby.

He put a cigarette between his lips and reached for the lighter that was in the same drawer. Living with a baby – *his* baby – was not going to happen now so there was no point in giving up one of life's pleasures, was there?

That was what the phone call he'd just made had been about. He'd rung his acquaintance who owned the house in Vence that he had taken Laura to view, thanked him for giving him a personal first refusal, apologised for having taken so long and then delivered the news that he was not going to purchase the property after all and would now put it on the open market.

It had been an awkward call to make.

Embarrassing.

But those feelings were nothing in comparison to how the call from Laura had left him feeling.

He'd been shocked by that.

Angry...?

Yes... Noah flicked the lighter and held the flame to the end of his cigarette. Of course he was angry. He was as angry as he had been when he'd discovered that Laura was pregnant and she hadn't had the courtesy to tell him or allow him any input into choices being made. He drew in the smoke and then blew it out in a dismissive kind of huff. She hadn't even had the decency to *call* him last night. She'd left an audio message instead. Something he could only listen to and not say a word.

Noah lifted his hand to take another puff of his cigarette but his hand stopped before it reached his lips. Instead, he stubbed it out in the ashtray on his desk and reached for his phone. Maybe he should have let the message be automatically deleted but something had made him tap the 'keep' option as he'd stared, stunned, at the empty screen long after the recording had ended.

Laura's voice, with its lilting Scottish accent, sounded as if she was actually in his office when he tapped the Play button. Like she had been the very first time he'd laid eyes on her.

'I'm so sorry this has taken so long, Noah, and I'm sorry to be just leaving a message, but I would never be able to say everything I need to say if I heard your voice.'

Her voice wobbled.

'The first thing I want to say is thank you. Thank you for wanting me to live with you in Vence and finding that beautiful house that would be so perfect for a family. I wanted to say yes from the moment you said you wanted to take care of me and the baby and that we could raise her together, but something stopped me and I finally realised what it was.'

There was a moment's silence then, as if Laura was taking a slow, deep breath.

'I wanted to say yes so much, but it wasn't so much that I wanted you to be a part of your daughter's life, it was because I wanted you to be a part of mine. Because... I love you, Noah. I know you won't want to hear this but I'm completely in love with you. Maybe you've guessed that already. I know you don't feel the same way. That you can't feel the same way. And I understand why, I really do. And I know how big this offer of living together is for you.'

He could hear the intake of a new breath this time.

'The problem is that, for me, loving someone who can't love me back would be only living half a life and it would be too hard. I don't want our daughter to live like that, either. She deserves more than that. I deserve more than that and... and so do you, Noah. It breaks my heart that you can't take the risk of letting yourself get close enough to someone to accept this kind of love or be able to return it. Maybe, one day, you will, but I can't make the biggest decisions of my life based on nothing more than hope. Because this isn't just about me.'

Another silence, but it was a kind of sound – the sound of an imaginary door closing?

'I put my apartment on the market two weeks ago and it sold remarkably quickly. I'm going to stay with my mother when the baby is born, but I'm trying to find a house to buy that I'll be able to move into very soon.'

Her voice wobbled again.

'I'll let you know as soon as it looks like something's happening. I would be okay with you being present for the birth if you want to be. Or to have you visit as soon as you can afterwards. I really want you to be part of our lives, Noah, and I hope we can always be friends, but… it's best for all of us if we keep our lives the way they were.'

A tiny silence suggested there was nothing more to say.

'*À bientôt*. I hope…'

The call ended on something that sounded like a stifled sob.

A sound that had to be ignored.

He wasn't going to allow sympathy for Laura to override what was happening. He was still angry. Buying that house and taking all the responsibility of being a father and partner had been the only real choice he'd been able to make and it had been rejected.

He had been rejected.

It was just as well he'd kept enough control to protect his own heart. It had been a mistake to think they could be that close. It was back to plan A. He really didn't need to feel guilty that he was not a part of that child's life on a daily basis, which could have become a deeply meaningful level, because Laura had made the choice to exclude him.

He would do what he was allowed to do in the way of financial support and he would be a father to his child.

From a safe distance.

Just the way he liked all of his personal relationships to be.

He reached for the packet of cigarettes again but then he stared at the box. Making a kind of growling sound deep in his throat, he crushed the packet in his hand and hurled it into the wastepaper basket.

He was done.

* * *

A week or so later and Noah knew he would never smoke again. He wasn't even remotely tempted to because he knew it would not provide any pleasure. Not that many things were providing pleasure recently, and some things that used to be a pleasure were, in fact, unpleasant.

Like showing a potential purchaser through that house in Vence this afternoon. The house that could have been his.

And Laura's.

The sooner it was sold, the better. Perhaps that would help him get back to his old life and not feel so...

Noah let his breath out in a sigh. He didn't have a word to describe how he was feeling, but it was pushing at protective walls that were there for a good reason, so it was better to not even try to analyse how he was feeling.

Maybe all he needed was some good company and he had that lined up for tonight with a rendezvous with Julien and Christophe to taste what was, apparently, a particularly good red wine from a small *appellation* in Bordeaux.

It wasn't so good that Julien was hosting the evening, however, but Noah couldn't let the link to Laura interfere with what was becoming a valued friendship. Even when Ellie pulled him aside almost as soon as he arrived *chez* Rousseau.

'Not long now,' she said. 'I'm sad that Laura decided not to come back to have the baby in France but I'm holding my breath to hear that she's in labour. It could be any day now. She told me she's hoping you might be able to be there for the birth?'

Noah shrugged. His response was just as noncommittal. 'It remains to be seen whether that's possible.'

'Just in case it is, can I give you this?' Ellie was holding something in her hands. Something small and brown. 'She left it in La

Maisonette. Maybe on purpose, because she thought she was coming back. It's a little teddy bear rattle, see?' She held up the soft toy and shook it. Then she pressed it into Noah's hand. 'Thank you...' Her smile was bright. 'And please excuse me. Theo's waiting for me to read his bedtime story. Enjoy your wine.'

Noah wanted to enjoy his wine, which was, as promised, excellent.

He wanted to enjoy the company as well. Julien and Christophe were on good form, putting the world to rights as well as discussing the merits of this wine, like the notes of black cherries and spices.

Right now they were discussing an unseasonably severe storm that might brush western France before barrelling towards the UK and Ireland, particularly Scotland. Noah was listening but not saying anything – even when the others glanced in his direction at the mention of Scotland. He could feel the lump of the small teddy bear, having been shoved into the back pocket of his jeans. He was thinking of Laura, getting ready to have the baby any day now. The thought that a storm might be heading in her direction was disconcerting – an external factor being added to a very internal tension that had suddenly been unleashed.

Because Noah had suddenly realised what the word was for how he'd been feeling ever since he'd received that voice message from Laura. The pressure of trying to shore up those protective barriers had become too much and they had crumbled.

Invisible, that's what the word was.

Exactly the way he'd felt after Elise had died.

Because she'd been the only person he'd really mattered to.

The only person who had loved him as much as he'd loved her.

Like Laura loved him?

Was that why he'd felt so different in her company? Why it had felt so different to make love to her?

Why he'd started feeling invisible again because that voice message had told him that she was gone from his life in any truly meaningful way? They would be living in separate countries. He might never get any time alone with her ever again. Worse... she was being forced to give up on loving him because he couldn't love her back, and that made it too hard.

He had kept himself shut away and, by doing so, he had hurt Laura.

How remarkable was it that he could hold his glass up without his hand shaking? He could swirl the ruby-red wine around inside the glass and admire the *larmes* as the drops ran down from the rim like tears. He could even take a small mouthful and hold it in his mouth as if he was trying to taste every note.

When he wasn't aware of any of them.

What he could *really* taste, perhaps because it was totally filling his head – and his heart – was the knowledge that whatever barrier had held that word back from him had also been hiding the truth that had been there all along.

He loved Laura Gilchrist just as much as she loved him.

He was *in* love with her. Maybe he had been all along, ever since the first moment he'd seen her.

And she was about to give birth to their baby.

What the *hell* was he doing *here*?

'*Excusez-moi, les amis*,' he said to Julien and Christophe. '*Mais je dois partir. J'ai vraiment besoin d'être ailleurs*.'

He really did need to be somewhere else.

But could he get there in time?

24

‘Good heavens, Laura... what are *you* doing in here?’

‘It’s my office, Colin,’ she responded. ‘Is there a reason I shouldn’t be in here?’

Laura turned from where she was dusting the shelf. Dusting the award for Regional Estate Agent of the Year for Oban, Argyll and the Isles, in fact. The silver plaque wasn’t the least bit tarnished yet, but the urge to clean everything was becoming almost compulsive.

‘Ah... does being due to have a baby any minute count as a reason?’ Colin Armstrong was shaking his head in disbelief. ‘Or the fact that we’re facing the worst spring storm in living memory? I just heard they’ve closed both Glasgow and Edinburgh airports. Apparently the last flight in had a pretty hairy landing.’

‘I’m on my way home,’ Laura said. ‘Or rather, my mother’s home, where my bag is packed and ready to be taken off to hospital at a moment’s notice. Which I’m not, according to my midwife when I saw her about ten minutes ago. It might be my due date but this baby is not showing any signs of following the rules. It could take another week or more and I'll be bored stiff if I have nothing to do but look out the window at all this rain.'

The sudden rattle of wind and rain on the office window almost sounded like an echo of the way Laura had been feeling for weeks now. Ever since she'd made the decision not to go back to France. Not to spend her life hoping that, one day, Noah would feel the same way about her as she felt about him. She had focussed, instead, on preparing for the birth of her baby. Sorting her work obligations, shopping for baby supplies, attending antenatal classes and midwife appointments. And cleaning. Lots and lots of cleaning.

'Get yourself home,' Colin ordered. 'I'm sure you can find something to clean there when you're safely inside away from this storm.' He looked at the feather duster in her hands. 'Is this part of what they call the "nesting instinct"?'

'Probably...' Laura dropped the duster onto her desk. 'Fine... I'll go home.' But she narrowed her eyes at her boss. 'What were you going to do in here, anyway? It's still my office, isn't it, even if I am officially on maternity leave?'

'I was going to put this on your desk.' Colin held up a Manila envelope. 'It's a house that will be coming on the market in a month or so and I knew you would be poking your nose through your office door again well before then.'

'But I've handed over my listings. I might well pop into the office but I'm not planning to be back at work by then.'

'I thought you might like to look at this yourself. You haven't liked any of the other suggestions I've made about a baby-friendly replacement for your apartment.'

'No...' The house hunting had definitely been disappointing. Maybe because Laura couldn't forget about that gorgeous property in Vence that Noah had taken her to see. The one that had given her a glimpse into the dream of the family life it felt like she'd been craving her whole life. 'Is this another terraced house with noisy neighbours and a garden the size of a pocket handkerchief?'

'Quite the opposite. Only a ten-minute drive into town but you'd never know that you weren't in the middle of the countryside. Probably not modern enough to suit your style, though.' He turned away. 'I'm doing this as a favour for a friend I play golf with. He's left the keys with me and some photos he had taken recently because he's off on a cruise for the next month. He's asked me to do a valuation and put together some ideas for a marketing brochure by the time he gets back.'

'Can I have a look? Marketing brochures would be something I could play with at home before I get back to the office properly. Babies do sleep sometimes, I'm told.'

Colin grinned at her. 'I'm sure your baby will sleep at exactly the prescribed times – if she takes after her mother.' He handed her the envelope and Laura opened it to take out a photograph.

'Ohh...'

'What, you don't like it?'

The little stone-built cottage she was staring at looked like the house she'd grown up in, but it was in the country with a big garden and a forest of trees around it. It looked rather like a Scottish version of La Maisonette, in fact, with grey stone instead of golden and a slate roof rather than the terracotta pipe version.

For the first time in weeks, Laura felt a tiny glow of something that had nothing to do with the extensive to-do list she was ticking off. This felt like a whisper that something good could be just around the corner.

'I *do* like it,' she said softly.

It was, in fact, quite possibly exactly what Laura hadn't realised she'd been looking for when she'd started the hunt for a home of her own to raise her child in.

'Where is it?'

'Out Glencruitten Road, past the golf course.'

'I love that area. My dad used to take us out to see the cathedral of trees in the Glencruitten woods, and we went fishing once, in one of the lochs out that way.'

Just the two of them, father and daughter, because she was the oldest.

'I might just do a drive-by on the way home.' She looked out the window. 'It looks as if the rain might be easing off a wee bit.'

'That's not a good idea. Just go home,' Colin advised. 'Take the keys with you. The house will still be there tomorrow. Or the next day. Or however long it takes this storm to blow through.'

'Okay...'

Laura was in her car minutes later. She checked that her seat was far enough back to accommodate her belly and the seatbelt straps were between her breasts and well under her bump. She glanced at the envelope that was now lying on the passenger seat. She didn't want to wait days to have a look at this cottage. It was only a few minutes' drive away and surely it wouldn't hurt just to take a peek. To see if there was any basis for the feeling that this was the start of something that could lift the heaviness she was fighting. The prospect of something positive to look forward to might make all the difference when she was in labour.

Without Noah. He might have sent her a message to say he would visit as soon as possible, but he hadn't taken up her invitation to be present at the birth of his child. She would have her mother with her but Laura knew she would still feel alone.

She found herself indicating a turn that was not going to take her directly to her mother's house. It wasn't as if Jeannie was waiting for her. She was at work at the medical centre until late this afternoon.

Laura wasn't going to do anything stupid. All she wanted was to look at the little stone house in real life. She wouldn't even get wet if she didn't get out of the car.

* * *

What was the expression he'd heard used in English?

Noah Dufour looked down at his hands gripping the armrests as the plane's engines howled in protest at slowing down so fast. Or was it the wind outside that was howling?

Whatever. Looking at his hands reminded him of the expression.

It had certainly been a 'white knuckle' ride. The turbulence and the 'go around' abortion of the landing at the last moment had been *terrifiants*.

'Sorry 'bout that, folks.' But the pilot's voice sounded as if he'd enjoyed the challenge of landing this aircraft on the second attempt in vicious crosswinds. 'You won't be surprised to learn that we're the last flight that will be landing here for a wee while. Welcome to Glasgow.'

The woman on the desk of the luxury rental car agency did not sound as if she was enjoying the challenge of the weather.

'You're not heading anywhere near Aberdeenshire, are you? The snow gates are closed on the A93 and there's traffic chaos with a truck rolling on the A9 going into Perth.'

'I'm heading for Oban,' Noah assured her. 'I'll be very careful, but I have requested a four-wheel drive.'

'I'm sure you'll be more than happy with the latest Range Rover we have available for you. Let me get the paperwork sorted. Have you got some ID with you?'

'Yes, of course.' Noah reached into his jeans pocket for his driver's licence. He had to stoop to pick up something else that fell out at the same time. A small, soft teddy bear.

'Aww...' The woman gave him a misty smile. 'That's *so* cute...'

Noah had Jeannie Gilchrist's address and that seemed like a good place to start looking for Laura. According to the built-in satnav in the luxury off-road vehicle, it should have been a two-hour drive to get to Oban, but it was going to take at least twice as long in the slow traffic and appalling weather conditions that seemed to be getting steadily more intense. He had the radio on in the car but he was focussing on his driving more than listening to the news bulletins and experts discussing the unseasonably stormy weather.

'...there could be gusts of wind up to or even greater than sixty miles an hour, which is nearly a hundred kilometres an hour.'

'Is it dangerous for people to be outside in winds like that?'

'Most definitely. There's a high risk of being blown over and injured. Tree branches or even trees may come down. Unsecured objects could become missiles...'

* * *

It came from nowhere.

Laura had been sitting perfectly safely in her car, looking at the little stone house, which was every bit as attractive in real life as it had been in the photograph, despite this awful weather. She was only going to stay for a minute because, if she was honest, the drive along the narrow tree-lined roads out of Oban, with the leafy twigs swirling through the air and hitting the windscreen, had been scarier than she'd anticipated and the gusts right now were enough to rock her car so hard it made her wonder if it might tip over. That was more than enough incentive to release the handbrake and put her foot on the accelerator, but she heard the terrifying sound of cracking wood at exactly the same moment. The trunk of the falling tree missed her car but some of its branches didn't. The largest one caved the roof in over the back seat and the level of light was cut dramatically by the spring foliage covering all the windows except the one Laura had been staring through. She was unable to move. All she could see was the little stone house. The house that reminded her of France.

And Noah...

It was possible to release the safety belt and reach for her handbag on the passenger seat. Her fingers closed around the familiar shape of her phone at the same time as she felt the muscles in her abdomen beginning to tighten. It would only be another Braxton Hicks contraction, she reassured herself. It was less than an hour since she'd seen her midwife for the check up and been told there was no sign of her going into labour anytime soon. She still needed to call for help, however. Being stuck in a car under a tree was not a good place to be.

She tapped the phone screen to bring it to life.

She tapped the telephone icon and then the three-digit emergency number. She didn't expect an immediate answer – they were probably inundated with calls right now. But she didn't expect complete silence, either.

The phone wasn't even ringing.

It took only a tiny shift of her gaze to realise why. She didn't have even a single bar of reception.

Laura squeezed her eyes shut as she pulled her coat around her and huddled into the car seat.

She'd never felt this alone.

'*Noah...*' It was supposed to be just a thought. A squeeze of pure longing. But she heard his name cross her lips. '*I need you...*'

* * *

Noah breathed a sigh of relief when he finally reached his destination in a quiet street in Oban. He'd had some concerning moments on the drive from Glasgow, with parts of the road flooding, having to get round a couple of abandoned cars that had clearly been involved in an accident and dodging a sheet of iron that came loose from a farm shed and took off like a kite. He had been very impressed with the capabilities and handling of the vehicle he'd hired.

The neat little grey-stone cottage with a slate roof, where Laura was planning to live with her mother after the birth of the baby, looked homely and welcoming. Except that there was no one to welcome him. No one answered the door.

He hadn't told Laura he was on his way. Partly because it had been such a rush and, although he'd secured a last-minute ticket after racing to the airport, they had been warned there was a possibility that they may get diverted or have to turn back due to the incoming weather system. Mostly it had been because he wanted to surprise Laura. He wanted to see the look in her eyes when she saw him because that would tell him exactly how she felt about him. He was confident he knew how much she loved him but...

...he wanted to see it for himself. Unguarded. Utterly honest.

Getting back into the car, Noah pulled out his phone. He had the address of The Property Centre on numerous emails, along with Colin Armstrong's phone number. It would be unwise of Laura to still be working at this stage of her pregnancy but he wouldn't put it past her. If she wasn't there, his next stop might have to be the local maternity hospital – if there was one. What if she was somewhere in Glasgow and he'd driven right past?

He fired off a quick text, despite the flickering level of reception.

Laura? Where are you, ma chérie?

25

Colin Armstrong answered Noah's call on the first ring.

'No... I sent Laura home hours ago. She shouldn't have been here in the first place. She said it wasn't going to happen, but did you know she was due to have her baby today?'

Noah gritted his teeth. 'She's not at home. I'm parked outside her mother's house and there's nobody here.'

There was a moment's startled silence on the other end of the line and then it crackled and Colin's words were blurred. Reception seemed to be dodgy, probably due to these high winds.

'...just checking... Hang on...' There was a long silence. 'Her mother's still at work at the medical centre. She said Laura would have called if she needed to go to the hospital.' There was another short silence and then a sound like a groan. 'Oh... *no*... she wouldn't have done that.'

'What? Gone to the hospital without telling anyone?'

'No. Gone to see a house that I gave her the keys to this morning. She said she wanted to have a look but I told her it wasn't a good idea.'

Noah was looking up at a leaden sky. The wind and rain had dropped for the moment and he could feel an almost ominous stillness outside the car. Then he saw fat, flakes of snow beginning to drift down and stick to his windscreen.

'Give me the address,' he demanded.

It wasn't that far but it was startling how isolated it began to feel as soon as he left the outer edges of Oban behind. He found himself passing a golf course and farmland, with roads too narrow to allow for two directions of traffic even if they weren't cluttered with broken branches from the trees on both sides of some stretches. He reached a fork in the road but he'd lost reception on his phone completely now and there was no satellite navigation to assist him. With a silent but desperate plea that he was making the right choice, Noah bumped the car over several large branches and kept going. Until he couldn't go any further. A huge tree had been completely blown over and it was blocking the road and almost covering a small car with its canopy.

A small car that was parked right in front of a small stone cottage – like the one Colin had described. The one that Laura had expressed a desire to go and see.

Noah left his car right where it was, in the middle of the road. He left the driver's door wide open as he jumped out. He forced his way through the smaller branches until he got to the driver's door.

And what he saw in Laura's eyes was far more than he'd expected to see.

There was astonishment, of course. Shock, even, that quickly gave way to relief. Joy, even, judging by the way her eyes filled with tears. There was fear there as well, but more than anything else he could see exactly what he'd been dreaming of seeing ever since he'd almost fled from Julien's house last night to get to the airport and wait for the first available flight to Scotland.

He could see that he was the person Laura wanted to see more than anyone else in the world.

The person that she loved.

He had to hold her. He might never want to let her go. There was a branch that was making it impossible to open the door and it was thick enough to present quite a challenge to break, but Noah found a strength he didn't know he had and, with his entire body weight behind that, the branch snapped with a satisfying crack, high enough to make it possible to wrench the door open. He helped Laura out of the car and wrapped his arms around her and they stood there, the foliage of the fallen tree not providing enough protection from the snow that was falling even more heavily. Soft white flakes were catching in the waves of Laura's hair as she made sounds that were like words but so broken they made absolutely no sense.

'*Tout va bien*,' he told her. '*Je suis là*.' He kissed her, in case she wasn't understanding what he was saying. And then he kissed her again. 'You are safe, *mon coeur. Et... je t'aime... je t'adore. Je suis là et je ne te quitterai plus jamais*.' Somehow he'd lost the ability to translate what he was saying but it didn't seem to matter. When Laura lifted her face it looked as though she understood him perfectly.

'You're here,' she whispered. 'And I love you. I love you *so* much, Noah... I... I...' Her face crumpled and her fingers were digging into his arms with a force that was painful, but it was Laura who cried out.

'Oh, *mon Dieu*,' Noah said. 'Is it the baby?'

Laura nodded, unable to speak.

'We have to get you into my car. I can get you to the hospital.'

But Laura shook her head. 'There's no time...' She took a gasping breath. 'The contractions are too close now...'

'You have the keys to this house, yes?'

'In my bag...'

'*Ne bouge pas.*' Noah had the keys in his hands seconds later. He held the smaller branches back to give Laura a pathway through the foliage, opened the gate to the cottage garden, then scooped her into his arms to carry her to shelter.

* * *

The living area of the cottage was tiny. And cold. But there was a couch and a blanket draped over the back of it. Noah grabbed the blanket and wrapped it around Laura's shoulders.

'You're shaking. I will light the fire. Can you lie down?'

'I think I need to stand up at the moment.' Laura pulled the blanket around her. She walked to the back of the couch and leaned on it, knowing that another contraction wasn't far away. She'd been timing them over the hours she'd been stuck in her car. They'd been fifteen minutes apart to start with and lasting only about forty seconds, but the last two had only been six minutes apart and they'd lasted so long she'd almost forgotten how to breathe.

She'd been so convinced she was about to give birth, in a car, entirely alone, and she'd been terrified. She'd seen the headlights of an approaching vehicle through the screen of the branches and leaves and she'd hoped with all her heart that it was someone from the emergency services. If she could have waved a magic wand and had her greatest wish come true, the vehicle would turn out to be an ambulance and some skilled paramedics would be by her side in seconds. Until she saw Noah's face at the window and knew that the greatest wish she would ever have in her life was to be with him. To be held by him.

And... maybe somewhere, somehow, it looked like a magic wand had been waved because, judging by the look in his eyes, she could add being *loved* by him to the list.

He was crouched in front of a fireplace that had been left piled with pine cones and kindling twigs and there was a basket of neatly cut logs beside the hearth. Even seeing the flames start to flicker made Laura feel warmer but she was still shaking. An odd, rather violent kind of shaking. And then another contraction began and Laura gasped in horror as she felt the wetness soaking the legs of her maternity jeans. She could feel something else, too. Something she'd never felt before, but she knew instantly what it was.

'The baby's coming,' she said in alarm. 'I can feel her *head...*'

Noah was there. Right beside her. 'What do you need me to do?'

'I... I think I need to get on the floor. You'll have to take my jeans off... We're going to need some towels...' She had to stop talking as the contraction built. She couldn't even move to get onto the floor. All she could do was lean into Noah's arms and hang on for dear life.

Things got a little blurry for Laura after that, but she found she was on the floor on her hands and knees, in front of the fire, with soft towels beneath her and more in a pile beside Noah. He took hold of her hand.

'Feel this,' he said, his voice awed.

He took her hand and put it between her legs and she could feel her baby's head had been born. She could feel the damp whorls of hair under her hand and Noah's hand on top of hers. They could both feel their baby being born as a final contraction built and their daughter slipped out into her father's hands and into the world.

'She's not crying.' Laura twisted her body so that she could see what Noah was doing. If felt like her heart was about to stop beating. 'Babies are supposed to cry.'

Noah was wrapping the newborn in a clean towel, being careful of the umbilical cord that was still attached. 'She's looking at me,' he said. 'Her skin is pink and she's breathing. I think she's good… maybe she's too happy to cry?' He gently put the baby into Laura's arms as she lay down on her side.

She opened the towel and pulled up her jumper so that the infant could be against her own skin.

'*Non*…' Noah's voice sounded suspiciously clogged with tears as he knelt beside Laura. 'I don't think she's good.'

Her swift upward glance was fearful but Noah was smiling.

'I think she's perfect,' he whispered.

He leaned down to place a heartbreakingly tender kiss on Laura's lips. He touched his daughter's head with the tip of his finger but his gaze went straight back to Laura's.

'Just like her mama.'

Noah took cushions from the couch to make it possible for Laura to sit up enough to cradle her baby against her breasts, and he covered them both with a blanket and then sat with one arm around Laura and the other on the baby's back so that it felt as if he was holding them both.

It felt as if a family had just been born.

They knew they might not have long like this. From far away, they could already hear the faint sound of a siren.

'I love you, Noah.'

'*Je t'aime aussi*,' he said. He pressed a kiss to her hair this time. 'I thought I could stop myself. That it would keep me safe if I didn't let myself love you but... I've never been safe, Laura. Not since the first moment I saw you.'

'Same,' Laura whispered. She looked up to catch his gaze. 'We can keep each other safe from now on, can't we?'

'*Tout à fait*,' Noah murmured. '*Et notre poupée*.' He bent his head enough to kiss their baby's head.

They could hear vehicle doors slamming outside the house now. Flashing lights were being reflected in the windows. Their precious time alone was over.

But Laura was still looking down at the baby in her arms. The tiny girl who was quietly gazing back at her parents. Then she looked up and found herself falling into the love she could see in Noah's eyes.

Those eyes suddenly widened. 'I almost forgot,' he said softly. He reached behind him and pulled something from his pocket.

'Ohh...' How had Laura managed to forget about that little brown bear? The very first thing she had ever bought for her daughter because it was '*parfait pour un bébé*'. *Her* baby.

'We got a call.' A paramedic was coming through the door. 'We heard that you might need us.'

Laura was watching Noah tuck the little bear into the folds of the towel wrapped around the baby. A baby girl that now had both her mother and her father to adore her – and each other.

'It's great you're here,' she told the paramedic. 'But I think we've got everything we could possibly need already...'

EPILOGUE

If you were truly lucky, dreams *could* come true, and this time it was undoubtedly Jeannie Gilchrist's turn to be the lucky one.

It was Christmas Eve. She was back in France and her whole family was together.

A family that was getting steadily bigger.

Theo Rousseau was four years old now, a serious little boy most of the time but, right now, he was making his cousin Lili laugh out loud as he made tiny puppets on the end of his fingers pop up from behind the arm of a chair. And wasn't the sound of a baby's laughter the best sound in the whole world?

Lilou Elise Dufour was nearly eight months old and she was, of course, the most beautiful baby in the world. She had her mother's golden-red curls that were a soft cloud around her head but she had her aunty Ellie's quick smile and the sheer *joie de vivre* that she had reclaimed. Or did that attitude to life, for Lili, come from her papa?

Jeannie wasn't sure if she'd ever seen a happier man than Noah Dufour. Or a more charming one, come to that. And, oh *my*... the way he looked at Laura sometimes made her own heart skip a beat. No wonder Laura had melted into a version of herself that Jeannie had always dreamed her oldest daughter could become.

She'd known love like that herself, long ago, and any sadness that it had been lost was being washed away by tears of joy that it was happening for her girls. First Ellie and now Laura. There was just Fiona who was without a partner in life now, but at least she wasn't going to be alone for Christmas this year, having finally come, with Jeannie, to visit her sisters.

There was a burst of laughter from the kitchen of this wonderful house in Vence that was Lili's home. She might have been born in a snowstorm in Scotland, but who could blame her parents for wanting to raise her in the soft sunshine of the South of France? Preparations for the Christmas Eve feast were well under way and both Julien's mother and grandmother were in the kitchen supervising the cooking, with Laura and Ellie helping. Noah and Julien had gone down to the cellar some time ago to fetch the wine to accompany each course of the fabulous dinner to come, but they'd been gone so long Jeannie suspected they might be tasting them all to be sure of their choices.

Fiona was still missing as well, having gone on some mysterious mission that she'd told Jeannie wouldn't take long.

It was Ellie who appeared first from the kitchen, wiping her hands on an apron that barely covered the bump of her advancing pregnancy. There was a family joke that Ellie had fallen pregnant at the same time Laura had been giving birth to Lili, but below any teasing was a strong current of joy. All the stronger, in fact, because of what had been overcome to get to this wonderful new phase of her life.

The front door of the villa opened at almost the same

moment and Fiona came in, her cheeks pink from the cool winter afternoon.

'Where on earth have *you* been?' Ellie asked.

'Someone had to go and give the donkeys their Christmas Eve carrots,' Fiona said. 'And I took them some ginger biscuits, too. They love me the best now.' She put a bunch of keys down on a side table. 'Margot's really cool to drive,' she said. 'Thanks for letting me use her while I'm here. I can see why you don't want to get rid of her, even though she's a totally unsuitable car for someone with a baby.'

Jeannie loved the little red 2CV car as much as everyone else. Maybe she'd be brave enough to try driving it herself on this visit.

'She's part of the family.' Ellie was heading towards her sister, clearly intent on giving her a hug. 'Just like you are.'

Laura came into the room from the kitchen as Lili let out another shout of laughter. She held up her arms with a squeal of glee as soon as she saw her mother, and Laura was scooping her daughter into her arms as Noah and Julien appeared through another door. Noah put down the bottles of wine he was carrying and went straight to Laura and Lili. He made them both laugh as he wrapped his arms around his family and danced a few steps to the Christmas music playing in the background. Jeannie reached for the tissue tucked into the sleeve of her cardigan as she saw the way Laura and Noah were looking at each other as they danced. She could *feel* the love between them.

From the corner of her eye as she dabbed it with a tissue, Jeannie saw the way Fiona had slipped out of the briefest of hugs from Ellie. 'I had a quick look inside La Maisonette, too,' she heard her say – as if she was trying to change the subject.

'It's a bonny wee house, isn't it? Here's the key.' She held out the large, cast-iron key.

'It's a spare key,' Ellie told her. 'You can keep it, if you like.'

'Why would I want to do that?'

Ellie caught her mother's glance and smiled at the almost imperceptible nod Jeannie found herself giving.

'You never know,' she told Fiona, 'you might need it one day.'

* * *

MORE FROM ALISON ROBERTS

ACKNOWLEDGEMENTS

Many thanks, as always, to my wonderful editor, Megan Haslam, whose instinct for pace and focus in a story are always on point.

Helen Woodhouse has, again, excelled in providing a meticulous copyedit for this book and I must give her the credit for the clever, French-flavoured pun she added to my grouping of the heroes of this series as the Three Musketeers.

Thank you to all the other people in the Boldwood team who have been working on my behalf. Wendy Neale in Sales, Marcela Torres in Marketing, Ben Wilson and Kathryn Smith in Production, the designers who are creating magic with covers in the background and Rachel Sargeant's final touch of proofreading.

Thank you all so much.

I would also like to acknowledge and express my heartfelt appreciation for my amazingly talented writing family – the Maytoners – so named because of the location where we held our first annual writing retreat in Australia more than fifteen years ago.

Carol, Kelly, Fi, Trish, Linda, Meredith, Barb and Anne – thank you all so much for the encouragement, support, commiserations and celebrations over so many years. I love you all!

ABOUT THE AUTHOR

Alison Roberts is the author of over one hundred romance novels with Mills and Boon, and now writes romance and escapist fiction for Boldwood.

Sign up to Alison Robert's mailing list here for news, competitions and updates on future books.

Follow Alison on social media:

facebook.com/rosie.richards.75
instagram.com/alison_roberts_author

ALSO BY ALISON ROBERTS

A Year in France Series

Falling for Provence

From Provence, With Love

Medical Romances

The Doctor's Promise

Doctor Off Limits

The Surgeon's Surprise Baby

A Kiss Before Midnight

Printed in Dunstable, United Kingdom

66062361R00170